The Lie of the Land

a novel by

Jaspar David Utley

UNAM
PRESS
UNIVERSITY OF NAMIBIA

University of Namibia Press
www.unam.edu.na/unam-press
unampress@unam.na
Private Bag 13301
Windhoek
Namibia

First published:	2017
Cover design:	Nambowa Malua
Cover map:	From *Kriegskarte von Deutsch-Südwestafrika*. 1904. *Blatt Keetmanshoop*. Berlin: Dietrich Reimer. Reproduced by courtesy of the National Archives of Namibia.
Frontispiece map:	John Kinahan
Design and layout:	Vivien Barnes, Handmade Communications
Printed by:	Times Offset (Malaysia)

ISBN   978-99916-42-35-2

Distribution
In Namibia by Namibia Book Market: www.namibiabooks.com
Internationally by the African Books Collective: www.africanbookscollective.com

For Nahum and Sharon Gorelick

'Old sins cast long shadows'

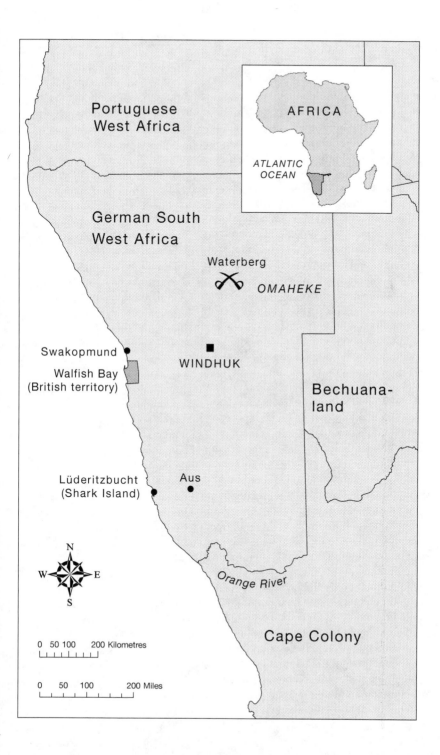

Portuguese
West Africa

AFRICA

ATLANTIC
OCEAN

German South
West Africa

Waterberg

OMAHEKE

Swakopmund

Walfish Bay
(British territory)

WINDHUK

Bechuana-
land

Lüderitzbucht
(Shark Island)

Aus

N

W   E

S

Orange River

Cape Colony

0   50 100   200 Kilometres

0   50   100   200 Miles

One

'You'd better come in.'

I've seen warmer eyes on an African puff adder.

Her face was as unyielding as if it had been carved out of granite. Thin fair hair was scraped back from her forehead in a severe bun. A faded brown dress covered her from neck to toe. In contrast, a small lace ruff at her throat, adorned by a red stone brooch, seemed almost frivolous. Her faded blue eyes stared at me contemptuously. They took in my homespun suit and heavy boots and glanced at my tanned face.

'Come in now, before the wind blows the dust inside,' she sniffed.

She was as inviting as an open grave but the autumn streets of Munich were even more unappealing, with a bullying wind shoving the leaves aside, and at least she didn't tell me to go to the Tradesman's Entrance: von Epenstein's letter must have had some effect. I went in and she slammed and bolted the door behind me. She pointed to the doormat marked *'Willkommen'* and I wiped my boots several times until she gave a curt nod.

I followed her down a dark, cold corridor deadened by brown and green wallpaper. It smelled of lavender with an underlay of wet dog. We came to a heavy door crafted out of some dark wood. They like that sort of thing in the Kingdom of Bavaria: it gives the illusion of strength and permanence. She opened it and indicated to me to go in.

'Wait here,' she said and was gone, closing the door behind her. I half expected her to lock it.

The room had an uncomfortable air about it as if guests were not expected to linger. Heavy brown velvet curtains were drawn across the

1

window and the only light came from an oil lamp perched on a side table. The furniture was as heavy and solid as the door and seemed afflicted with an epidemic of antimacassars. No doubt they were for decoration as I could not see the woman allowing anyone to wear hair oil in her house. Framed photographs of frowning relatives who looked disapprovingly at the cameraman covered most of the available spaces on the sideboard and the mantelpiece. Portraits of poor, mad King Otto and the other Otto, von Bismarck, took pride of place above the empty fireplace. To emphasise the coldness of the room, a large ornate and unlit potbellied stove stood in one corner. In Bavarian fairy tales, they burn people in stoves like that.

In short, it was a room that could have existed in a million homes across the kingdoms of Germany. Except for the wall opposite the fireplace. A huge head of a stuffed antelope hung on one side. The large curling horns and big ears were those of a kudu. On the other side was the head of an oryx, its long slender horns pointing towards the ceiling.

I examined the sjambok lying casually on an occasional table: no doubt a memento of Germany's civilising mission in Africa. It seemed in good working order. I was wondering what Webb had got me into when the door opened. The woman entered and held the doorknob while checking the room with a quick glance to make sure everything was still in its place.

'*Reichskommissar* Göring will see you now,' she said.

∼

Earlier, in London, Webb had been very affable, offering me a cigarette, and I knew something nasty was about to come up. Mind you, the Department specialised in nasty stuff so I wasn't too surprised.

'The people upstairs are very pleased with you,' he lied, absent-mindedly stroking his glossy, brilliantined hair. I have always suspected there were no people upstairs at all and that this cramped office he shared with a couple of filing cabinets was the entire Department. 'Your work in South Africa, especially at Mafeking, was outstanding and still no one suspects what you were up to: not the Boers, certainly not the Germans and not even us, come to that. Well, Baden-Powell may have had an inkling but he kept it under his large hat.' He smiled unconvincingly and touched his small moustache as if it were a talisman. Maybe it was. He also sported a deep tan, Indian army I guessed.

'So all that will come in handy.'

I grimaced. I'd only just started again on my research and I didn't know if the University would take kindly to my sailing off again. I was sure, however, that Julia would object.

'Come in handy for what?' I asked.

Webb took a long drag on his cigarette, blew a cloud of smoke in the air and then stubbed the thing out in a brass ashtray.

'What do you know about German South West Africa?'

A thin ray of sunshine that had managed to penetrate the fog slipped in through the window and glinted off one of his uniform buttons. But it didn't illuminate anything else.

'German South West? Well, I know that von Bismarck reluctantly decided that Germany should have some colonies after all and, among other places, claimed the area in the 80s.'

'1884,' said Webb. 'They didn't call it a colony despite sending in settlers. They said it was an Imperial Protectorate.'

'Really? What were they protecting? The place is mostly desert with no permanent rivers except on its northern and southern borders.'

'It's all that was left in Africa after we, the French, the Portuguese and the Belgians had taken what we wanted.'

Again Webb smiled. 'Oh, and we took over Walfish Bay before they could. It's the only decent port in the country.'

'That didn't stop them for long.'

Webb nodded. 'That's true. The Germans are a very industrious people. As you must know.'

I didn't rise to the bait. I may have had a German father but that didn't make me a German. Mind you, I had an English mother and that didn't make me English. I stuck with being British.

'Indeed,' I said. 'They've already got on with Swakopmund and Lüderitz as ports of a sort and settlers are pouring in. They'll make a go of it, all right.' I paused a moment. 'So what's bothering you about the place?'

He lit another cigarette by way of punctuation.

'In the war, you had dealings with the German Commando at Elandslaagte.'

'I was a member of the Commando, as you well know. On your instructions.'

'Quite. And Germany sent arms to the Boers.'

I nodded.

'So we have already had an instance of Germany interfering in our affairs. Now that they are developing a Protectorate, it won't be too long before they'll be a powerful influence in the area. And that could pose a bigger threat to our colonists in South Africa. They might even decide to take over Walfish Bay.'

I could see where this was leading.

'So when do I leave?' I said.

He stiffened. 'I haven't briefed you yet. Besides, you need to go to Munich first.'

I sat back in my chair. 'I'll have one of those cigarettes after all, if you don't mind.'

It took two more cigarettes before he was done.

~

Unlike the rest of the house, the *Reichskommissar*'s room was full of a dry heat. It was full of many other things as well, most of them dead, including more animal heads on the walls and several African curios. I half expected to see the stuffed head of a Hottentot. I noticed a small drum in one corner. Two large dogs raised an eyebrow as I entered but otherwise remained lying on the zebra skin that served as a carpet. Their master, wearing an old smoking jacket, also stayed sitting where he was on an over-stuffed sofa, one slippered foot resting on a stool made out of an elephant's foot. A pair of tusks formed a gong stand near to hand. A large curved pipe made of meerschaum shared a side table with a photograph of what I assumed were his Bavarian wife and children. He liked his comforts, did the master of the house. An empty cup and saucer next to a brandy bottle showed he had already had his coffee.

A letter was in his hand as he indicated me to sit on an uncomfortable carved ebony chair.

He was a portly, bull-necked man in his sixties with a huge grey moustache and a pair of piercing grey eyes. The deep sagging bags under his eyes made him look older than he was. I had the feeling that he didn't smile very often. Except, possibly, when saving Africa from its wildlife. He made no attempt to offer me a drink and went straight to the business at hand.

'You are a man who collects languages,' he reminded me. He held up a hand to silence my unuttered reply. 'And you wish to go to *Deutsch Süd-Westafrika* to study the language of the natives there.' I knew that, too. We had dictated the letter to von Epenstein, a friend of my grandfather. Göring's wife was rumoured to be his mistress and he had appointed himself godfather to the children. Heinrich tolerated him, even liked him, and von Epenstein was more than willing to give me an introduction to the old man.

'Learning the languages of the savages might well be a good thing as it will not be long before they fully accept German civilisation and our language. You must examine their heathen tongues before they vanish altogether.' He coughed or it might have been a laugh.

'I was there for several years, as you must know. I was the first *Reichskommissar*. Prince von Bismarck himself gave me my responsibilities.' I tried to look impressed.

'I managed to institute some kind of order in the place. It was not easy; the people there are unruly and uncivilised and cannot be trusted to keep their word.'

I knew that as Imperial Commissioner he had made many fruitless attempts to buy off the local chiefs. In fact, in many ways he had been a total failure, leaving the country with his tail between his legs. If I knew anything about him and his kind, real order would be established at the point of a gun.

'What do you wish to know? I can tell you about the tribes of savages that you will find there.'

'That would be most generous of you, *Herr Reichskommissar*.'

He nodded agreement.

'You will take notes.'

'You see,' he began, breathing heavily, 'there are many tribes with varying degrees of interest.' He held up his hand and began ticking them off on his fingers.

'Up in the North are the Owambo kingdoms. They could cause trouble but the outbreak of rinderpest – the cattle disease – has reduced them to penury. What is more, their land is unsuitable for settlement and they have no minerals. It is possible you will not come across any of them.'

I sat there, scribbling industriously.

'Next there are the Herero and the Nama. They are always in conflict with each other. The Nama came off worst in their latest encounter and are now in the South of the country. The Herero are the ones to watch: they dominate the centre of the country and they are resistant to our people acquiring land and cattle although their land is ideal for settlement. Our missionaries are doing sterling work to educate them to our ways.'

I waited while he coughed.

'Finally, there are smaller groups of little significance. The Damara are more or less the slaves of the Herero and the Bushmen have no standing with the other tribes. The mongrel Basters are our allies. That is all I can tell you. Oh, of course,' he added, 'there is the white tribe, the Cape Dutch.'

He looked at me over his moustache and I realised I was supposed to acknowledge that he had made a joke. I smiled appreciatively. I didn't let on that, thanks to Webb, I knew Göring himself spoke Dutch.

At that moment the door burst open and in ran a sullen-faced boy who must have been about nine years old. Clutching a small wooden rifle he was oddly dressed in the uniform of a Boer soldier which I guess had been given him by his father. He was followed into the room by a flustered nursemaid.

'I'm sorry,' *Herr Reichskommisar*,' she said as she tried to curtsey and grab the boy at the same time. 'I was tending to Alfred and ...'

'No matter,' said Göring, waving his hand. 'Boys will be boys, eh Hermann?'

The boy nodded but stared at me with hostile eyes. 'Who is this man?'

'A man who was a fine soldier in the South African war, fighting with our German contingent.'

'Did you kill any of the British?'

'Many,' I said, mentally crossing my fingers. That brought a short smile to his pudgy face.

'Now go back with Helga,' said the old man. 'I must finish my business with this gentleman.'

The boy threw me a salute that I gravely returned and left the room with his nurse. She looked extremely nervous and I briefly wondered if the sjambok would be wielded later on.

'My apologies,' said Göring. 'Now where were we? Ah, yes. As I said, I laid the foundation for what has followed. Now there are more German settlers farming the land, with herds of cattle.'

Most of the cattle had been swindled away from the Herero but he forgot to mention that.

'The over-population of Germany will be solved there and in our other colonies. I feel honoured to have been part of this noble enterprise.'

'I also hear many missionaries have followed the settlers.'

He grimaced.

'I suppose they are necessary, if only to convert the natives to our way of thinking and thus make them more docile. But they have the habit of interfering with military matters. Sometimes they give natives the idea that they are equal to us and this will lead to insubordination and even uprisings. We must keep an eye on them.'

Finally, he reached under a pillow on the sofa and produced another envelope which he handed to me.

'This is an introduction to the present authorities. I think you will find this will make your researches easier.'

The old man was being exceedingly generous; von Epenstein must have laid it on with a trowel.

'Tell me,' he said suddenly. 'Why are you working in England and not here in Germany? We have the leading linguists in the world working here.'

I nodded. He was right.

'Because the British have their Empire and countless languages are spoken there: those languages are easily accessible in London.'

'I see. But you have lived in South Africa.'

'Yes, sir. There are many German people there.'

'Your work in the recent war in South Africa has not gone unnoticed,' he added.

How he knew that, I had no idea but it couldn't do me any harm. Or so I thought. One of the dogs broke wind as I left the room.

The woman was no sweeter when she showed me out. She didn't even say goodbye. She certainly didn't express the desire to see me again. The feeling was mutual. I also had the feeling that she had seen right through me but all that mattered was that I had what I wanted.

This time, Webb had asked me not to meet him in the War Office.

'They have spies watching the place all the time,' he explained. 'A repeat visit might arouse suspicion. You may be sure that the Germans also have a network in South West, so you can't be too careful.'

So we had tea together in a greasy little half-lit café in Soho that smelled of fried onions while I told him all about Göring. He was in ill-fitting mufti and for some reason it made me notice what bad teeth he had.

'That sounds pretty good,' he said, offering me a cigarette. He then passed me an envelope across the stained tablecloth.

'Your ticket,' he said. 'You sail for Walfish Bay in a couple of days. Keep the same papers and identity as you used in the war. You'll have plenty of time on the boat to perfect your story and to work out where to start looking and listening. There is not much in the land between the coast and Windhoek so I suggest you begin there. I've told our man there in Walfish Bay that you'll be coming and he'll supply you with some cash but otherwise you're pretty much on your own. You won't be able to send any message so you'll have to save everything until I debrief you on your return.'

'No messages? Not even a cry for a help?' I smiled.

'Especially not that.' He wasn't smiling at all. 'Trouble's brewing in the colony. There's been an uprising among the Herero. It's been going badly for the Germans with settlers being murdered and with so few troops there. But things are likely to change as they are already pouring thousands of troops in. And that makes your mission even more urgent.' He scratched behind his ear. I had a dog that did that. 'By the way, the Germans have already set up a banking system and of course they use German currency. I have opened an account for you. The details are with your ticket.'

'So let me get this straight. You are sending me into a remote territory where I might possibly find myself in the middle of a war. I am supposed somehow to find out if the German top command is intending to invade South Africa and then, without any lines of communication, I am supposed to get this information back to you.'

'That's about it. However, if you do find something out you must head straight back to Walfish Bay and tell our man there who will get the information to Cape Town from where it will be telegraphed to London. Any other questions?'

I shook my head and we shook hands.

'Oh, incidentally,' he said as I headed for the door. 'I know there is no need to say this but those on high have asked me to remind you of where your loyalties lie. I mean, you being half German and all that. Sorry.'

I took this in the way it was intended.

'From your accent,' I said, 'I'd say that despite an overlay of a minor public school, you have Irish connections. My loyalties are as firm as your own. Good day.'

His face went as white as it could under his Indian tan but he said nothing.

I took a passing cab to my flat. Now all I had to do was say goodbye to my parents. And Julia?

~

As always, I tried to push that thought to the back of my mind. Julia was becoming a problem. She was beautiful enough, tall and elegant with the palest skin I've ever seen. Her figure, though concealed and corseted, was more than clearly desirable.

'She comes from a very wealthy family,' said my mother on several occasions, 'and she's a good girl. No gallivanting about and that sort of thing.' By which my mother meant she was still a virgin. 'Her mother and I have been friends for years.'

After we had met, arranged by our families, it was rapidly assumed that an understanding existed between us. Assumed, that is, by everyone except me.

Neither of us had ever raised the subject of a future together. The last time we had met had been a failure. We were sitting on a bench in the park. Not too close together, of course, and with her aunt clearly visible on two benches along to give our meeting propriety. It had rained that morning and the clean air was enriched by the scent of a nearby lavender bush. Julia looked even more beautiful than ever.

I began with a safe question. 'How is Betsy?'

Immediately her face became animated.

'Oh, she's wonderful and so clever! Only last week, when I was a little unwell, she came into my room and immediately cheered me up.'

Betsy, of course, was her dog, a loathsome Pekinese.

Julia chattered on in this vein for some minutes, including giving me the latest news on her horse, whose name I forget. All I needed to do was smile, nod and occasionally gasp with amazement. I knew I was deceiving her but it was my protection against what I was beginning to feel was a trap. Eventually her enthusiasm petered out and with a nervous smile, she asked me about my work at the University.

'Oh, much the same as usual. Professor Smythe is becoming more eccentric each day. Just last week, when I was in the library, he entered wearing his pyjamas and slippers.'

'Goodness! Did he walk through the streets dressed like that? Wouldn't he catch cold?'

'I suppose he might,' I said.

An uncomfortable silence settled between us. She fixed her beautiful eyes somewhere over my left shoulder.

Normally, when we met she asked me about my time overseas. During my participation in the South African War we had, for obvious reasons, been unable to write to each other and when I returned my welcome had been nothing more than friendly. There was never a move by either of us for anything more than a chaste kiss on the cheek when we met and parted.

In short, we were not in love although I had the impression she wouldn't have minded being my wife as long as I settled down in the country. That was the problem. I had no inclination to settle down at all. She seemed content to leave it at that but I was wrong.

'Who are you?' she said suddenly.

'I'm sorry?'

'I mean, I know what you do and where you've been but I know nothing of how you think and feel about me, about anything. You make clever remarks about this and that but it's as if you are wearing a mask. You can see and watch other people but they can never see you. I can't see you. All the time I feel you are hiding from me.'

Her delicate fingers trembled as she clutched her reticule, barely large enough to hold a handkerchief, and her eyes still failed to meet mine. A tear trickled down her cheek. Her aunt must have had the sight of a buzzard for she rose from her bench and marched towards us with set jaw, holding her umbrella like an assegai.

I decided to speak the truth. 'I don't know. I have always hidden my true thoughts and feelings even when I was a child. It helped me survive school but, to be honest, I've never had close friends.'

'And am I a close friend?'

The aunt's arrival saved me from replying.

Julia rose and offered me a weak smile.

'You must come for tea,' she said.

I watched the pair move away, ashamed at my sense of relief.

~

As for my parents, well, they made no complaint when I announced I was leaving again on my travels. They knew what business I was engaged in. Webb, of course, had commanded me to tell no one of my secret work, including my family, but I trusted my family more than I trusted British Intelligence. They knew of my work in the South African War and when I told them of my new mission – a grand word for a leap into the unknown – they looked sad but nodded acceptance. Mother fussed about as I packed, making sure I had clean underwear while making me promise to eat properly. My father said little but, in a very British way, shook my hand several times and gruffly told me to take care of myself.

As for Julia, I decided I wouldn't have time to meet her to say goodbye. Instead, I would write her a long letter explaining why I had to go abroad again. That would postpone further awkwardness and save either of us from acute embarrassment. Besides, I had a boat to catch.

Two

Fog. A huge rolling bank of fog that wouldn't have been out of place in the London I had left behind. Fog so thick that there was no way we could land. And given the treacherous nature of this coast, we had to lay some distance offshore waiting for the fog to disperse before we could make our way into the harbour.

It had been a rather ordinary journey until now: even the Bay of Biscay had behaved itself and all along the West African coast we had escaped any sign of inclement weather. The sole intrusive element had been the shrill hymn singing of two ladies from the London Missionary Society who were destined to run a school somewhere in the Gold Coast. They had shut themselves up in their cabin for the duration of the trip, praying and singing. The ship's complement to a man felt relief when we finally reached Cape Coast.

The slave citadel, a gleaming white perversion of a fairy castle, a British flag hanging limply from the summit, dominated the town but I watched with some interest as the surf boats ploughed through the sea towards us. Even more fascinating was the sight of the two ladies sitting in a boat, ramrod straight, as the near-naked surf men, their blue-black bodies glistening with sweat and spray, dug their paddles into the waves as they rode them back on to the shore. I could hear no hymn singing this time, mostly because the paddlers were chanting as they worked but I assume there was a fair amount of praying. I hoped they were also praying that the fever wouldn't strike too soon. When the ladies disembarked, they made no effort to look back and wave but strode grimly towards the town. I felt a twinge of sympathy for the school children waiting for them.

As for me, apart from trimming my beard and moustache so that it looked more like a German Imperial than a Boer farmer from the back of beyond, I spent a lot of time wondering what I had got myself into. The more I thought about it, the more absurd it seemed. So I decided to concentrate on learning the languages.

Since I was small, I'd had an ear for languages coupled with a gift for mimicry. When friends and relatives from Europe visited the family, I listened to their accents and learned much vocabulary in the process. I was already bilingual in German and English and soon discovered that once I had mastered two languages, it was that much easier to learn another. These days, I was picking up new languages as a dog acquires fleas. In South Africa I'd learned a smattering of Zulu, Cape Dutch and some Hottentot – these last two should stand me in good stead in German South West.

Now I stood at the rail smoking a post-breakfast cigarette and staring into the blank cloud of mist that lay between me and Walfish Bay. I wondered when it would lift and when the sun would reappear.

'About mid-morning,' said a voice at my right shoulder. I didn't turn round. After weeks together on board, I knew every voice. This came with a thick Glaswegian burr that was owned by a surveyor sent out at the request of the Cape government to examine the roads of the port and its surrounds. He was one of those short wiry fellows that had formed the backbone of the Highland Light Infantry in the South African War.

'I was wounded at Magersfontein,' he'd said when I tentatively asked about his slight limp. 'It was nothing compared to what happened to some of the lads. Not exactly a picnic, if you know what I mean.'

'But you're still in this part of the world.'

'Aye, it grabs you by the throat after a while. There's a bit more sun here than back home in the tenements.'

He was a friendly enough companion on a boat that would never qualify as a luxurious liner.

'Morning, Mac,' I now said. 'So this damned fog won't last forever.' The smell of Kennedy's pipe was somehow reassuring. My father smoked a pipe.

'No. It's always like this. You see, the sea is ice cold on account of the current that comes up from the Antarctic. And the shore is hot on account of it being a desert. The cold meets the heat and, och, there's your fog. It rolls inland for miles and miles. I gather whatever manages to live there couldn't exist without the moisture the fog carries in. And when the sun takes over again, the fog will creep back out to sea, and we'll soon see land.'

'We have fog back home. Why don't we just steer our way through it?'

Kennedy laughed and spat over the rail into the grey swell below.

'Because this is the most dangerous stretch of coast in Africa: ships have been wrecked here for centuries. You can still see some of the wrecks lifted up high and dry on the dunes. We don't want to join them. The desert stretches miles inland. Anyone who is wrecked on this coast and makes it ashore has little chance of staying alive. That's why they call this the Skeleton Coast.'

Kennedy was right. Two or three hours later, the fog lifted dead on cue and there, before us, was Walfish Bay.

The first thing I saw was the curve of an immense lagoon, already shimmering with a heat haze. A brilliant blue sky was reflected in the sea and in the distance I could see huge sand dunes marching right down to the sea's edge. Nearer to the boat, distorted by the haze, were large flocks of flamingos. Two pelicans glided above us, heading for the shore.

As we approached the harbour, I could see a small cluster of wooden huts on one of the spits that curled round the lagoon.

'Walfish Bay,' remarked Kennedy, knocking his pipe out on the rail.

'It doesn't look much,' I said.

'Believe me, you're right, it isn't. The Germans at Swakopmund are already building a better place there although they've no natural harbour and the place is little more than a large beach.'

'How far away is Swakopmund from here?'

He turned and looked at me.

'Are you thinking of going there?'

I've always believed in telling as much of the truth as possible, saving the lies for special occasions.

'I am.'

'It's about twenty miles as the crow flies but it'll take you some time. You'll probably need to ride at the edge of the sea.' He paused briefly. 'What's your business there?'

I smiled. 'I have some business with the Germans and I don't fancy a long ride in an ox cart to Windhoek from here and then back down to the coast.'

He shrugged.

'You'll cross the border round about the Swakop River, though it moves around a bit. They'll check your papers there.'

I nodded.

'How long have you been working in Walfish Bay?' I asked.

'Two years. This is my second tour. And my last, with any luck.'

'So you've nearly done the job.'

He spat over the rail once more.

'The job's finishing me. It's the sand, you see. Whatever you do with roads or even, heaven help us, a railway, the sand always blows over them. It's a nightmare job. I've recommended we give up on the idea of a railway and the Cape Government want me to take one last look. Well, it's their money. Once we're done, I'll find a billet down south. Now that's God's country.'

It was late in the afternoon before I finally went ashore. I immediately made my way, after following Kennedy's directions, to a hut set back from the sea. The whole town consisted of nothing but wooden huts plonked on the sand and which served the port and its workers. There was little to distinguish this one from any other save for a heavy-duty steel shutter that was now lifted and a weather-beaten sign outside that indicated that it was a grog shop owned by a fellow called J. Morrison. I pushed at the door and went in, shaking the sand off my boots.

There was a single badly-trimmed oil lamp that lit the room revealing several shelves lined with bottles of liquor. A strong smell of spirits hung in the air. A red-eyed and rake-thin Hottentot had just bought a bottle of cheap gin. He grinned at me stupidly, revealing a mouth with more gaps than teeth, and staggered outside. I was then alone with a tall, broad-chested red-bearded fellow dressed in rough corduroy trousers held up by red braces and a blue flannel shirt. His face looked as if it had been sculpted by wind out of solid rock. His eyebrows were so bushy that they dominated his face. He said nothing and waited for me to speak.

'Mr Morrison?'

He nodded.

I looked around to make sure we were alone.

'I'm looking for a rare single malt,' I said. Webb had chosen this as a coded introduction, observing that the chance of there actually being malt whisky in Walfish Bay was highly unlikely.

Morrison scratched his beard.

'Are you now?' he spoke at last. Another Scot, they seemed to populate the entire Empire. 'Well, what brand do you favour?' He stared at me with shrewd blue eyes.

'Glenturret,' I answered. 'You cannot better it.'

He reached out a hand.

'Welcome,' he said with a perfunctory handshake.

He left the counter and walked over to lock the door, having first placed a CLOSED notice on it.

'Come inside,' he said. 'I'll be obliged if you take off your boots first, if you please. You can leave your bag by the door.'

It was a cosy little room, neat and clean and smelling of beeswax polish. There were a couple of over-stuffed armchairs and a small round table in front of a fire-place ready for lighting. A copy of 'The stag at bay' hung over the mantle shelf. He followed my gaze.

'It gets awful cold at night here. You'll find that out for yourself soon enough. Now sit you down.'

I sat in one of the chairs as he fussed about with glasses. He returned with a bottle in one hand and the glasses in another. He held up the bottle for my inspection. It really was a bottle of Glenturret Malt Whisky. Webb had got that wrong, for a start. There clearly was Glenturret in Walfish Bay. I wondered what else he might have botched.

After we had sipped appreciatively, Morrison stretched out his legs.

'Well, let's get down to business. I've arranged for you to go to Swakopmund tomorrow. The horses are round the back.'

'Horses?'

'You'll need a guide. Thomas will take you.'

'Thomas?' I felt stupid repeating everything he said. He didn't seem to mind. I think he relished the company.

'He's the fellow you saw just now.' Morrison must have seen something in my eyes. 'Don't worry, he'll be sober in the morning; he has a head like iron. He also knows this place like the back of his hand.' He bent forward. 'Now, listen. You've come just in time. Something big is happening over the other side. They've been landing more and more troops. There are rumours that the native uprising against the settlers is not going too well for the Germans. It's turning nasty. I'm not surprised. The natives have had their lands taken away from them. Just like the Highland

Clearances.' He bared his teeth in a mirthless grin. 'The Germans have been none too gentle about it and have stirred up a lot of resentment. It'll be a bloody business.'

He replenished my glass though I should have liked something to eat as well. It seemed a lifetime since I'd last eaten on the boat.

'It's risky your staying with me but there's a place you can bed down a small way from here. It's rough but warm and the food's passable. The widow who runs the place is my friend. She knows to hold her tongue.' Again, he bared his teeth. 'Leave from there in the morning as soon as the fog clears. The British border patrol has been notified to stay out of sight. You won't see them but they'll be there. Once you find the border, you can walk the rest of the way. The Germans won't let Thomas in; they don't like the natives at the best of times but if there's trouble they'll completely batten down the hatches. The border moves around a bit while the Germans and us squabble over which patch of sand they wish to claim. Thomas will bring the horses back with him. With any luck, the Germans will take care of you.' He seemed to find the ambiguity amusing. 'Once over there you're on your own.'

'So Webb told me. He also said I have no way of getting in touch with you except in person.'

'That's true enough. Remember that German South West Africa is an enormous country. The railways are only just beginning and there's no telegraph network. Don't send a message, it could be intercepted. You'll have to do your best. Good luck.'

He made my mission sound even more ridiculous. I was beginning to think I would find out nothing and end up dead in the process, shot as a spy.

The afternoon turned into evening as we sat and consumed more of the whisky. Morrison lit the fire and we studied the flames as he told me a little about himself.

He was clearly normally a taciturn fellow and his oath to say nothing of his secret duties made conversation awkward. Once, however, that malt had mellowed and loosened his tongue, he told me something of himself.

He had left a poor crofter's family and, like so many others, he had ventured to this part of the world to make his fortune. He had had no luck with gold or diamonds down south but had quickly realised that he could make more from trading with treasure hunters than from looking for himself. There being a chance of prospectors moving into South West, he had decided to try his luck with a fresh clientele.

Eventually, as conversation ground to a halt, I wished him luck as we bid each other goodnight, though if anyone needed luck, it was me.

Soon after, clutching the bottle in one hand and a lantern lent by Morrison in the other, I followed his directions. It was already turning cold. The sky was filled with a million stars but I guessed that by morning they would be hidden by the incoming fog.

Once, as I trudged between wooden shacks, I saw a shadow up ahead dart behind a hut and I froze. Then I heard a snuffle and a strange cry and I guessed it was only a jackal. After a short passage through the packed sand that passed for a road, I came to the widow's hut.

I expected it to be dark and silent but as I approached, I could hear music. Loud, even jolly music. Perhaps she was a merry widow. I knocked on the door. The music continued playing and I knocked again. The cold was beginning to seep into my bones as I knocked for a third time.

The door opened and a beam of light spilled out on to the sand. The music sounded louder as it echoed into the night. I thought I heard the sound of a woman's voice shrieking with laughter. A blast of warm air, smelling of fish, hit me in the face. A huge ruffian, swaying slightly, asked me in Cape Dutch, and none too politely, what I wanted. There was no sign of a merry widow.

'I've a message for the widow Huxtable,' I said.

'Round the back,' he burped and slammed the door. I rather liked the warmth but I guessed it would come at a price and the sovereigns sewn into my belt were for less frivolous pursuits.

The back door took only one knock to be opened but after a great deal of noise from a bolt and chain. A tall raw-boned woman, wearing a shawl around her shoulders, stared at me. Her hair was ginger tinged with grey. She looked anything but merry. Maybe she had a sister living in Munich.

'James Morrison sent me.'

She opened the door wider.

'Come in. And don't bring any sand inside.' Her accent was American. New England, I thought. Walfish Bay had an international community.

I followed her down a corridor into a small parlour equipped with a rocking chair, a small desk and a driftwood fire in the grate. Through the wooden wall I could make out the laughter and music in the rest of the house. I raised an eyebrow. She smiled grimly.

'Whalers,' she said. 'My man was a whaler and it killed him. Now they give me a living. They're good customers and rarely give me any trouble. We have to scratch to survive here, Mister, and morals don't come into it.'

I shrugged.

'It's no business of mine,' I said.

'That's true enough. Now, James said you wanted a room for the night. It's clean and the bed's been warmed.'

I reached for my pocket.

'It's already been paid for. Are you hungry?' She pointed to a small table in the corner with a place set.

Suddenly, the whisky rebelled in my stomach and all at once I was ravenous.

'Yes, please.'

'There's some cold meat and bread. It's all I have.'

She stood and watched as I ate. Perhaps she was concerned that I would make off with the cutlery. The bread was stale and the unidentifiable meat was tough. It was delicious. She showed me the location of the ablutions and my room.

'Thomas will be here about ten in the morning. There'll be bacon, eggs and coffee for breakfast.'

'That's very kind of you,' I said.

'I know.' And with that she wished me goodnight. In candlelight, I poured some icy water from the pitcher into the bowl and washed my face and hands, drying them on a threadbare towel.

The sheets were warm and still feeling the motion of the boat I dropped into a deep sleep on the first night of my mission.

I awoke to a stern knock on my door.

'Breakfast will be on the table in ten minutes.'

It didn't take me long to wash and dress and trim my beard. I had already decided that shaving was something I could do without in a land where water is scarce. I packed my carpet bag, large enough to hold all I needed while travelling, and went downstairs.

Mrs Huxtable was as stiff as ever as she shovelled breakfast on to my plate. The eggs were overdone and swimming in grease and the bacon tasted as if it had been marinated in a salt-pan. But the coffee was good and I wolfed down a couple of cups before it was time to leave. There was no sound from next door. Mrs Huxtable nodded an expressionless farewell as I said goodbye.

Thomas was waiting for me outside, holding on to the reins of two scrawny horses. He seemed perfectly sober and flashed me a toothless smile. I tried out a couple of words of Hottentot on him and his eyes opened wide. He replied, getting his tongue round the clicks in a way I knew I'd never master.

'The master speaks my language!'

'A little,' I said. 'Is Thomas really your name?'

'No, sir, it is ...' and he reeled off a series of clicks and plosives that defied reproduction. 'I'll call you Thomas,' I said.

After establishing that I was British and neither German nor Cape Dutch, he relaxed.

The fog was still hanging around as we mounted and headed for the shore. It was bitterly cold and I was thankful for my thick English jacket and my cap. Thomas had an old towel round his shoulders and a threadbare woollen cap to cover his peppercorn hair.

We soon left the shacks of the port behind us as we trotted through the wet sand on our way north. Tall dunes were on our right and the swell of the sea on our left. The air was damp and salty. I had to remind myself that there was no land between this coast and that of the Americas.

Once we spotted a large brown shaggy creature on the sand, the size of an Irish wolfhound. It turned and snuffled and giggled at us, slavering at the mouth, before loping away with a sort of limp. I realised that it was the same sound as I'd heard in Walfish Bay. The horses shied at the sight of it and we struggled for a while to control them.

'A *strandwolf*,' said Thomas. It was, I thought, a huge species of hyena. I had caught a glimpse of impressive teeth and jaws and decided I was happy for it to leave us alone. 'It won't hurt you unless you're competing for food. They usually eat whatever is washed up on the sand. There are not many of them left.'

The breakers crashed on to the shore at our left and the dunes rose up higher on our right as we traversed the narrow strip between them. There was no one about. Once we disturbed a pelican and I also saw a skein of cormorants skimming the waves.

Thomas chatted away happily as we rode along, telling me about his people and how they had fled the Cape because of their treatment by the Cape Dutch. I was happy to listen to him for it meant he was not quizzing me about the purpose of my journey. At one point, he suddenly reined in his horse.

'Why have we stopped?' I scanned the dunes and the sea for signs of the Germans.

'You are a civilised man. You know something of our language. May I ask a favour?'

'Of course.'

'The Germans and people in Cape Colony call my people Hottentots. I do not like the name. We call ourselves Nama. Would you please use our name?'

I smiled.

'I promise.'

After about twenty miles, having seen no sign of the British side of the border, we were suddenly stopped by a crude wooden barrier ahead, behind which stood a small group of German soldiers in the khaki uniform of the colonial *Schutztruppe*, including the slouch hats with their distinctive rosette. Their horses were tethered to one side. By this time, the sun was climbing the sky, the fog had disappeared and my jacket was slung across my saddle.

An officer signalled me to dismount while casting a dark look at Thomas. The other men had raised their rifles and were clearly on edge.

'Stop where you are!' yelled the officer. 'This is German territory. What is your business?'

'I have an official document that explains why I am here.'

He hesitated. 'Advance and show me your documents.'

His men were still aiming their rifles at me and I had no doubt that they would fire if the order were given.

I trudged through the sand towards them and across the barrier handed the officer my letter from Heinrich Göring. His mouth opened and he read the letter at least twice before barking an order at his men. They lifted the barrier and allowed me through. I said a silent prayer to the German respect for authority, especially when put in writing.

I turned to wave to Thomas but he, with my horse following him, was already on his way back to Walfish Bay without a single look behind him. I was on my own.

'Welcome,' said the officer with a salute. His men lowered their rifles.

I was in German South West Africa.

Three

The dunes on the German side of the border were no neater, no more disciplined than those on the British side. The colonial powers may have drawn a line in the sand but that was all it was. The desert was unmoved.

I was lent a horse and, accompanied by a taciturn trooper, I carried on between the sand and the sea until we reached the shallow brown estuary of the Swakop River. Our horses trod carefully between the scrawny plants and sand islands to the other bank. It was more a river in name than anything else for I saw little sign of water. According to Thomas, it is more often than not just a dry bed and only when the rains come, and that is seldom, does it flow with the murky brown water that, according to Thomas, gives the river its name: push out the shit.

The dunes had flattened out and a short ride took us across the sand to the town of Swakopmund.

What a difference from the ramshackle nondescript cluster of wooden shacks that is Walfish Bay. Here it was all bustle, order and efficiency. Men were rushing about carrying planks and pots of paint to half-finished buildings. There was an air of the American West about the place.

Despite the lack of a natural harbour, there were ships anchored everywhere out at sea. Many of them were unloading soldiers and marines and building materials on to barges that then crashed their way through the surf on to the beach. These were in turn being transported to the town proper.

The streets already had wooden pavements and several buildings had been constructed in an unmistakeably German shape. A Bavarian style railway station and a narrow gauge line that snaked its way through the barren desert and hills all the way up to Windhoek showed just how much the new colony was being shaped. The Germans may have come late to having African colonies but they were clearly determined to put all other nations in the shade. Webb's fears about our South African territory might have had a point after all.

The trooper took me straight up the beach to the sandy hills on which the main town was being constructed. The smell of fresh bread and coffee drifted out from one building which had cream cakes on display in the window. A general store was next door, selling everything from galvanised buckets to beer mugs. A sign indicated the way to a brewery. I was impressed and, to my surprise, a little proud of German zeal and organisation.

Swakopmund was still a small town with about fifteen hundred civilian inhabitants and it took us no more than a few minutes to cross the embryonic streets and up a small sand hill. Almost immediately we were at German military headquarters.

I was ordered to sit on a wooden bench and hand over Göring's letter and left kicking my heels for a long while. I took the opportunity to cross over to a window and look out at the activity outside. I watched the long lines of soldiers and wagons heading for the station. Something was happening for sure. I was also becoming nervous about having to wait: it was looking too easy and my story about collecting native languages sounded thin even to me.

I sat down again on the bench and wondered if I could make a run for it. But then at last an orderly appeared and deferentially handed me back my letter and invited me to follow him. Old Göring's letter still seemed to be working its magic and it later transpired that the delay was caused not because they were suspicious of me but because they didn't know what to do with me. Apparently responsibility for my future was being passed from one officer to another. Well, after all, they did seem to have weightier matters on their hands. Eventually they had found a civilian who had some authority yet had links with the military chain of command. His name was Gans. Maybe the soldiers passed me over to him as some kind of joke: *Gans* means 'goose'. Not a very good joke, to be sure, but soldiers are not normally regarded as great wits.

He didn't look like a goose; his marked overbite made him more of a rodent. In fact, he reminded me somewhat of Webb. I thought he had been shipped in fairly recently by the pale look of him. He had the faint air of a policeman: the kind that stops you in the street and asks you for your papers. That made me once more uneasy. He asked me if he could study my letter which by now was rather grimy and crumpled.

After a period of time during which he gnawed his lip and sniffed, he handed it back to me.

'I am not sure there is any way we can help you,' he began slowly. 'Our settlers are at present under threat and our brave soldiers are preparing to defend them. There is no place for academic research. You are wasting your time.' The way he said it implied that it was his time that was being wasted.

I didn't bother to reason with him; that would have got me nowhere. Instead I took a step forward and suddenly shouted at his pasty face.

'Germany is a great country,' I bellowed, 'and because of its colonies it is about to become an even greater one. It will be built on foundations not only of military strength but also of the newest developments in human knowledge. Knowledge comes from research and I am contributing to research, as *Reichskommissar* Göring has recognised. What are you contributing, *Herr* Gans?'

His mouth dropped open but no noise came out. He was busy recalculating his position. You see, his official life was all about establishing who gave orders and who obeyed them: that was the Prussian ethos that was rapidly spreading like a cancer over the whole of Germany. Strut or grovel – that was the choice the system forced him to make. He grovelled.

'My apologies,' he stammered. 'I misunderstood what you were saying. What do you need?'

'I need to get to Windhoek. See to it. Now.'

That was how, after a cup of excellent coffee and a pastry in town at the newly-opened baker's shop, I found myself waiting at the station in a queue with scores of newly-recruited marines. They were joking with each other and bragging about what they were going to do to 'the natives'. I listened in but learned nothing about where they were going and what they were going to do, for it soon became clear that they had no idea themselves. Soon the queue shortened as we were jammed on to a train. And what a train it was. It resembled nothing I had seen before. It was a miniature train, much like a larger version of the ones played with by children. It consisted of several open wagons drawn by five or six locomotives and it was about to embark on a long, slow and hot ride up to the escarpment.

Within a few minutes of lurching and steaming out of town we were in the vastness of the desert. I glanced back and the town appeared so small, so insignificant, so impermanent that the task the Germans had set themselves of occupying and taming the country suddenly, in spite of their drive and enthusiasm, seemed immense.

The stony desert stretched on for ever. Apart from the green line of trees that marked the course of the Swakop River, there was nothing but a few sparse bushes on each side of the track as far as the eye could see. There was a line of hills in the distance but no sign of habitation. The soldiers soon grew bored and chatted among themselves or tried to sleep.

As we slowly climbed up from the sea, it grew warmer and many of the troops loosened the necks of their tunics or took them off altogether and travelled in their shirt-sleeves. One or two tucked their handkerchiefs under their hats to protect their necks from the sun. They resorted more and more often to taking long drinks from their canteens. The sides of the wagons became almost too hot to touch and I could smell the hot metal of the men's rifles.

The desert landscape was broken only by the stations at which we stopped to stretch our legs or take on water for the engines. The station more often than not was a whitewashed single-storey building on one side of the track accompanied by a water tank and a windmill. The stationmaster always appeared and met us, no doubt pleased to see another human face. His job had to be both hot and lonely.

At first I enjoyed the names of the stations and wrote them down in my note-book. 'Welwitsch', what on earth did that mean? 'Jakalswater', I could make a good guess at that. At a station named 'Sphinx', an inquisitive young marine next to me, who was sitting a little apart from his fellows despite the cramped space, could restrain his curiosity no longer.

'Sir, what are you writing?'

'Here, take a look,' I said, anxious to show I was not recording any secrets.

I told him of my profession and supposed mission and he was only too willing to break the monotony of the journey by telling me his story.

His name was David Bruck and he had lived with his family in a small village in Schleswig-Holstein. He was a slight doe-eyed young man with the makings of a sparse moustache and the scars of acne. To my eyes, they were more genuine than the ritual sabre scars on the cheeks of some of his officers. Most of his fellows, he said, were from families of shoemakers or blacksmiths or similar trades: his father was a jeweller who had ironically escaped from the Russian Pale to avoid military service.

'As Jews,' said my new friend, 'we had no rights except that of dying for the Tsar. My father understandably does not like my joining the marines but finally accepted the argument that we owed it to the Germany that had provided us with sanctuary. My mother said nothing but she cried a lot. She has the gift of prophecy or as some would say, second sight. She had had a vision of my destiny in which she had gathered that I would die in Jerusalem. It gave her some comfort that I was going to Africa.' He laughed and took one of my cigarettes. 'I have no plans to go to Jerusalem. My future is with the new Germany. I don't even speak Yiddish like my parents, only German.' His German was indeed that of an educated man. I guessed that made him pretty unpopular with his fellows. Perhaps that explained why they sat a little apart from him and regarded me with some suspicion. Or there could have been another reason.

'Have you met any hostility in Germany to your being a Jew?' I asked. 'I've heard stories, if you know what I mean.'

He stiffened. 'I am a German soldier. We are all comrades here.'

'Of course,' I said, 'but I was thinking among the German people as a whole.'

'Well,' he said after a pause. 'I've heard that down in Bavaria, there is some talk against us but that is all that it is. Just talk. It's not so bad up where I come from although I was called names at school. You know, 'Christ-killer' – that sort of thing.'

I was intrigued. 'What is the cause of this?'

'It's the Bible.'

'The Bible?'

'Yes, you see, many people accept the words of the Bible as being absolutely true. And it says that we are the Chosen People. So they believe it is true and hate us for it. That is my explanation, anyway.'

I hadn't thought of anti-Semitism in quite that way before. But my job was to find out the German intentions towards South Africa. Perhaps David would let something slip.

'What do you think about this war that is coming?' I asked.

He then told me that everyone in Germany had heard stories of how the natives in the Protectorate were killing German settlers and taking their land. He and the other marines were all eager to take revenge.

'Ever since we sailed from Wilhelmshaven, we have thought of little else. It is our duty,' he said sternly, 'to teach these people a lesson they will never forget.'

He knew little of where they were going and who they were going to fight. I doubt if he even knew much about the place. He certainly stared with open mouth at the dry, rocky country through which we were slowly ascending. It was obvious that he couldn't give me any information. When I reached Windhoek somehow I should have to get to the people in power. And I had absolutely no idea in advance how to do that. I would take the opportunity when it arose.

At one point, we passed through a landscape where the stones and sand were crossed by long black outcrops of shiny curved rock. The result, I guessed, of some volcanic upheavals of aeons ago.

'Like the spines of dragons,' said David a trifle uneasily. 'How are our people going to farm here? I can see only small tufts of yellow grass and no real soil. It is not ideal country for farming.'

'Or anything else,' I suggested. 'For a start, water seems in very short supply. We have crossed over several small river beds that look as if they have not seen a drop of water for centuries.'

'It must be more fertile inland,' he said uncertainly.

'Perhaps the natives could work the land here,' I said. He took this seriously.

'I think their labour will be needed to build the new colony.' That didn't bode well, then, for the natives.

I also learned that the Germans, ever since the death of our Queen, had been steadily building new ships.

'We want a fleet that will rival the Royal Navy. How can we have an Empire equal to theirs if we do not have a navy large enough to defend it?'

So the Germans wanted an Empire to rival ours. That wasn't news. The Kaiser had been saying it for years. But would that include South Africa? Were they really interested in taking over the diamond fields in Griqualand? As I knew from my own experience, they certainly had been more than happy to sell guns and ammunition to the Boers. Well, I now had the chance to find out. But these soldiers didn't know and maybe even the officers wouldn't know, anyway. Possibly only the Kaiser had any idea and he was spoken about in Britain as being highly unstable. I had no wish to create suspicion about my activities so I was content to chat with David about life in Schleswig-Holstein.

After what seemed a lifetime climbing up from the coast, we gradually entered land that sustained more and more grass and quite a few trees and as we approached Windhoek we saw more signs of life. We had caught sight of a couple of ostriches and once a zebra but little else. The marines were quite disappointed, they had expected at least lions and elephants.

Suddenly, there was a burst of excited cries: some of the marines had spotted a few warthogs, their tails sticking up like lightning rods, browsing in the burnt grass by the side of the tracks. Then, further on, there was more excitement as someone pointed out a troop of baboons in some thorn trees.

Suddenly, all talking stopped: we were approaching a farmstead, the first we had seen. An abandoned farmhouse. It was burnt out and a couple of freshly-dug graves were visible under a water tower. A group of jackals scattered at our approach. The soldiers aimed their rifles but the jackals were already slinking away in among the thorn trees.

The soldiers had found the war they had been looking for.

David muttered to me about the atrocities that the natives had been inflicting.

'We have heard stories back in Germany how they cut off the private parts of our wounded men while they were still alive. They are totally uncivilised.' He grinned mirthlessly. 'We shall civilise them.' And he clutched his rifle until the knuckles of his hand turned white.

The silence lasted all the way up to Windhoek. The soldiers disembarked at the station and I said farewell to David. I spoke to a junior officer at the station who pointed out the *Schutztruppe* headquarters and the German Command. Now my story would be tested by professional soldiers.

The city was surrounded by hills whose green and purple colours were a great relief after the khaki of the desert. There were trees and plants although the ground was still bare rock covered with sand. Many houses of German design had already sprung up on the lower hills within the city and there was a bustling air to the place that was augmented by the military activity that was visible everywhere one looked. Tents had sprung up below the fort and everything from machine-guns to cannons were being assembled. I could also see several heliographs: given the limitless amount of sunshine in this country, with their movable mirrors they would be the most efficient way of sending messages. A great number of horses were tethered under some trees out of the sun. I could smell their hot dung as I passed.

The atmosphere at this elevation was warm but the air was dry and thin. Windhoek was several thousand feet above sea level and I found it tiring to walk in the sun up a hill from the station to the Fort.

It was an impressive place, with four crenellated towers at each corner and with high stone walls. The imperial flag fluttered against the bright blue sky from a tall pole. It dominated the city and was meant to although I noticed a cornerstone for a church had been laid not far from the Fort. From what I had heard from Göring, the country was already buzzing with missionaries so no doubt the native inhabitants would soon be colonised body and soul just as they had been in South Africa. However, I was looking to tap into the missionaries not only for my research, which I had already decided to pursue in earnest, but also for information. If anyone had their ear to the ground, it would be them as well as any traders I might come across.

I found my way inside the Fort and after being stopped several times by sentries, I was led into the office of a senior adjutant who had his back to me.

He was as thin as whipcord and his bronzed neck and hands indicated that he was no newcomer to the country. He was working on some maps which I tried, unsuccessfully, to read upside down.

As I entered, he looked up impatiently.

'Yes?'

Then suddenly his face changed.

'My God,' he said, 'Is it really you?'

His voice gave him away. Although he was a German and spoke German, there was a twang to his vowels and diphthongs that indicated long term exposure to Cape Dutch. And it was a voice from the past, my past in the recent war in the south.

'Hartmann!' I said. This was a stroke of luck, finding someone who knew me.

Hartmann stood up and strode across the room, holding out his hand. He was as I remembered him, tall, slim and elegant with a small trimmed moustache. He had the reputation when I knew him of being a stickler for discipline but with a keen sense of duty and an excellent field-commander. It seemed the Germans also appreciated his gifts for I noticed that he had been promoted. The bright blue eyes gleamed intelligently in his tanned face.

'It is good to see you again, my friend, and the beard suits you,' he said, shaking my hand with the firm grip I remembered so well.

'And I am pleased to see you, Hartmann.' My handshake was genuinely warm. Hartmann could well be the key to open the door to my mission. If he had a key role in the German campaign against the Ovaherero, then he might also be party to any intentions to invade South Africa. As a former comrade in arms, he might just reveal to me any vital information. I was anxious to start asking him questions so I could guide the conversation that way. 'How did you get here? Last time I saw you, you were in South Africa being chased by English cavalry.'

His face darkened.

'We managed to get away in the confusion,' he said.

'We?'

'I was with Weiss. He had links with this country so we eventually ended up here. There's a great future in the South West for Germany. We're both still fighting though now we have a different enemy.' He let go of my hand. 'Come, join me in a drink and tell me why you are here.'

As he poured a schnapps, I explained my declared mission and showed him Göring's letter. He read it and handed it back to me and smiled.

'You always were a bookish fellow. Even when we fought at Elandslaagte, you always had a book with you.'

I smiled back. I didn't want to linger on the subject of that battle. He persisted.

'Did you know we were betrayed? Someone told the English of our position.'

Of course I knew. I was the one who'd got a message through to the British commander. I'd given a verbal message in Zulu to one of the miners from the town. But I registered surprise all the same.

'Really? That is hard to believe.'

'Yes but it doesn't matter. Now we have other things to think about. These damned natives.'

'Tell me,' I said.

And I heard the same story of settlers, of broken treaties, of stolen cattle, of burnt farms, of murdered farmers and of reprisals. Then, to my surprise, Hartmann suddenly stopped. He lowered his voice.

'And we have been getting nowhere,' he muttered. 'We have recently had a bad defeat at Oviumbo. Governor Leutwein is bungling the whole campaign. If we are not careful we could lose all that we have built up here.' Then, raising his voice again, 'come and have a spot of lunch at my place.'

As we walked, he pointed out how fast the town was developing. 'You've already seen the Fort and I assume you noticed the cathedral. The court house is also under construction; we must have order here.'

'You have a prison, then?'

'Of course. And down there is the camp we are preparing for prisoners of war. There they shall learn to work for the glory of Germany.'

There was a gleam in his eyes that revealed something of the fanatic within. It was a look that was becoming more common all over Germany. These days even the most intelligent Prussian has a touch of the bully about him. The Kaiser was not the only German who had dreams of ancient glories.

His place was a newly-constructed bungalow on the outskirts of town. It was set in a garden full of sturdy bushes, probably imported from Germany. I preferred the honesty of the local thorn trees on the stony hillock at the back. The plants were tended by a surly young black man, barely out of his teens, who stood back as we passed: Hartmann said something to him that I couldn't hear but I was distracted by the sun glinting on a rather unusual row of large white stones forming the border of one bush. I nudged one with my foot and immediately stepped back with a small gasp. It was a bleached human skull.

Four

As fast as a striking mamba, Hartmann's arm whipped out and struck the young gardener full in the face. He must have worn a ring, for immediately a fierce cut appeared on the lad's cheek. He staggered back a couple of paces, tripped over his rake and landed on his ragged rear upon the stony soil. His face was contorted with fear and pain.

'You fool,' said Hartmann in a dispassionate voice. 'I told you to dig that thing up. Do it now. And all the others and then clean them and pack them in the box I gave you. And if you damage them, I'll damage you.'

He kicked the boy, who scurried off, and indicated to me to follow him into the bungalow.

'Idiot!' He threw his hat across the room aiming at an ornate hat stand. He missed. 'Lazy, stupid idiot. These people are useless. You ask them to do something and they either make a meal of it or get it wrong. Pah!'

I sat down in a heavy armchair with a springbok hide as a cover.

'Boy!'

Another youth, naked to the waist, came running from another room.

'Lunch! Now! For two.'

The boy crouched there, open mouthed, indecision and fear fighting for dominance.

'Bread, meat, beer. Quickly!'

I sat and watched and said nothing, letting the scene play itself out. Hartmann snorted and flung himself into another over-stuffed armchair. His chair was decorated by the skin of a cheetah.

'I'm sorry about that,' he said, not sounding the least bit apologetic.

'The army top brass have been after me – and my fellows – to stop us using those things outside as garden ornaments. Some kind of scientist has arrived from Berlin, a Doctor Fischer, who wants the skulls for scientific study; apparently he intends to examine them for physical signs of degeneracy in these savages.' Hartmann snorted. 'He actually wants to prove they are animals and inferior to us Germans. Such nonsense and a total waste of time. We already know they are not far above the apes. What else is there to study? We should concentrate on getting rid of them. Which is what I wanted to talk to you about.'

'Where do they come from?'

'What?'

'The skulls, where did you find them?'

He grinned mirthlessly. 'I didn't find them, I claimed them. After a skirmish a few months ago, I had them cleaned and brought here. A lot of the fellows did the same. After all, we had great sport hunting them down.'

The boy returned carrying a tray with two beers, some *brötchen*, a hunk of cheese and a small plate of salami. His hand shook as he laid out the crockery. It was fine bone china and there was a delicate lace cloth on the tray. It contrasted oddly with the rest of the room. Hartmann waited for him to turn to leave but not before swiftly glancing at him. I've seen that kind of look before. So that was where his inclinations lay. It was no concern of mine and I mentally shrugged and turned back to Hartmann.

'Are you not concerned that these boys might attack you? Especially if those skulls ...'

He laughed and stood up. In a wall mirror, decorated with native beads, he inspected his moustache and scars. Satisfied at what he saw, he turned and sat down again.

'My *Bambusen*? No, they are Damara. They used to be the virtual slaves of the Herero – and it's the Herero we are fighting. No, I'm pretty safe and, in any case, I have this with me all the time.' He took his pistol from its holster and placed it on the embroidered table-cloth.

I glanced around the room whose white-washed walls were stained brown from tobacco smoke. It was furnished with the usual massed skulls of antelope – kudu, oryx, impala and a couple of water buffalo, interspersed with festoons of ostrich eggs, hanging like balloons. On a side table was the large shell of a tortoise, next to another table with a couple of half-full decanters.

More skins, including one of a leopard, were flung over a sofa. Two large oriental fans were displayed incongruously on another wall. I idly wondered if Hartmann had shot their owner. It struck me yet again that most people who have spent time in Africa return with hunting trophies of one kind or another. How long would it be before there would be nothing left to hunt? But then there were always people. I reached for some cheese and bread.

'So what do you want to tell me?'

Hartmann grimaced as he drained half of his glass of beer. 'It's the war. It's not going very well. Leutwein, the Governor, is too hesitant. We need a firm hand here if we are to solve the problem once and for all. The settlers are not happy, I'm not happy and, most important, Berlin is not happy. The word is that they are on the verge of appointing a new leader, someone strong and not namby-pamby. We should hear who it will be any day now. I mean, we marched south to meet and defeat the stupid Bondelswarts rebellion and immediately we have had to turn round because the Herero took advantage of our absence to start causing trouble to the north of here. But with a new leader I'm sure we shall march and make good use of all the men and materials we are accumulating. And when we march, you shall come with me and collect your languages in the same way as the scientists are collecting information about these savages. More beer?' Going with Hartmann was ideal for my purpose; that way I could establish if all those men and all those guns really were for use against the Ovaherero.

I didn't learn much more from Hartmann after that. Apart, that is, from repeating the old stories about British atrocities in the late war.

'They tried to exterminate the Cape Dutch in those camps, everyone knows that, although they claim they were just holding them there to isolate the men. What nonsense.'

He stubbed out his cigarette and drained his glass.

'What is more, they are saying in Berlin that it is common knowledge that Jewish finance was behind the British war effort. They're behind everything, of course. His Majesty the Kaiser has been known to say as much.'

I'm sure the young marine, David, would be delighted to hear that.

'I believe the Tsar of Russia has much the same views,' I added.

'No doubt, no doubt. And he is dealing with it by pushing them into Germany. Have you read the Protocols of the Elders of Zion?'

I nodded. Of course I had. It was a crude forgery, dreamed up somewhere in Russia, possibly by the Secret Service, the Okhrana. It claimed that there was a world-wide conspiracy by Jews to take over the world.

'It just proves that the scum are preparing to take over. Well, we'll see about that.'

I said nothing. You cannot reason with people who believe what they want to believe.

'Now,' said Hartmann, 'you'll need somewhere to stay and I think I know just the place. There's a missionary and his wife who have a spare room and I know I can persuade them to put you up until we start fighting.'

That was a relief as I had no wish to bunk down with him. Fortunately, he felt the same way.

'I'll take you there,' he said. 'I don't hold too much with missionaries as a rule, they give the natives ideas above their station. But old Reinhart is a fine fellow and has colleagues all over the country that you could stay with. What is more, you'll be safe at the mission stations when we travel as rumour has it that the Herero have said they will attack only German settlers and soldiers and leave missionaries and the English alone, damn them. I doubt if they will keep their word but they seem to have held to it so far.'

It didn't take us too long to walk across the city to Pastor Reinhart's bungalow. It was pretty enough and, as far as I could tell, there were no skulls in the front garden.

Hartmann introduced us and left abruptly, as if anxious to get home. I don't think he was hurrying back to do the washing-up.

Reinhart was a jolly looking fellow with kind eyes, a large paunch and a huge white beard. His wife, on the other hand, was stick thin but very friendly and welcoming. Their house was simple and unadorned except for a small crucifix on one white-washed wall. No heads of beasts here. There were scores of photographs, presumably of relatives, scattered around on any free surface. Neither were there any servants. Mrs Reinhart brought in coffee and homemade biscuits as we sat and talked of nothing in particular as strangers do, until we came to the native uprising.

'It must be heart-rending for you to witness this war,' I said, taking another biscuit.

The pastor and his wife exchanged glances. He sighed and put down his coffee cup.

'You will find out sooner or later,' he said. 'It is like this. Not all of us missionaries are of the same opinion. Some, seeing the attacks on German families and in many cases having buried them, have called for the soldiers to bring down God's wrath on the natives. Others are appalled at how their native converts have had their land and cattle taken from them by the settlers and, in addition, have been cheated by traders. It is a sorry business.'

I thought that was all they were going to say when his wife spoke up, blushing as she did so.

'Governor Leutwein addressed us all recently. He made it clear that the natives should either work for our German settlers or be restricted to rather limited reserves. The main aim of the government, he said, was to prepare the country for colonisation and that the natives are only of secondary importance.' She lowered her eyes and touched her Bible that was lying on a table next to her. 'We pray for all of them. I am afraid that some of the mission stations where you are going will not care too much about the natives, apart from their souls, and will pray for a German victory.'

She blushed again and rushed out to the kitchen muttering something about coffee.

Reinhart closed his eyes and after a few seconds I realised he was praying.

I didn't ask them which camp they were in and they didn't say. But they did ask me to pray with them. I've had to do it before and as I was their guest I made no objection. And, anyway, the coffee and biscuits were really rather good.

I stayed with them for over a week. Most of the time I spent tracking down people from different tribes and starting on trying to pick up their languages. It wasn't easy as I had few interpreters to assist me in the early stages and, above all, most of the people I spoke to were wary and tried to stay away from me. As everyone assumed I was a German, that wasn't surprising at all. At least they didn't attack me.

Most of the time I was left to my own devices and I spent many hours in the small garden at the back of the house. There was little soil and it consisted mainly of thorn trees growing on a stony hillside. Very biblical. There were a few flowers and vegetables but they were constantly under attack from mousebirds and large rodents, the rock hyraxes. It was pleasant to sit there in the shade, looking at maps, writing up my language notes and reading a hopelessly optimistic pamphlet that the pastor had written about the country. Apparently God would see that all would turn out well and that the people of the South West would all be united in worship of Him. In my view, He had rather a big task on His hands.

On the eighth day, I had just finished my breakfast when a message arrived from Hartmann. I was to go at once to the Fort. The new General had arrived.

I was sorry to say goodbye to the Reinharts; they were decent people who were worried about the direction that the country was taking. They refused any payment for my stay and, in anticipation of this, I had bought them some small gifts in the city. They were as pleased as punch and I could have sworn I saw a tear in the corner of *Frau* Reinhart's eye. She handed me a small bag of biscuits and biltong for the journey.

'My husband made the biltong,' she said shyly. The pastor himself embraced me and handed me a letter.

'This is addressed to my colleagues,' he said gruffly. 'I have asked them to give you what assistance they can. In particular, I have pointed out that the more people who learn the native languages, the more we can translate God's word for the benefit of the pagans in this country.' I couldn't have put it better myself.

As I made my way to the Fort, I sensed a new atmosphere among the troops. There seemed to be an air of excitement and the soldiers were running at the double and smiling as they did so. I'd seen that before. It was anticipation of war among soldiers who'd had little experience of it. From what I'd heard, up to now this had been a guerrilla war where you don't see the enemy until they swoop down, kill some of your fellows and ride off again. It had been like that in South Africa most of the time. The enemy didn't play fair and seldom offered a conventional pitched battle. On the other hand, the Ovaherero didn't have machine guns. Either way, it would be long and bloody. If these young fellows hoped for a quick victory, they were almost certainly in for an unpleasant surprise.

I waited for a train of overloaded bullock carts that had come up from the coast to plod past and then I entered the Fort. It was even more hectic here. Field guns were being cleaned and inspected. Ammunition boxes were being manhandled by soldiers on to ox carts. Troopers were grooming their mounts. Soldiers were everywhere at the double. The excitement was palpable.

Hartmann was pleased to see me. He had a cigar in his mouth and was rolling up maps. A rifle stood in the corner, newly polished and a pair of binoculars perched on his desk.

'Come, come!' he cried. 'Leutwein has been forced to accept a real soldier to lead the troops.' A note of awe crept into his voice. 'Have you heard of Lothar von Trotha?'

Indeed I had. He had first made his mark in the German contingent to Peking, to help put down the Boxers. Actually, the Germans were the last of the eight foreign powers to arrive in China but that didn't stop them from acting in a way that raised the eyebrows of the others, none of whom were angels. My cousin is still living off the proceeds of the loot he handled for the British contingent. But the Kaiser had given orders for the Germans to act without mercy and kill all the Chinese revolutionaries and take no prisoners. Of course they obeyed their orders. And von Trotha was among them. That was just the start of his career.

'He already has had a great deal of experience in Africa,' said Hartmann. 'He knows these people and how to deal with them. He proved that in German East Africa.'

His handling of the native uprising there was notorious for the utmost severity with which he had put it down. General von Trotha was just the man to bring civilisation to the South West. Hartmann seemed to think so, anyway.

'The man is a legend,' he said. 'It is an honour to serve under him. We shall take the fight to the enemy and in his own territory. One good thing Leutwein did do was to herd the Herero north at the Waterberg. Now the Herero shall feel the full might of the German Empire.' So maybe that conventional pitched battle was going to happen after all.

He went on in this manner for some time as he packed his gear. I'd heard it all before which meant I could try and work out how I could observe the war without actually getting killed by one side or the other. I needn't have worried, Hartmann had already thought about that.

'The General has graciously agreed to take you with us. He at first thought you might be a burden but I told him of your fighting prowess in South Africa and he has agreed that you should bear arms with us.'

'That is truly generous of him,' I said. I should have been an actor. Hartmann hadn't finished. 'He also welcomes your study of the native languages. You will be able to interpret for us and persuade any prisoners to surrender if they value their lives. You may also interrogate the prisoners. If there are any.'

So I was going to war whether I wanted to or not.

'We leave in an hour,' said Hartmann. 'Be ready.'

Waterberg, I gathered, was about 200 miles north of Windhoek. It was basically a large mountain complex and the Ovaherero tribes and their beloved cattle were gathered around the springs at its foot. It was going to be a long slow and very hot journey.

The troops were assembling in a long train that would head north. As well as the mounted troopers, there were ox wagons full of soldiers, food, water, ammunition and machine guns, in short all the necessities of modern life. In addition, there were the field guns. A crowd of civilian onlookers, including women and children, were watching the small army and waving handkerchiefs. I even heard a few shouts encouraging them to take revenge for the loss of good German lives.

I heard a voice cry out my name. I turned and saw young David hurrying towards me. He was wearing two bandoliers of brand-new leather ammunition pouches across his chest.

'Hello,' he cried, panting a little in the thin air. 'I hear you are joining us. What is more, we shall be in the same section.'

His face, now reddening with the sun, displayed a wide grin. 'Yes, at last the war has begun! We are marching towards the enemy!'

I could not resist trying to bring him down to earth.

'There are other enemies you must watch out for. Malaria, typhoid, they will kill or disable as many troops as the Ovaherero. Keep yourself clean and cover yourself at night.'

'Of course! But look at our magnificent forces!'

It was certainly a formidable body of men. Yet, as we moved away from the city and into the stony veldt, it seemed small and insignificant.

The landscape was dotted with thorn trees and yellow grass and small hills were visible through the heat haze. There was little sign of human habitation. A tree covered with a huge nest of weaver birds stimulated some interest as did a hornbill gliding overhead but the overall atmosphere was shaped by the lowing of oxen, the jangle of harness, the cracking of whips and the constant shouts to keep in line.

In a matter of moments of leaving the city, the smart uniforms of the soldiers and the glossy coats of the horses were all covered in a coating of dust that was kicked up by boots and hooves. I was not in a German uniform but had kitted myself out in a plain khaki shirt and trousers with leather boots. I had no intention of providing a target for an Otjiherero rifle. My hat had been given me by Pastor Reinhart. I looked more like a cowboy than a soldier, which suited me just fine.

There was also no road to speak of but a badly defined trail snaking through the veldt and leading who knows where. As we went further north, the trail grew wider and dustier and there were piles of cattle droppings everywhere. We were following the path of the Ovaherero, thousands of them by their spoor. Some of the soldiers began to look a trifle uneasy and their eyes were constantly on the lookout for signs of an ambush.

We did come across some villages but they were deserted save for a dog or two. The soldiers burned them down anyway.

As time passed, the dust became thicker as did the flies swarming around the horse and ox dung.

About a quarter of the way to the Waterberg, I saw my first Ovaherero 'in the wild'. A group had been found wandering lost in the bush and had been rounded up by some troopers and brought in for questioning. I was summoned to assist with interpreting. David looked as if he wanted to come with me but the messenger made it clear that Hartmann had asked only for me. I wiped some dust off my face and lips and swigged a mouthful of water from my water-bottle.

It turned out that they were only old men and women. According to Hartmann, this was why they had been taken in. If there were no young men, then it meant they were off fighting. So these wretches were guilty by association.

'It is possible that they know if any bands of the enemy are waiting to ambush us. It is the kind of cowardly thing they do.'

Hartmann led me through the maze of ox wagons and troopers to a group of thorn trees that gave little shelter from the sun. The prisoners were huddled together in a vain attempt at protection.

The women were naked to the waist and wore cow hide skirts. On their heads was a peculiar tall leather headdress that resembled a sort of three-horned hat. They carried themselves well but were clearly frightened by the sight of so many armed men. None of them looked us in the eye and kept their gaze firmly fixed on the dust at their feet. Pastor Reinhart in Windhoek had said the Ovaherero women were often abused by settlers and traders and these people had obviously heard the same stories.

The old men were bags of bones but all of them had distended stomachs. The war had not treated them well. They would obviously be a burden to any force and had been abandoned by the main Ovaherero army. They stood around the women as if they could protect them. Much good would it do them.

Just before I started talking to them, Hartmann grabbed my arm. He was visibly excited.

'We are being given a great honour,' he said. 'The General himself has stated that he desires to witness the interrogation. You will be introduced to him.' He obviously expected me to express awe and wonder and I did manage to nod gravely.

As I waited, I began thinking of how I could overcome Webb's ban on communication and get a message to him without compromising myself or my mission. It was already clear to me that Webb had sent me on a wild goose chase. There was no obvious sign at all that the Germans wanted to go south. They had more than enough on their hands putting down the natives here.

All I had managed to do was carry out Webb's other order. Every day on the pretext of finding out about local tribes, I picked out a soldier who looked as if he had been in the country for some time.

'You must know a great deal about this country,' I'd begin and then while he was still smirking with flattery, 'what can you tell me about the local tribes?'

Anxious to display his knowledge, he was ripe for other questions.

'It's fortunate we have a garrison there.'

He'd nod or shake his head. This way I began building up a map in my head of German forts, relay stations and garrisons.

During one of these interrogations, David had suddenly appeared. It is fortunate I have good peripheral vision, a necessary weapon in a spy's armoury.

'Still conducting research, sir?'

'Indeed,' I replied. 'The languages and their distribution are even more complicated than I had imagined.'

He nodded. I would have to be even more vigilant in future.

I still hadn't figured out how to contact Webb when there was a ripple of anticipation and straightening of uniforms among the soldiers guarding the prisoners. Out of sight of their officers, they surreptitiously polished their boot caps on the backs of their trousers, threw back their shoulders and stared straight ahead. Hartmann barked an order and then their ranks parted and I came face to face for the first time with General Lothar von Trotha, the hero of Peking, the scourge of East Africa and now soon to be the saviour of German South West Africa.

Five

At first sight he looked like a caricature of a Prussian officer, with a Kaiser moustache preening itself above a stern mouth. He was costumed in an immaculate khaki field uniform, including highly polished riding boots and a new slouch hat. One leg was thrust forward and one hand was posed on his hip while the other held the inevitable whip. I assumed the stance must have taken hours to perfect in front of a mirror. To my eye he looked as if he lunched well. All in all, he would have made a splendid recruiting poster.

Berlin maidens might swoon and dream of him at night but to me he represented all I disliked about Prussia. His eyes suggested he didn't smile much although they projected intelligence. The whip and the boots, in particular, spoke volumes: he was yet another bully albeit one who was no fool. You don't become a general just by being a bully. As it turned out, he was much worse than a bully. After all, you don't pacify East Africa just with a whip. A demonstration soon followed.

He pointed the whip at the group of wretches and asked no one in particular what information they had to offer.

Hartmann was there in a flash, ever ready to give keenness a bad name.

'The interrogation was just about to begin when you arrived, my General.' He pointed at me. 'This is the man I was telling you about.'

I was granted a glance in my direction and a slight inclination of the General's head.

'Begin.'

'What does the General wish to know?'

He awarded me a flinty stare and impatiently tapped his boot with his whip.

'Ask where their men are. Ask exactly where the Herero have gone. Ask what weapons they have. That sort of thing.'

In the limited Otjiherero I had picked up, I asked the questions. Each was received with an uncomprehending silence. All I received in return were wide eyes and trembling limbs. I could smell their fear. I asked again, gently using what polite expressions I knew, hoping against hope they would say something that would satisfy the General although I already guessed that he was the kind of man who would never be satisfied.

'Please tell us where your people are. I am sure they are long gone by now but this soldier wishes to know for sure. I see no cattle. Have they gone too?'

One old man who had lost his mind started mumbling to himself, rolling his eyes and grinning at the sky but the silence of the others hung between us. It was broken by the General.

'Flog them,' he said. 'Loosen their tongues. We need to continue our march and I cannot waste any more time.'

Hartmann eagerly barked an order and some of the soldiers grabbed the prisoners and pushed them to the ground. An old man, who was already bent double with age, was hauled to the tree and tied to it. The skin at his wrists was bleeding before it even began. The women began wailing and despite commands to stop, they continued throughout the flogging like Hell's version of a celestial choir.

A soldier stripped to the waist and I noted the sharp contrast between his tanned face and neck and his white skin blotched with sweat. He grinned and raised a short whip. It was a sjambok, made out of rhinoceros hide and capable of stripping the skin from a man's back in two or three strokes. I'd seen it used in South Africa. I'd seen one in *Reichskommissar* Göring's house. I guessed Göring and this Omuherero were about the same age. The old man would talk or die. I already knew it might be both.

The first blow etched a dark red stripe on his bone-stretched skin and his breathed whistled as he cried out. The cries of the women turned for a moment to deep groans. The second blow crossed the mark of the first in an obscene cross. The old man voided his bowels.

'Enough,' said the General, pinching his nose against the smell. 'Ask

45

them again.' Hartmann looked disappointed but ordered the flogging to cease.

I asked the questions again as commanded. One woman, her empty breasts hanging flat against her chest, stood up and took a step towards me. The soldiers raised their rifles but I indicated them to hold their fire.

'We know nothing,' she whimpered, 'nothing at all. We are poor people who have lost our cattle. We have been left behind to fend for ourselves. All we know is that everyone, all the men and women and all their cattle, have gone north with Paramount Chief Maherero. All the clans had been summoned. Those of us here have been left behind because we are all too sick to travel. We have no idea of what other plans there were or what weapons the men carried. These words are true. I beg you to leave us alone and go on your way.'

I gave the gist of this to von Trotha, stressing their innocence and ignorance.

The General thought about this for at least thirty seconds.

'Are they telling the truth?' he said to me.

'I believe so, sir.'

He pondered for another thirty seconds.

'Very well. Their usefulness is at an end. They have admitted that their families are fighting against us and that makes them all traitors and enemies of the Empire. In any case, they are half-starved and not fit for work. Hang them.'

Hartmann ordered a cart to be drawn up under the tree. The prisoners were made to stand on the cart while rough nooses were placed around their necks and slung over branches of the thorn tree. The old man, blood streaming down his back, was held up by two of the women. The keening and moaning had stopped. The mad old man was still grinning and mumbling even as the noose was placed around his neck. Hartmann smiled as he gave the order. A soldier whipped the horses and the cart drove off, leaving the Ovaherero dangling. I distinctly heard the flogged man's neck snap. He was the lucky one.

As we rode on, David joined me. He was looking distinctly green. I turned round and saw all their bodies, men and women, swinging from the thorn tree. One or two of them were still kicking. I found myself glad that no children had been captured.

'Is this what you expected from the war?'

David licked his dry lips.

'These people have killed innocent German farmers,' he muttered.

'Really? They didn't look capable of killing anyone.'

'The General did the right thing,' he said and rode off.

I looked up, shielding my eyes against the sun. Already a couple of vultures were riding the air above the tree. I was now certain I would see many more of them before the war was over. A trooper captured the heroic scene with a large clumsy camera and tripod before we were dismissed.

A dust-devil suddenly sprang out of nowhere and whirled past us, causing one or two troopers to flinch nervously.

As the days went by, we pushed further into Otjiherero territory. We passed more burnt villages and witnessed more hangings.

I shouldn't have slept at all but in war you tend to grow a hard shell round your feelings. Otherwise you lose your senses. I've seen it happen too many times. So I slept like a log but one night I was woken at dawn by the young soldier, David. We had not spoken much since that first execution but when the troops were divided into sections, he stayed with me and sometimes nodded at me across the lines of men and horses. When we did speak he asked me about life in Britain and my time in South Africa. That morning, when he shook me awake, I saw by the expression on his face that something was wrong.

'Sir, sir,' he said. 'Come quick, we need your advice.'

'We?'

'The doctor, sir, I am assisting him.'

I had not met the doctor. I didn't even know there was one. Now I was to meet him and Lord knows what for.

David led me through the stirring of the camp and I had just a moment to take in the beauty of the sun bursting in the morning sky. There is nothing like a morning in Africa, each day is a new birth.

On the outskirts of the main group of tents was the sick bay, another tent to which the sick soldier had been taken. Standing next to the tent was an officer I had not seen before. David introduced us, somewhat incongruously as if we had been at a tea-party.

'Sir, this is Doctor Strauss.' My civilian dress meant I was not entitled to a salute. We shook hands.

Strauss was a gaunt figure, dressed like all the soldiers in creased khaki. I took him to be middle-aged but it was difficult to tell. He was another new arrival from Germany. There were no medical epaulettes on his uniform.

'I didn't know we had any doctors in this column,' I said.

It quickly transpired that Doctor Strauss was very competent in his field and had even had papers accepted in professional journals on several diseases. He told me so himself. The only problem was that they were the diseases of animals.

'I am a veterinary surgeon,' he explained. 'I was selected as part of the force to take care of the horses and oxen.'

I could see why his face was etched with worry. Horses were one thing but now he was dealing with the diseases and sicknesses of men and not just any men, but soldiers.

'Soldiers do not expect to get killed or wounded; that always happens to the fellow next to you. Even less do they expect to fall sick. What is more, this is a foreign land and has its own foreign and frightening illnesses.'

That is very true. I have seen diseases that could ambush one silently and deadlier than a native warrior.

A soldier I did not recognise lay inside the medical tent, his body racked with fever. The tent was stuffy and smelled of sickness. It did little to ward off the heat that was already rising although it was not long since dawn. The soldier's uniform was soaked with sweat and he was tossing and turning on his camp bed.

'At first I thought it was malaria,' said Strauss, chewing his moustache. 'This area is less dry, especially since we have moved further north and entered the heartland of the Hereros. They have abandoned this land for their withdrawal to the Waterberg. Here they kept cattle and the waterholes that enabled them to survive. And with the waterholes came the mosquitoes. That's why I considered malaria but now I'm not so sure. Quinine seems to have no effect. This marine appears to think you might know as you have lived in this part of the world.'

'May I ask a question?' I said.

'Of course.'

'Why is there no doctor with these troops?'

Strauss snorted.

'There was one but just before we left he was run over by an ox cart.

He is back in hospital in Windhoek.'

From Strauss's tone, I guessed he thought the doctor to be lucky.

I took a look at the sick soldier. There are many causes of fever and Africa nurtures many fevers. I had no idea at all what was wrong with the fellow.

'If it had been rinderpest, I'd have diagnosed it and been able to treat it,' he said with a grimace. 'So what to do? This man is a highly skilled heliograph operator and replacing another who was bitten by a scorpion near the Waterberg. If he dies, it could upset the General's battle plan.'

Not to mention upsetting the General himself.

It was then that David intervened and proposed what I thought was a good idea and it recalled what Pastor Reinhart had told me about a network of missionaries.

'One of the troopers who has lived in this country says there is a mission station not too far away,' David said. 'He has given me very clear directions as to its location. We could ride there with the sick trooper and a small guard to see if the pastor can help. He will be much more familiar with the symptoms and the cure. These missionaries treat the natives all the time. At the very least he might be able to diagnose what is wrong with the fellow.'

Strauss's mournful face lit up.

'Excellent!'

'We shall have to get permission from the General to ride ahead,' I cautioned.

Hartmann was in his tent, having his boots polished by a young trooper. The acrid smell of a cigar clenched between his teeth caught at my throat as I entered.

'Hail!' he cried. 'Come in, my friend. I am almost done.'

There were no other chairs so I had to stand while the trooper finished his work which was rewarded with a curt nod.

'Get out!'

The trooper stood, saluted and scuttled out of the tent in one seamless movement.

'Let us go for a stroll while we chat,' he suggested.

'What about your clean boots?'

He raised a surprised eyebrow.

'What about them?'

'They've just been cleaned.'

He raised an astonished eyebrow. 'There is much dust here but there are also many troopers. Now what do you want?'

Solders were stirring all around us as we walked. The smell of wood smoke indicated breakfast was not far off. A whiff of coffee tantalised us.

'The General seems to be a man who knows what he wants,' I began by way of breaking the ice.

'Of course. What is more important, he takes firm action to make sure he gets what he wants. The Empire needs more men like him. You saw how he dealt with the rebels. By the way, he is impressed with your conduct. Most civilians would have been overcome with weakness.'

'War blunts the sensibilities,' I replied.

'Absolutely, and a good thing, too.'

I then explained about the sick heliograph operator. Hartmann stopped and frowned.

'We must have the man. Good communications are essential in any war.'

'So will you agree that we should take him to this Mission that the soldier mentioned so we might have a chance to cure him?'

Hartmann threw away his cigar butt.

'The Jew boy is right. Of course you must go. Thank you for suggesting this course of action. I shall bring it to the attention of the General.' I wondered about his description of David as 'a Jew boy'. How did he know?

And if things went wrong and the trooper died, David, the vet and I could be scapegoats. I expected nothing less from Hartmann.

'Very well,' I said. I was not a German soldier and if things became tetchy I could always take my leave.

Hartmann must have read my mind. 'And for the duration of this campaign, you are under military command,' he said. 'The General insisted on awarding you that privilege.'

'How very kind,' I said as Hartmann transferred his attention to his boots. No doubt another soldier would soon be called to give them a polish. I strolled back to give the good news to the vet.

And so it came to pass that soon afterwards I found myself riding on an ox cart driven by a heavily-bearded Boer and containing the sick man, with David and three other soldiers for protection, towards the mission station that would bring an interesting test of my abilities.

The countryside was deserted. We passed abandoned native villages with only yapping half-starved dogs as inhabitants. Otherwise, there was just burnt grassland, thorn trees and the dry red soil of Africa. Not for the last time I wondered why the Germans had wanted to come here. I could not see a farmer making a living unless he owned a farm larger than any in Europe.

We surprised some guinea fowl, which make good eating, and warthog which do not. An occasional bee-eater glided overhead and once in the distance I heard an elephant rumble his presence. I also knew there were lions, leopards and cheetah in this country. It was hostile in every sense of the word.

The sun was hot enough for us to pause every now and then to drink from our water bottles. Once we were relieved to come across a waterhole and the men and their horses quickened their pace. Even as one of the men dismounted I called out.

'Wait!'

The soldier looked up. He had already gone down on one knee to drink. 'Wait? Why?'

'It may be poisoned. Possibly the Ovaherero have left us a gift. Allow me.' Guerilla fighters had been known to poison wells. Equally undesirably, animals frequently urinated in the very water they drank from.

The soldier stood back, holding tight to his horse which was skittish at the smell of water. I leaned down and gingerly passed a few drops over my lips.

'It's all right,' I said at last. 'It's not fouled but I suggest you drink small amounts. I shall boil my share before I refill my canteen. You should do the same.'

We built a small fire and boiled the water while the horses drank their fill.

As we moved on, I was looking for landmarks but in every direction the view was the same; dry yellow grass and fierce thorn trees.

'Are you sure we are on the right track?' I said to David.

'My information said we should come across two hills that resemble a woman's bosom,' he said, lowering his voice. 'The Mission is on the south side. It has a windmill powering a water pump; you really can't miss it.'

By mid-day, the heat haze made it difficult to estimate distances and even to make out physical features. A tree would suddenly loom ahead of us and a huge pile of rocks that seemed to be miles away, in the end would turn out to be rather modest in size and quite near at hand. And then I saw them.

Jutting proudly out of the surrounding country, the two soft green mounds could be nothing but breasts. Even one of the soldiers pointed out the resemblance though in a crude manner. Whereas I, fresh from reading Mr Haggard quite recently, named them in my head as Sheba's Breasts although I doubted there would be any diamond mines nearby nor a White Queen. Well, not quite. And there would certainly be breasts.

The oxen and horses must have smelled water for they lifted their heads and increased their pace. Through the dust and heat haze, a water pump became visible and then a squat stone house and another building alongside that I assumed was the church. It had hitching rails outside for parishioners. A garden was scratched out in the dry soil. Dwarfed by the hills the buildings seemed, like everything else in this continent, impermanent and insignificant.

As we approached, a figure appeared at the door of the house, gun in hand. Another rifle poked out of one of the many windows of the house. It was built more like a fortified post than a mission but no doubt that made sense in hostile territory. We halted the caravan and I walked towards the house, holding out my hands to show I was unarmed. My civilian clothes, I thought, might stop the inhabitants from automatically thinking of us as dangerous. I was greeted by a couple of nasty looking hounds straining on a leash held in one hand by a bare-headed clergyman who, with the other, pointed his rifle straight at my belly.

'Stop there!' he said. 'Who are you? What do you want?' He did not sound pleased to see us. Who could blame him? That was not the interesting thing about him. What struck me most of all was that he spoke truly execrable German. So bad, indeed that, clearly, he had to be an Englishman.

'Good day, sir,' I said in a cut-glass British accent.

He blinked and I thought for a terrible second that he was going accidentally to let slip the dogs.

'Oh, yes, good day to you,' he stammered in reply.

North Country by the sound of him; Lancashire, I'd say. Hollow-cheeked and with stooped shoulders, he had a cadaverous look about him. He would have made an excellent undertaker and, considering what was going on around him, he may have had to be one from time to time. He was wearing a waistcoat and collarless shirt and dark trousers as if we had caught him in the middle of preparing to go to church.

'I am sorry to trouble you, sir, but we have a man here, sick with a fever. We hope you may be able to help us.'

I said that fairly quickly so as to make it clear that we were not talking about a war wound. Who knows where his sympathies lay? The Ovaherero supposedly had sworn to leave the missions alone but there were always exceptions in any war.

'Of course, of course,' he said. 'Let me just tie up the dogs. Then I'll help you as much as I can. I have some medicines but not a great deal. The war has affected our supplies. Tell your men to bring him on to the verandah. He'll be more comfortable there.'

We unloaded the sick soldier on to a makeshift stretcher that we had fashioned out of thorn branches and empty sacks of horse feed and carried him to the house. The parson had called for help and a couple of Ovaherero women appeared and hastily carried the soldier into the shade of the veranda. The women were startlingly dressed in the prim clothes normally worn by German housewives. Civilisation had already begun out here in the veldt. The rest of us were also seated there while cold water was brought for us to drink. Another native lad watered the animals. Apparently, none of us were to be allowed into the house itself but it was cool there and at least we had somewhere to sit other than on an unyielding army saddle or inside the sweltering ox-cart.

The Boer, without asking for orders, drove the cart off and, once his oxen had drunk their fill, untied them from the cart and let them graze freely under a thin group of trees.

The men carrying the stretcher had reached the verandah when the door of the house opened and I saw why the parson had made it clear it was out of bounds.

Six

The soldiers abruptly stood still as if turned to stone. Only the parson continued with what he was doing, rolling up his sleeves in preparation for the work ahead. He was dark and dour and burnt by the sun but the vision that appeared in the doorway of the house was anything but. She was delicately fair-skinned with blonde hair that was almost white. When she saw the soldiers, she relaxed and lowered her rifle and released the full force of a smile that could be felt at a hundred paces. Where he was as thin as a rake, she was a hymn to the flesh and while she was dressed demurely as befitted a member of a parson's household, when she moved you could sense the full body flowing beneath her clothes. Her eyes were for the most part lowered but once she flashed a quick glance at me. The eyes were a mocking grey.

The parson turned round and saw her.

'Ah,' he said. 'I need some hot water and carbolic soap.'

She glided back into the house and gave the sun a chance.

The parson started examining the sick soldier while I helped David and the others set up a small camp around and under the ox cart. Some gathered thorn branches to form a makeshift barrier around the camp. One went off to dig a latrine some way downwind of both the soldiers and the Mission. They worked swiftly, despite the heat, and were constantly looking around them. Their rifles were not far from hand for there was always the chance of a surprise attack. We would all have been safer inside the stone house or the church but the parson was adamant. He looked up from wiping the brow of the sick soldier.

'This place is a sanctuary,' he said, 'and I cannot have it defiled by armed men. I will give you food and drink and treat your sick. I would do this for anyone for that is God's command.'

'Including the Ovaherero?' I said.

'Yes, even them. They are murderers and thieves but they are still the children of God.'

That would have been news to Hartmann and the General. I had heard them describing the natives as sub-human.

'Have they tried to harm you in any way?'

He hesitated. 'Not me personally but some of my German flock who are farmers have seen their families killed and their cattle stolen or killed. On the other hand, many of the natives have had their land and cattle stolen from them by settlers and unscrupulous traders.' He paused. 'And their wives and daughters have in some cases been defiled. However, I am not here to judge but to do God's work. Now please fetch me some more water from the pump trough. This man is still burning up with fever. Use that bucket.'

The woman came out of the house, minus her rifle, carrying a bowl of hot water and some soap and towels. Like a midwife, I thought.

I did as he instructed, conscious all the time that the woman's eyes were at my back. A sudden thought caused me to pause a second, daughter or wife? She was much younger than him but that meant nothing in a land at war.

I swung round with my bucket and cast a quick glance at the woman and her hand. Yes, that was a gold band, she was married. Lucky pastor.

First he washed his hands with the carbolic soap and hot water and dried them on a towel. That was a good sign; I'd known wounded men who died from being infected by the surgeon trying to heal them.

He bent over his patient and began examining the sick man's skin.

'Ah!' he said and sat back on his heels. 'As I thought.'

I leaned forward.

'Is it bad?'

He plunged the face cloth into the bucket of cold water and once more bathed the man's face. Given his fever, I half expected to see steam arise.

'It's not malaria,' said the parson. 'But I am fairly certain it is tick bite fever.'

I didn't think the General would be pleased to hear that.

'Tick bite?'

He pointed at the man's skin.

'See that rash? And that black mark?'

To me it looked like any other insect bite but I could see a black spot at the centre.

'I see it,' I said. 'Will he recover?'

He wiped his own face but with his forearm.

'Unless there are complications, yes, and he is a strong young man. He should get better. The fever will break soon and he will mend very quickly.'

'Good. And thank you. Will the others get the fever?'

He smiled wanly.

'Only if they get bitten. And before you ask, the best prevention is not to get bitten. Tell them to keep their sleeves rolled down and their trousers tucked into their boots.'

He looked up as David approached and switched to his fractured German.

'Ah, you can now keep an eye on this chap for me. Keep bathing his forehead. There is not much else we can do but wait. I think the worst is over now and he should be better tomorrow.'

He turned to me and said shyly in English: 'Would you like to come into the house and have a proper cup of tea?'

Damn! The fellow thought I was British. I should have injected a dash of accent into my voice. That's what comes of trying to be too clever by half. Now I should have to disillusion him. On the other hand, I was going to breach the fortress and get to know the woman.

'If it is not too much trouble for you and your wife.'

'My wife?' he said with a raised eyebrow as he ushered me indoors. 'I'm afraid my wife passed away last year.'

'I do apologise,' I stammered, 'but the lady I saw at the door was wearing a wedding ring.'

This time he burst out laughing and was about to answer when she entered the room carrying a tray of tea. I noted she had changed her clothes.

'Allow me to present my cousin, Amelia,' he said. 'My widowed cousin.'

She blushed and put the tray down with a clatter. She smiled weakly somewhere over my right shoulder and hurriedly left the room.

'So where do you come from in England?' as he indicated for me to sit down.

'Milk and sugar?'

He was relishing the ritual as if he were back home in Britain.

'I'm afraid we live humbly here,' he said. 'You must be used to better things back home.'

I took time over drinking my tea, which tasted as if made from brackish water, as I considered my answer to his original question. In the end, I told him everything except the truth. That I was a German studying and living in London and that although my father was from Germany, my mother was from Britain.

'That explains your excellent English,' he said. My explanation seemed to satisfy him though I think he was a little disappointed that I was not a compatriot.

'And which part of Britain do you come from?' I said, more to verify my guess at his origins than from any real interest.

'I was born in London but brought up in Manchester. If you'll excuse me a moment …'

As he left the room, I patted myself on the back and sat back in my chair. The house was simply decorated and could have been an English cottage. I had a look round the room while the parson and his cousin busied themselves elsewhere. Apparently they had no servants. There were no horns or stuffed heads on the wall but there was a sampler hanging there encouraging us to put our Faith in the Lord. My mother used to say that but that was a long time ago. There were also a couple of shelves of books in a corner.

Then he returned and sat down and told me more about himself in slow Northern vowels. I thought I detected the faint smell of alcohol. Was the parson a secret drinker?

'I was sent to this country by the London Missionary Society nigh on ten years ago,' he began. 'Then, when the German influence grew and grew, all missionary work was handed over to the Rhenish Mission. They're in charge now but they have let me stay, especially once my wife passed away. That was upcountry in my last mission. My wife is buried there behind the church.'

He hiccupped and I could definitely smell liquor.

'Before all this trouble began, I was having some small success with the natives. I won't claim they were the most steadfast of worshippers and they still clung to their fire-worship and obeyed their chiefs in everything, but some days we had a respectably sized congregation. But now, those that aren't dead have moved north with all the others. In the meantime, my cousin, who was widowed by a snake bite, moved in as my house-keeper and to keep me company. Apart from a few helpers from the other tribes, we are pretty much alone here.'

Although it was clear he hadn't had anyone new to talk to for a long time, after a while our conversation stuttered into silence. He drank the last of his tea and I made a move to go back to join the others.

'You know, you are welcome to stay here for the night,' he said nervously. 'We have a spare room and if you don't mind leaving your men. The heliograph man will recover, I assure you.'

'They are not my men,' I said kindly. 'I am a civilian and I'm here to act as an interpreter. That is all. And, thank you, I should very much like to stay.'

He flushed with what I assumed was pleasure and called for his cousin and explained the situation.

With her eyes still lowered, she said she would make preparations for a meal and for my stay. It was the first time I had heard her speak. She had a low voice that I found very attractive although I couldn't place her accent. But then I found everything about her attractive.

I went outside and explained things to David. He was chatting to the old Boer smoking his pipe by the ox wagon but broke off as I approached and explained the situation.

He gave a sly smile and I noticed for the first time how big his ears were.

'I'll tell the others,' he said. 'I'm sure they will approve.' Again that rather knowing smile as if he could read my thoughts.

The Boer knocked his pipe out on one of the wagon wheels.

'We'll be safe enough,' he said. 'There's no kaffirs within miles of here. I'd have smelled them if there were.' He stuffed some biltong into his mouth and sat back, staring at the horizon. I stopped and looked around myself. The green breasts towered promisingly over us and there was still a heat haze over the veldt that seemed to stretch without end in all directions. The sky was clear except for a hawk of some kind gliding overhead. I could see why the Afrikaners loved this continent with a deep spirituality and why they had fought so hard to stop us taking it from them.

He didn't look like a man for conversation but as he'd spoken first, I took this as an offer.

'They're new to Africa,' I said in his own language. 'Most of them have come straight from Germany.' He raised an eyebrow at my use of Cape Dutch. It was a very hairy eyebrow on a very hairy face. Like many Boers, he had grown a full and extremely bushy beard but his eyes were a piercing blue, the colour of the Dutch serving dish that my mother used to keep in the kitchen dresser. He held out a gnarled bronzed hand.

'Du Plessis,' he said. 'You speak the *taal* well. How did you come to learn it?'

'I was in the German commando in the war,' I said.

His grip was strong, as you would expect from a man who controlled a team of oxen.

'Huguenot ancestors?' I asked.

'*Ja*, on my father's side but Dutch on my mother's. She was a Viljoen.'

'How did you come to be in German South West?'

He relit his pipe. This was a man who did nothing in a hurry. He puffed a few times until the thing was lit.

'You know about the *Dorslandtrekkers*?'

I nodded.

'Originally from the Transvaal?'

'Right. In the eighties, realising the damned British were encroaching on their land, they left, heading to southern Angola. But they didn't get on too well with the Portuguese so they came here and set up their own republic, Upingtonia. It was centred around Grootfontein. I was a small boy at the time. Then there was trouble with the natives, first the Herero and then the Owambo from the North. Their chief, Mpingana killed our leader, William Jordan, and the Republic failed and was absorbed into German South West. The Germans gave us protection but many of my people left and went back to the Transvaal but I stayed on here. I like the place. It's almost empty.'

He was not looking at me but at the hills and the sky. In my experience, most of the Boers are always restless, anxious to move on after a while, looking for the Promised Land, but this one seemed to have found it. Or at least, a temporary version which, I suppose, is all we ever settle for.

That night she came to me in my room.

Supper had been a subdued affair. Outside the soldiers had lit a huge fire under the stars and were roasting a buck that du Plessis had somehow managed to find, track and shoot. Inside, we ate an overcooked piece of beef with some rather miserable vegetables consisting mostly of squash but one normally wouldn't expect much more in this semi-desert of a country. Lord knows where the beef had come from because I had seen no sign of cattle at the Mission. No doubt bought and salted from a neighbouring farmstead. However, we ate off the parson's best china with Sheffield plate cutlery.

The conversation was polite and rather stiff in that way the British have made their own although the parson did admit his name was Edward. But Amelia made up for it all. She chattered on so much but the parson made no attempt to admonish her. He seemed more intent on emptying the wine carafe.

'I'm sorry,' she said, 'but it's so long that I've met someone who speaks good English and knows London.' She turned to me with a shy smile. 'We know so little German that life is sometimes a matter of sign language. I do know a little Herero, though.'

She had changed her plain day dress for a more formal one that was alarmingly deep-cut and emphasised by the silver cross hanging from her slender neck. The parson didn't seem to mind when I complimented his cousin on what she wore.

'My cousin has so few opportunities to dress properly,' he said, finishing yet another glass of wine. Once Amelia leaned over to replenish my glass and I caught a tantalising glimpse of her full bosom.

Poor as Edward's conversation was, I did indirectly learn more about the Germans and their intentions towards our own colony.

'This seems quite a barren country,' I said, 'compared to the British colony down south. I wonder that we are so keen on it. Agriculture and animal husbandry will be much more difficult.'

Edward nodded.

'It is hard but your people are extremely industrious. I do not doubt that they will succeed in making the country productive. You are investing so much time and money in it.'

I hesitated before taking the plunge. 'Is there any sign of gold or diamonds here as there seem to be in Griqualand?'

Edward shook his head.

'Not that I am aware of,' he said 'though I am sure they are looking.'

'The British are fortunate with the riches they have discovered in South Africa.'

He just nodded and at this point Amelia asked me about the latest fashions in London and I tried to recall what Julia had been wearing when I last saw her. In fact, I found it difficult to remember Julia's face at all. After that, the conversation dried up completely and we all decided to retire. I don't think they drank wine very often for Edward was clearly affected as he bade me, 'Good night' and stumbled a couple of times as he left the room.

~

My room was sparsely furnished but it had a bed with a good mattress, possibly new and free of bedbugs. There was a washbasin and a jug full of clear water on a homemade washstand. There was a crucifix on the wall directly above the bed.

I had barely clambered into bed and was about to blow out my candle when there was a soft knock at the door. I wrapped a towel around myself and cautiously opened the door a fraction. It was Amelia.

'Hello?'

'May I come in?'

She was wearing a sweet smile, a long dressing gown and holding a flickering candle.

'Er, yes, of course.'

She slipped into the room and I closed the door behind her. We had been whispering but I doubt that the parson would have heard anything in his drunken slumbers. I pulled the towel tighter.

'I'm afraid there's nowhere to sit,' I began.

It didn't seem to bother Amelia whose gown was off as quickly as if she were preparing to save a drowning child. She dived under the bed clothes and pulled them up to her chin.

'Are you going to stay there all night?' she breathed. 'You'll catch cold.'

I needed no further invitation. I dropped the towel.

As soon as I joined her, in no time at all her hands and lips were all over my body. The warmth and scent of her skin were more than I could bear. I pulled her to me.

She was an inventive lover and at one point I fleetingly wondered if she had worked her husband to death. There was almost no end to her demands and my needs. Finally she paused for breath. I lay there panting while she rested on one arm as those grey eyes looked amusedly down into mine.

'Thank you,' she said sweetly in the same tone of voice that she might have used if I had passed her the sugar.

She might have chatted a great deal at supper but that didn't mean she had exhausted things to talk about.

'Tell me about London,' she said.

I told her about the shops and the foggy streets and some of my work at the University, though that was of less interest to her.

'Do you have a family?' she asked.

'My parents are dead,' I said. 'I'm alone in the world.'

'Oh you're a poor orphan. Let me make it up to you.'

So she did.

Finally she asked me what I thought of German South West Africa.

'It must seem boring and dull after the excitement of London.'

'It has its own beauty,' I replied 'and its name is Amelia.' She seemed content with that and reached for me once again. This time we were not in so much of a hurry and we lingered over each other's bodies on a new voyage of discovery. Afterwards, she lay there with her head nestled in the crook of my arm.

'Tell me again what you are doing here,' she asked. 'You are a cultured man, why are you mixed up in this war?'

'Because I believe in the German plan to colonise this country. We have as much right as Britain and other European countries to have colonies in Africa. It is our destiny to make this country great.'

My mother always said I should have been an actor. Amelia seemed to be satisfied by this twaddle for she gave me one last lingering hug.

'I like you,' she said finally. 'Now I must go in case my cousin wakes.' She slid out of the bed and in what seemed like a second put on her nightdress and gown and blowing me a final kiss, she was gone, closing the door as silently as I had opened it.

I lay there musing a while. After what had happened, I still knew very little about her except that I could deduce it was some time since she'd been widowed. I also thought of Julia who had talked of nothing except marriage yet showed no sign of wanting or needing intimacy. Above all, however, I wondered why two people who professed to know little or no German had several well-thumbed German books on their shelves. And I would have liked to know how they knew that the sick man was a heliograph operator. I'd said nothing about it and none of the soldiers spoke English.

~

I was still mulling this over at breakfast, which was a sedate affair enlivened by excellent coffee. The parson chewed a trifle gloomily on his homemade roll, no doubt regretting the night before, while Amelia sipped her coffee demurely at the same time stroking my foot with hers.

We were interrupted by a knock on the door. It was David. He hadn't shaved and his uniform was rumpled as if he had just been roused out of bed. 'We have to strike camp and join the main column,' he said excitedly. 'The General has ordered the advance and our helio man is weak but the fever has gone and he is now well enough to move. We leave within the hour! The real war has begun!'

Seven

One of the men hawked and spat out a throatful of dust.

'Quiet!' hissed the lieutenant. 'Obey your orders. Stay silent at all times.'

From then on, there was only the clink of metal, the sound of boots moving through the red earth and the smell of crushed vegetation.

It was dark and cold and we had been moving only at night, much of it uphill. There were just thirty-eight of us. We were carrying supplies, including ammunition and equipment, along the top of the Waterberg.

It was not just any old mountain or even one peak but a huge plateau running from the south east to the north west, rising out of the plains and broken up into several smaller outcrops. Our route would take us about twelve kilometres along the top of the plateau with the aim of setting up a heliograph station. Once established, we would be able to report to our forces far below on enemy activity.

Suddenly, there was the sound of something crashing through the bush. Immediately the column froze, waiting, listening. The noise could be anything from a startled buck to a hungry leopard. I gripped my rifle tighter.

'No shooting!' hissed the lieutenant, as if reading my thoughts.

Out of the darkness came a groan and then a familiar stench.

'Private Neff,' said David in my ear.

Neff was the heliograph operator who had been treated by the pastor. He had never completely recovered and recently, like many others, had come down with dysentery. It seems he had made an emergency stop in the bush.

We chuckled, covered our noses, and waited for him to emerge.

Eventually, buttoning up his trousers, he rejoined the column which gave him a wide berth as we travelled on.

We were being guided by an Ovaherero man who could speak a little German. He was missionary trained for he called himself Philemon who was, I gather, a character in the New Testament. Philemon may have been a Christian convert but the troopers treated him as just another native. I was the interpreter for the group, which was led by a Lieutenant Auer von Herrenkirchen; the name says it all – another German aristocrat. David was also there as my assistant. In the dark, he never moved from my side.

I touched Philemon on the shoulder and he jumped as if he'd been shot. I bent down and whispered into his ear.

'Is it far?'

He shook his head. 'Just another hundred paces.'

I moved forward and intercepted the lieutenant. He cocked his head and raised an eyebrow.

'A hundred paces,' I breathed.

He nodded.

It was bitterly cold, just above freezing. Most of the men were not only worried about the cold and the enemy but also about scorpions and other night creatures. As we trudged on, we could hear rustlings in the bushes and animal or bird cries. This made the men nervous and I was relieved that they had strict orders to maintain silence. The last thing we needed to do was disturb the animals and alert the Ovaherero down below. I was worried not only about snakes, especially puff adders, that are too lazy and slow to get out of the way but also the biggest killer of all – mosquitos. Malaria had already incapacitated several of our men up here and killed one but in the cold they were presently inactive.

The air smelled of dust and sweat; none of us had washed for days. The journey had taken two nights and during the days we had holed up out of the sun and out of sight but now we were approaching our planned position.

The aim was to set up the station just back from the rim of the plateau where the heliograph could catch the sun and flash messages to the troops, but not be visible to the Ovaherero encampments. The battle would begin once the sun had risen. There was not long to go.

The parson and his cousin had watched us prepare to leave. Amelia had even made up small food parcels for the soldiers and the Boer and presented them personally with a little curtsey.

Her cousin had dressed formally for the occasion and just before we departed said a prayer in English that I translated into German. I'm not a praying man but a brief smile from Amelia encouraged me to say the words. She gave me my own gift of some sandwiches.

'To enable you to keep up your strength,' she said innocently. The memory returned of the curve of her breast and of her smooth buttocks cupped in my hands. I licked my dry lips.

'You're very kind,' I said.

Her eyes smiled at me and for a split second I thought she might jump me there and then and start all over again.

'May you have a safe journey.'

The sun was already rising high in the sky by the time the wagon was hitched and the horses fed and watered. We steadily left the farm behind as we headed north and a last glance back showed the parson and his cousin walking back towards the small church. Behind the church the massive green breasts of the hills reminded me of what we were leaving behind. I doubted there would be much pleasure lying ahead of us.

~

As daylight burst upon us, I could see the Ovaherero far below. Their main force was spread across several camps below us at the foot of the main outcrop and to the south east. I estimated they numbered about 50,000. Philemon agreed but said that only maybe four to six thousand were armed warriors, the rest being women and children and, of course, their cattle. They had brought their wealth with them, thousands of cattle, gathered around the waterholes. Our forces were heavily outnumbered and consisted of about 1,500 troops but they were equipped with the tools of civilisation: 12 machine guns and 36 cannons. The Ovaherero, on the other hand, had rifles, some of them very old and mostly acquired from traders in return for tribal land and cattle that weren't theirs to give. There were still plenty of spears and clubs in evidence.

'Why did they come here?' I asked Philemon. 'They are now open to attack.'

He glanced at me nervously. 'They are not expecting a battle,' he said. 'They have had enough of fighting and came here to get away from the Germans. The land now belongs to them. The great chief is expecting to negotiate a peace treaty.'

I nodded slowly. It was too late for that.

Soon after daybreak we had finished our work and while the soldiers began signalling the main forces, I lay down on my back and watched the sky. A couple of expectant vultures rode the air above us as the day warmed up. David approached me.

'What does our Herero guide think of the coming battle?'

I glanced across to where Philemon, wrapped in a ragged blanket, was lying on his side under a thorn bush. All I could see of him was his dust-covered hair and his cracked bare feet.

I shrugged. I had been doing a lot of shrugging recently. As usual I was reluctant to express an opinion or take sides; neutrality was my preferred option in nearly every circumstance. The guide, I thought, hadn't had that luxury. He had made his choice and was now grieving for its consequences.

'If he has any sense,' I replied, 'he'll be glad he won't be down there.'

David laughed scornfully.

'These people are all cowards!'

'You think so?'

'Of course. So far they have avoided meeting us in battle and have instead attacked from ambush. That is what cowards do. Now we shall fight like men, face to face, and we shall crush them under our feet.'

So that's what they teach them during training.

'Look,' I added, 'when it comes to it, and people are dying in agony with their balls shot off, and you're shitting yourselves with fear it might happen to you, you'll be glad as Philemon that you're up here. I know I will.'

I knew he wanted Germany to win the battle. It probably would. I, on the other hand, didn't really care who won or lost. I had seen enough of warfare to know that there would be a steep price to pay whoever came out on top.

'Are you also afraid?' I could see his high opinion of me draining away.

'I'd be stupid not to be: that way you don't do something silly and let down your comrades. Being afraid is not the same as being a coward. And when you see the aftermath of a battle, it's only natural to be relieved you weren't in the thick of it. My advice is just do your duty and don't try to be a hero: the world is full of dead heroes.'

'I'm not afraid of dying for my country,' he said stiffly and walked off. Maybe he felt invulnerable and actually believed in that prophecy of his mother about dying in Jerusalem. For his sake I hoped so but in my experience prophecies are just a kind of wishful thinking.

The heliograph was now in position and I crawled forward to a point on the escarpment where I could look down on the Ovaherero emplacements below. I borrowed some binoculars from David. From up here I had a vulture's eye view of what would soon be the battlefield. The strange thing was, there didn't seem to be any emplacements, just a series of gatherings. As far as I could see, they were clearly not on a war footing. Either they had not known of the German approach or they were not expecting a fight. It looked as if Philemon was right.

If the Ovaherero hoped that von Trotha's forces would go away and leave them alone on their ancestral lands, then they had another think coming.

It seemed to me that it was the biggest error the Chief had made since firing that first shot long ago in Okahandja.

I wriggled back and reported on what Philemon had said to Auer.

'Excellent,' he said. 'That will make our victory more certain. God will be with us today.'

'Is there any doubt?' I asked innocently.

'Not really.' He hesitated. 'Our battle plan is almost foolproof. But you have been in war before so you know there is no such thing as a perfect plan.'

That was true. The British had learned that lesson in the first years of the South African campaign and the Boers had learned it even more painfully towards the end.

'The Ovaherero certainly have the numbers,' I offered. If I was to succeed in my mission, I needed the Germans to make a habit of confiding in me.

'You are an educated and cultured man,' he replied, 'so let me explain.'

He unsheathed his bayonet and drew a rough map in the red crumbling soil.

'Here are the three main groups of Herero in a sort of triangle, spread over a distance of about 40 kilometres. We have encircled them with a line about 100 kilometres long. Our forces will advance in six columns from several directions and close in on them and destroy them. Those we do not kill will be made prisoner and will work for us to build the new colony of South West.'

I could see only two flaws. Firstly, the German force was simply not large enough to encircle the enemy completely. Secondly, the ground that would form the battlefield was comprised of thick bush. Not only would that make it difficult for von Trotha's forces to see the enemy but it would also hinder them from seeing each other.

'A simple but effective plan,' I commented.

Auer smiled.

'We think so,' he said. 'Now we shall wait for the signal to start then we shall have the honour of co-ordinating the attack and reporting on its progress.'

Oh, how the Prussians love using the word 'honour' when in the business of slashing each other's faces or killing people.

The attack began on August 11th.

David was anxious to join in the action and suggested we go down the escarpment. Auer had no objection.

'You have performed your task,' he said. 'There is no reason why you should not have some fun.'

Fun? So it was his first major action as well. He made it sound as if he were planning to hunt wild boar. Perhaps that was how he saw it.

We scrambled down to the plains much quicker than we had climbed up. Unencumbered by equipment and in daylight, carrying only a water bottle and a rifle, we ran and slithered down the path winding down the mountain. All the same, covered in dust and sweat, it took us at least an hour or so to reach the bottom by which time the 'fun' had already begun and the battle was in full swing.

The noise was staggering though I could see little of what was going on. Machine-gun fire hammered away, punctuated by the individual fire of the field guns and rifles. Even as I stepped off the path from the Waterberg, a horse was hit by a bullet from an Otjiherero rifle and the air echoed with its screams. An officer to my right was shouting orders but whether or not his men heard them or could see him was doubtful given the noise and the swirls of dust.

It was blisteringly hot and I was already regretting leaving the cool of the plateau when out of the melee appeared a group of armed horsemen. Nama horsemen. One of them, the leader, rode up to me.

'Stay back,' I warned David. 'Leave this to me.'

The man's face was expressionless as I began to speak. His rifle I noticed was slung across his saddle easily in reach. I carefully kept my hands away from mine.

'*!Gâi tses!* – Good day,' I said in his language, just in case he had thoughts of shooting me.

'Good day. Who are you?'

That is always a tricky question and answerable only with another.

'What are you doing here? Is this your battle?'

The man scowled down at me as did his fellows.

'Yes and no. We are here fighting against the *Herero‖khaasi* because our Captain has a treaty with the Germans.'

'And you are not happy about that?'

He was clearly wondering whether or not to trust me.

'You are a German?'

'Yes and no.'

That drew a grim smile on his dusty face.

'I am not a soldier in this war,' I added.

'Good. Let me tell you this. Despite our Captain's orders we are leaving the battlefield.'

'Why?'

'Because the German soldiers are out to kill all the *Herero‖khaasi*, they said so to our face. They also treat us badly and at least one of them has said that we will be next. We are sure that is correct and we shall tell our Captain to prepare our people for war.'

I saw no reason to doubt him.

'God go with you,' I said.

'I hope so. There is no sign of God in this battle, that is for sure.'

'Farewell.'

They rode off away from the battlefield, leaving behind the cries of the wounded Germans and Ovaherero.

'What was that about?' said David, 'and who are they?'

'Friends. And they are going home.'

He had the good sense to ask no more questions and we turned our attention to the battle.

From high up on the escarpment, the opposing forces had been arrayed on a biblical landscape, with the Ovaherero and the Germans spread out as on a map. Close at hand it soon became clear that what Auer had called a battle was rapidly turning into a series of skirmishes in the dusty, stony brush.

Once, in the melee, we came across a wounded German soldier and a dead Omuherero. It was clear that the soldier had shot the Omuherero for his rifle lay by his side and a bullet-hole, still bleeding, was visible in the native's chest. We dismounted to tend to the soldier.

As we approached, we could see his hands were crossed over his stomach. There was blood on his fingers. I knelt beside him and raised my water-bottle to his dry cracked lips. His eyelids fluttered and he groaned at the exertion of raising his head. I looked down to see how badly he was wounded. At that moment, he dropped his hands and I gasped. He had been holding in his entrails and now they spilled out with a gush of dark red blood on to the dust. He looked at me once with a look of bewilderment, coughed and with a horrid gargle, died in my arms. David was being violently sick over a bush. He had found the 'fun' he was looking for.

We decided to leave the soldier there.

'Shouldn't we bury him?' asked David. 'We can't leave him for the beasts.'

'Do you have a spade? I don't.'

'We could use our bayonets.'

'In case you hadn't noticed, there's a battle going on. We could end up as dead as he is. A detail will pick him up as soon as the fighting is over. Come on, let's follow the guns.' There was no discussion about the body of the Omuherero warrior.

~

The main German aim was to capture the Ovaherero watering places and by nightfall, despite several setbacks and some German casualties, the columns had closed in on the Ovaherero and their main watering holes had been captured. We had passed several Ovaherero corpses, many of them

71

armed only with spears. Despite their superior numbers, the Ovaherero seemed to have been acting only in defence, giving way before cannons and machine guns. They died where they stood. No one would bother to bury them; the jackals and vultures would take care of them.

There were women and children among them, lying battered and broken in the dust and suddenly I was consumed with anger. This was not my war but the Germans', compatriots of Beethoven, Bach, Schubert and Schumann were acting like savages.

Among the smell of powder and blood the Germans could also taste victory. David, however, was not a happy man. Standing on a dead horse, he had his telescope to his eye and was looking towards the south east.

'No!' he cried. 'They are going too far. Their orders were to stop at the agreed point.'

I took his place on the horse and also looked into the heat haze. The dust was beginning to settle as the battle moved away from us and I could see what David meant. The western column had pressed ahead in its pursuit of the Ovaherero, not knowing what had happened to the south east. There the German column had failed to close the gap in the encirclement with the result that the Ovaherero were pouring through the gap and fleeing the battlefield. Men, women and children in one huge flood of people. The shooting was fading away, drowned out by the thundering hooves of the cattle. I could hear their cattle lowing as they were driven away in a huge cloud of dust.

'Damn!' cried David. 'The General must stop them!'

But it was too late. The rout was in full flow as the Ovaherero nation fled to the east. Some German troopers were following them but the main German force had stopped.

All around us now we could see the detritus of battle. Cartridge cases, abandoned spears, dead horses and cattle and the corpses; hundreds of Ovaherero corpses, many of them shredded by machine-gun fire. The air smelt of gunpowder, dust and blood.

'They're getting away!' cried David. 'Why are we not pursuing them?'

'I don't think there's anything von Trotha can do about it.'

After fighting all day in extreme heat, his men and their horses were exhausted and needed to recover.

And that wasn't the end of it but just the beginning. A voice spoke up behind me. It was Philemon, his hair still covered in dust.

'My people are going into the Omaheke,' said the guide. He didn't seem too happy about it.

'The Omaheke? What's that?'

He averted his gaze and stared at the parched red soil.

'It is the great sand,' he said.

'The great sand? What's that?' asked David.

I knew the answer.

'It's the desert between us and the British territory of Bechuanaland.'

Philemon nodded mournfully. 'There is no water, no grass. My people will die. It stretches miles and miles towards where the British are. There is nothing there. My people have avoided dying in battle only to die in the desert.'

He sat there in the dust and began pouring it over his head.

'Come,' I said. 'I will make sure you are not harmed.'

He shook his grey head and began weeping.

'My people are dead,' he said, 'and I was part of it. Now I am dead, too. Go on your way. As for me, I have no way to go.'

We left him there.

As von Trotha's forces rested and night fell, they counted their losses: 26 men killed and 60 men wounded. No one knew the extent of Ovaherero casualties. No one cared. Their bodies were sprawled all over the battlefield in their hundreds, lying where they had fallen, to be left for the hyenas and jackals. It had been not so much a battle as a mass slaughter.

David ran up to me.

'We are going down to join the chase in the morning! Come and get ready or you will miss the chase.'

~

Some of the forces that had chased the fleeing Ovaherero had already returned. David grabbed the arm of one trooper and asked him what had happened.

The trooper was covered in dust and drank water from his canteen until it was empty. He sat on a rock and rested his head in his hands. His face, under streaks of the inevitable dust, was grey with fatigue but there was something else haunting him. David and I sat by him.

'I was with Captain Bayer,' he began. 'We followed the path that the enemy had taken. It wasn't difficult. They had left a huge path through the bush, maybe a hundred metres wide. Wagons and cattle, together with thousands of people had flattened everything in their path. And as we went further, there were even more signs of the way they had gone. To help go faster, they had started to drop their possessions. We found pots and calabashes, all broken and abandoned. Then, in a bad sign, we found empty goatskins that they used to carry water. By then, we, and our horses too, were in need of water so we turned back. But there is no need to chase them any further; the desert will do our work for us.'

It didn't take long for the stench of rotting flesh hanging over the plains to attract the scavengers. We heard them all night long. At dawn, I went outside the tent for a cigarette. As the sun began to light the sky, there was a faint but persistent humming sound that I couldn't identify at first. Then I suddenly realised that I was listening to the sound of millions upon millions of flies. At that moment a huge sensation of revulsion hit me in the stomach.

I had been in colonial wars before. I had heard of the Indian Mutiny where savagery reigned on both sides and where the British soldiers took a terrible vengeance upon the mutineers and all those they thought had helped them. But this was different. The dead were not only those killed in battle but also their families and their cattle. The snarling of the jackals fighting over corpses and the humming of the flies was a vile hymn to the end of a nation.

Eight

A none too gentle but highly polished boot in the ribs awakened me. It was about two weeks after the battle. We had spent the time resting and replenishing our supplies. I had been chatting with the troopers and gleaned some information about forts and garrisons that were being established. I used a code in the form of a mythical native language that I was supposed to be recording and noted down my observations for passing on later to Webb. I was particularly interested in the number and location of horse relay stations that could be used to support any invasion of British territory.

Fresh troops up from the coast had swelled the numbers of the German forces and a cordon was now drawn up across the route leading to the Omaheke. A column led by General von Trotha himself had been assembled to go after the fleeing Ovaherero.

'Come,' said Hartmann. 'The General has not yet dispensed with your services. We leave shortly. Pack up your stuff and prepare to interpret as the General requires.'

Persuading myself that I was volunteering my services in the name of my mission, I went with them. My job was to be available in case we needed to talk to any stragglers. Hartmann was there, grinning like a dervish.

The column moved off at a cracking pace, with the ox carts containing water and ammunition following behind. As always the sun was stabbing down at us from a merciless blue sky. If the fleeing Ovaherero had had to endure this, I didn't give much for their chances. We stopped at the last waterhole before the Great Sand began.

When the horses had had their fill and we had managed a quick splash of tepid gritty water over our head and hands, all of us were assembled in disciplined ranks. The contrast between the several thousand fresh troops with their pale young faces and those of the grizzled, war-weary marines that I had accompanied on the train up from Swakopmund showed a new phase in the war. Would it lead south?

It was at this point that God briefly returned from his holidays. The Reverend Max Schmidt held a service. He gave thanks for the divine assistance given to the German forces and prayed for the souls of those who had died for their country. German souls, that is.

After the 'Amens' had died away and the troops had been stood down, General von Trotha summoned all his officers and kindly included me among them.

'It is a great honour for you,' Hartmann said. I suppose it was, for it gave me the opportunity to hear von Trotha seal the end of the Ovaherero nation. This came in the form of a proclamation 'addressed to the Herero people', though none were present. It didn't matter.

The General stood there, one leg placed slightly in front of the other and with his shoulders thrown back, a statue in the making.

He read out his proclamation as we stood around him.

'I, the great general of the German soldiers, send this letter to the Herero nation. The Hereros are no longer German subjects. They have murdered, stolen, have cut off the ears and noses and other members of wounded soldiers, and now they are too cowardly to continue fighting. I say to the nation: every person who delivers one of their captains to one of my posts as a prisoner, shall receive 1000 marks. Whoever brings in Samuel Maharero shall receive 5000 marks. The Herero nation must leave the country. If the people do not do so, I will force them to do so with our great cannons. Within the German borders, every Herero, with or without a rifle, with or without cattle, will be shot. I will no longer receive any women and children, but will drive them back to their people or will have them shot. These are my words to the Herero nation.

The Great General of the mighty German Emperor.'

A nation had been sentenced to death.

Von Trotha hadn't finished for he now addressed us. All ranks were to be told the contents of the proclamation. He specifically said that shots should be fired not at but over the heads of women and children so that they would run into the desert, for, as he said, 'the forces will bear in mind the reputation of the German soldier.'

To celebrate, the General then ordered some thirty natives to be brought forward. They had been caught near the edge of the desert and consisted mostly of old men, women and children.

'One of those is not Ovaherero,' I muttered to Hartmann. 'The short one with the darker skin is a Damara, a servant of the Ovaherero.'

Hartmann sniffed. 'That is of no importance. They are all enemies of the German Empire.'

My services were not required as the General was in no need of information. He gave an order. Ropes were slung over a tree and two men were hanged. The women and children were driven into the desert with copies of the proclamation in German and Otjiherero tied around their necks. Almost certainly, even if there were people who could read, none of them would still be alive.

I glanced around me. If any of the troopers were as appalled as I was, they took great care not to show it. It seemed to me at that moment that the Germany of Schiller and Goethe had been buried beneath the corpses of the Ovaherero. This new modern Germany, inspired by the Kaiser with his withered arm and preening vanity, and enthusiastically supported by so many, was one my father would not have recognised.

~

About a week later, Hartmann and I were with a section following up the Ovaherero who had fled into the Omaheke. It was now October and the weather was getting hotter by the day. Our aim was to make sure the Ovaherero were not scheming to return but given the heat, the desert and the cordon, that was unlikely.

David had stayed behind as we rode off. He had been assigned to other duties and looked at me as I mounted my horse. He signalled he wanted to come with me but I had no choice in the matter. I shrugged and rode off with Hartmann.

'I don't like that fellow,' he said. 'He's a Jew, of course.'

'I believe he is.'

'I can always tell. There's a kind of smell about them. He's not even from Germany. I know his sort. They wander the world sucking the blood from us. The British government is riddled with them and that is why the British Empire will eventually fall. The Tsar of the Russias has the right idea: he wants to be rid of them altogether. We were weak and foolish ever to take them in.'

The trail left by the Ovaherero was clear. At first, there was a vast area of sand that had been flattened by the hooves of hundreds of cattle. Then, as the trooper had described to me weeks before, there was the abandoned detritus of a people fleeing cannons and machine guns. Before long we came across the corpses of cattle, some of which were little more than skin and bone. Others had apparently had their throats slit.

'To drink the blood?' I guessed.

'Probably,' said Hartmann. 'Much good it did them.'

We found our first human bodies. No attempt had been made to bury them. They were a woman and child, lying where they had fallen. Skins already blackening under the sun, they were cradled together in a grotesque parody of sleep, their eyes already lost to scavengers and their lips drawn back in mirthless grins.

Then, we came across more and more corpses of people who had simply fallen, no longer able to move, their bodies twisted in the agonies of thirst and hunger.

We came across huge holes dug in a frantic hunt for water. More corpses indicated the extent of their failure. In one place, a desperate attempt at a well had collapsed on top of the men digging it; we could still see an emaciated and desiccated arm sticking out at the surface as if waving to us.

I was beginning to lose interest in my mission.

'We have seen enough,' I said, as we passed a pile of male bodies. This affected Hartmann even more than me.

'I'm not sure this is a good idea,' he muttered.

I must have raised an eyebrow.

'Don't misunderstand me,' he added hastily, 'The General is a great man but in my opinion it is wrong to kill all these people off. This is a huge land and our colonists are few in number. We need these blacks to work for us and build our colony. It could save us millions of marks.'

There was no answer to that.

After some hours, it became clear that there was no sign of any of the

Ovaherero attempting to return to German territory. They had all vanished into the desert. The General gave the order and we turned around.

'The remainder are either dead or have made their way to British Bechuanaland,' said Hartmann wheeling his horse. 'Either way, they are no longer our problem.'

~

Back in camp, however, we found a myriad of problems that were indeed ours. Africa is strictly neutral and takes no sides in the punishment it metes out to intruders.

The main battle was, we thought, now over and the threat of infected spear or bullet wounds had largely receded. However, many of the troopers were sick. Typhoid and dysentery were rife, especially among the new arrivals from Germany who, being constantly on the move, were remarkably lax in their building and use of latrines. What is more, insect bites were a constant irritant with the threat of malaria constantly hanging over us, especially those who were billeted near stagnant water. And those soldiers who neglected to knock out their boots each morning were quite likely to be bitten by venomous scorpions and spiders. No, Africa had no intention of making us welcome.

Inside the muggy air of the sick tent, army doctors were sweating as they comforted the men. Even as I entered the tent, I was brushed aside by two troopers holding up a third who was rolling his eyes and shivering with what smelled like fear.

'Snakebite,' gasped one of his companions.

'Lay him down there,' said a doctor, pointing to a blanket spread on the ground. 'Did you kill the snake? I need to identify it.'

The trooper shook his head. 'No, it was too fast for us. It struck at him twice and then slithered off very fast.'

The doctor sighed. 'What did it look like?'

'Well, it was brownish. Oh, and about two metres long.'

'Could be anything,' murmured the doctor.

'May I help?' I said.

He raised an eyebrow but raised no objection.

'Tell me,' I said, 'Did you manage to see the inside of its mouth?'

The bitten soldier raised himself on one elbow. 'Black,' he rasped. 'As black as Hell.' He slumped back on to the blanket.

I took the doctor to one side. 'Black mamba,' I said quietly. 'The bite is always fatal. He hasn't got long, poor fellow. Less than an hour.'

The soldier was now sweating profusely. I left the tent.

Outside I bumped into my old acquaintance, the veterinary surgeon. He was slumped against the axle pole of an ox cart, his eyes reddened with lack of sleep and his uniform stained and crumpled.

'Hello again,' I said.

He raised a weary head and slowly recognised me.

'Ah, the tick fever man. Hello. Got a cigarette?'

I gave him one and lit it for him. 'Thank you,' he said.

I joined him in the shade of the ox cart. 'How are the animals bearing up?'

He grimaced and there was a long pause while he lit the cigarette and inhaled deeply.

'Not too bad. The horses suffer of course. We should have brought up more camels. But they're better off than the troopers,' he said finally. 'It's an almost impossible task to keep up with their ailments. My comrades are doing what they can but, in all honesty, all we can do is give them some rest and clean water and isolate them from the others.' He sighed and threw away his cigarette. I left him to it.

~

David and his column had returned to camp and he, too, was not looking well. Although his sallow skin was now bronzed by his constant exposure to the sun, there were deep bags under his eyes as if he were not getting enough sleep. He was slumped in the saddle with an air of defeat hanging over him.

'I don't know what you've been doing,' I said as he dismounted 'but you need to take some rest. Are you sick?'

He sighed.

'No, I'm well. I've just been very busy.'

He was off duty so we sat together while I had a cigarette and he a glass of schnapps. He kept hold of the bottle as if someone might snatch it away from him.

'So what have you been up to?' I said.

He poured himself another schnapps.

'Medicine,' he said as he saw me looking at him.

'Medicine? For what? You said you'd not been sick.'

He wiped a hand across his face. Not once had he looked me in the eye. 'I'm not sick, not in the normal way.'

Then he told me.

'Not all the Herero were killed or driven into the desert at the Waterberg. Many, maybe 20,000, were still in their ancestral lands; in small groups, mostly. The General knew this and ordered us to find them and deal with them. We were to sweep the area moving towards the ancestral lands as we did so. We are called Cleansing Patrols.'

'Cleansing? Why "cleansing"?'

He looked at his empty glass and held it up to the sky like a telescope. I don't think he saw anything.

'Because that is what we do. Our orders are to find them and then to shoot them on sight.'

'Who are you talking about? Warriors? I'm not sure there are many of them left. They would have been with Maharero.'

'Anyone. Anyone at all.'

'Even though they may not have taken part in the battle?'

'Yes.'

I threw away my cigarette. It tasted harsh and bitter.

'You do realise, don't you, that some of these people probably didn't even know there was a war on. Lots of these villages are isolated and far off.'

He was no longer listening to me. He poured another schnapps. I hoped it wasn't helping.

'Once we found signs of a group that we said we would spare if they surrendered. We guessed that they were hiding in the bush, hoping that we would go away. Our commander called out again and one by one they came out of the bush, as scared as hell. The commander was smiling all the time but when they were all out, he stopped smiling and jumped to one side. We were waiting and our machine-gun opened up. It took only a few seconds and they were soon all dead. We left them where they lay. That was one of many such incidents.'

I knew he was going to tell me whether or not I wanted to hear him.

This was a man finding himself lost in darkness who had given up searching for a light.

He spat into the sand and continued. 'After a while the men adopted a motto, "Clean out, hang up, shoot down till they are all gone." We had few casualties for we were not fighting warriors, just people living in their villages. We'd move in, surround the village, set up the machine guns and, well, cleanse the place.'

'Easy targets, then. Good sport is it?'

That was the moment when he could have hit me. Perhaps he thought about it for I felt his body tense and I prepared to throw myself to one side. I wasn't going to fight him if I could avoid it. I might already have given myself away. I had to keep on his right side. After a second he relaxed and instead he drank some more schnapps.

'You would have done the same,' he muttered.

'Why would I?'

'Because you are no better than me.'

'Have you seen me kill anyone yet?' My voice rose as I couldn't help myself. 'Have I shot defenceless old men and women? Have I murdered children?'

He ignored that. There was more to tell. I began to feel like I was hearing his confession. Jews don't believe in Hell but David had created one all of his own. By now he couldn't stop himself. All of it had to come out. Perhaps he thought it would make him feel better. I hoped not.

'At one point we came across eight or nine sick Herero women who had been left behind after a skirmish with some mixed-race Basters who were our allies then. Some of the women were blind and they had been left food and water.'

David gulped down another mouthful of schnapps.

'Go on.'

'We heaped wood around the hut they were lying in and set fire to it.'

'You burnt them alive?'

He stared at the ground and nodded. 'I can still hear their screams and smell burning flesh.'

'And you think I would do that?'

'I don't know.'

He sighed. 'At a place called Otji-something or other the Basters handed over to us a group of prisoners. No order was given but we knew what we had to do. We had had our orders. We shot and bayoneted all the prisoners. There were over seventy of them.'

I had heard enough. I took his bottle and swigged a mouthful. It tasted like fire but it cauterised nothing. Now, having destroyed their songs and their gods, we were exterminating the people themselves like so many cockroaches.

I moved away. I felt sick and squatted on the sand.

At that point Hartmann rode up, the gleam in his eyes as bright as the polish on his boots.

'Don't rest too long,' he said. 'The General has ordered us to go still further into Hereroland. We are going south.'

'South?'

'Yes, we are done here. Now the battle has moved to the centre of the country.'

So we were moving south. Eventually, that would take the war much closer to South Africa. Was that the German plan? Maybe Webb was right after all.

Nine

Then the universe turned upside down.

I was dreaming of rain, the water splattering on my hair, running down my face and wetting my lips. I could smell it, as it soaked my clothes. But a stumble from my horse jolted me awake and my mouth was full of sand and my clothes stank after so many days in the saddle. The sun pressed down as I licked my parched lips. I reached for my water-bottle. I was bored.

As we slowly advanced across Hereroland, it was becoming clear to me that the Germans had no other interest except to exterminate the Ovaherero. My mission was, to all intents and purposes, at an end. The problem, as always, was how to get this intelligence to Webb. There was nowhere for me to go. All I could do was hope that an opportunity would arise for me to slip away from the German troops and make my way either to Walfish Bay or to South Africa. There seemed little chance of either.

It was then that I first saw Leah. They were about to hang her.

We were riding past Okahandja, the former centre of the now lost Ovaherero world, where the sacred fire had been extinguished and the graves of their ancestors had been violated. A group of stragglers had been rounded up by David and his men and among them was the most beautiful woman I had ever seen.

The sight of her instantly reminded me of something I had witnessed in Cape Colony where a pack of wild dogs had run down and surrounded an exhausted antelope. The animal, its flanks heaving, had stood there, wide-eyed, staring at the dogs about to rip it apart. At the time, I had wanted to step in and rescue the creature but had been helpless to do so.

This tiny woman, with her slight figure and huge eyes, was staring at the German soldiers with the same air of resignation, ready to accept her fate. This time I had the power to intervene.

Without thinking, I wheeled my horse round and approached David. The ropes had already been hurled over a branch and were being fashioned into nooses. Other soldiers were standing by and smoking cigarettes or playing cards, waiting to watch a scene they had seen acted out many times before. The prisoners were huddled together in a group in a vain attempt at protection. One of the women had a cross hanging from her wrinkled neck. The cross glinted in the sun. I doubted it was made of silver or any precious metal but a soldier wrenched it from her anyway.

David turned when he heard the hoof beats of my horse.

'Good day,' he said, smiling a welcome. 'You are just in time.'

'In time for what?'

'For the execution of these Herero.' He seemed to have overcome his earlier doubts and was enjoying this far too much. He had made his choice.

'What have they done?'

'They are Herero. You heard the General's order.'

I pointed to the woman. 'She is not Ovaherero.'

David frowned. 'No?'

'No. She's a Namaqua. Do you have orders to hang Namaqua?'

'What is that?'

'You'd call her a Hottentot.'

'So what? They are all the same to me. Who cares?'

'I care.' There, I'd said it.

David relaxed and bared his teeth in a knowing smile.

'Fancy her, do you?'

I maintained my patience. Anger would not help the situation. 'I'm trying to stop you getting into trouble. If you have no orders to hang Namaqua, then you are exceeding your authority. What would the General say to that?'

Personally, I thought the General wouldn't give a damn but I knew David would. After all, he was a German soldier in an army where orders are sacred. He hesitated for a few seconds.

'I see what you mean. Very well. It makes very little difference.'

He shouted an order. How he had grown up since that first journey on the train. Now he had the confidence of a corporal who had led men into battle. The soldiers cut the woman free and roughly shoved her to one side. She stood there making no attempt to leave, rubbing her wrists and staring alternately at me and at the ropes and the tree. The rest of the group fell to their knees, praying. She turned her head away at the sound of necks stretching and legs kicking and large tears ran down her cheeks. The stench of voided bowels drifted over the group of soldiers. None of them noticed.

When the dead Ovaherero had been cut down and left for the dogs, I rode over to her. She raised her head and looked at me. Her hair was covered with dust and her faded shift was patched and ragged. Her feet were bare. I leaned down and put out a hand. Her eyes locked on to me and slowly, hesitantly, her hand rose to meet mine. I pulled her up behind me. She weighed nothing, less than a young deer. She was clearly at home on a horse and her hands gripped me lightly around the waist. All this took place in silence. I had a sense that for the first time in years, and without thinking about it, I had made a commitment and taken sides without knowing what I was getting into. It was unsettling and exhilarating at the same time.

The first of many vultures, our regular camp followers, glided in and perched on top of a tree, waiting for us all to leave.

I suddenly realised that my instinctive action might have compromised my mission and thrown suspicion on me as betraying the German cause. Up to that moment I had deliberately remained inconspicuous, staying in the background unless called upon. Now I had exposed myself, and thereby risked drawing more attention to myself. I inwardly cursed myself at roughly the same time as I realised I did not care. Yet the reaction of David and the other soldiers showed that my rescue of the girl had had the opposite effect. In their eyes, because I had come away with loot, I was now one of them, part of the victorious army.

Like all armies, without exception, the German troopers compensated themselves for risking their lives by searching for plunder. They would ransack the native huts looking for gold or silver. The Ovaherero owned little of value to European eyes except for their labour and their women. The soldiers usually contented themselves with burning down the huts and violating the women before abandoning or killing them. They didn't take women with them as that would slow down their progress. I would have to keep close guard upon the Namaqua girl. Coarse comments, grins and obscene mimes confirmed my new found status among them. It was then that I felt a visceral surge of anger. They were now beginning to be the enemy. Her enemy and therefore my enemy.

Even Hartmann flashed a grin of approval and a wave when he saw me riding with the girl seated behind me.

'*Ach*, a prisoner of war! It seems I must offer you my congratulations. Well done!'

I think he may have winked.

'She is not Ovaherero!' I explained, perhaps a shade too vehemently. 'She is a Namaqua.'

This time he laughed aloud.

'She might as well be. Haven't you heard?' he cried, 'we are now at war with the Hottentots as well! Watch your back with her! Always keep a pistol by your side.'

~

It was true. Just at the moment when the Ovaherero were being defeated, the Namaqua under their leader, Hendrik Witbooi, foolishly attacked German supply transports. Von Trotha immediately ceased chasing the Ovaherero, left a holding force in the north and headed south. We went with them, the woman and me in a forward column. If anyone wished to know, I told them she was my assistant interpreter. But no one was interested: as far as they were concerned, she was mine to do with as I liked.

For some of the way, David and his section rode alongside. He seemed to have permanently attached himself to me. But I had the woman to think about. What was I going to do with her? I should have taken her back to her people but that was now nigh on impossible unless I could let her slip away once we approached her homeland. I took the opportunity of the long journey to learn more of her language. At least, that's what I told myself. At first, her answers had to be dragged from her but eventually, as I became a little more fluent, she relaxed and taught me. She was the most beautiful teacher I have ever had.

During the day, she rode behind me. At night, she curled up in a blanket beside our fire. I think she slept more on the horse than she did at night. I was constantly aware of her physical presence, especially the feel of her hands on my waist and the occasional brushing of her leg on mine.

I slept little at night. The stars were beautiful, the Southern Cross dominating the sky but my attention was on her. I believe she felt the same for if a horse whinnied or a sentry stamped his feet, she was awake in an instant and looked around to make sure I was there.

Once I awoke under a sky of a billion stars wheeling overhead and heard a faint whisper. Without turning my head I glanced towards the fire. The woman was there, facing a bat-eared fox that had entered the camp. They often drifted in and out of the encampment, looking for scraps of food. She was talking to it in a voice so low it could have been a trickle of sand. The fox stood stock still, its back to the fire, eyes fixed on the woman. She was on all fours, her head jutting forward, communing across species. I must have moved because suddenly the fox jerked its head and was off into the dark. Slowly she turned and looked at me, her eyes even larger in the firelight. A swift shy smile crossed her face and then she covered herself with the blanket.

Apart from me, that was the only living creature she spoke to. She certainly went nowhere near the troopers. Even then, she was scared, coming close for a second to snatch some food or a few words and then retreating to a safe distance. Nevertheless, over time I came to believe we respected each other. I kept her safe from the hands of the soldiers and she trusted my intentions.

In the southern hemisphere, this season passed for spring but I hadn't seen one day of rain. Water was rationed. The horses had priority but there was none for the woman. She shared mine and in any case drank very little. We would soon be in the heat of the summer and I thought of the Ovaherero dying in the desert. We saw few animals, save a small group of ostriches and a solitary magnificent gemsbok.

As we rode along and entered Namaqualand, the ground grew stonier like the desert of the Bible but there was little evidence of a God here. Our horses and faces and all our clothing were covered with dust. The men were continually cleaning their weapons, especially the machine guns, while keeping watch in case Nama horsemen swooped out of the low hills.

Slowly, in the saddle, and never face to face, I attempted to learn more of the nuances of her language. Over the next few days I tried to tell myself that it was the complicated nature of her native speech that made it unusually difficult to master although, in truth, I was too distracted by her voice itself. It was soft and warm and surprisingly deep at times. Above all, I was fascinated and infatuated by how she trembled with giggles at my attempts to master the clicks and tones of the Nama language. In fact, I began deliberately to make mistakes for the pleasure of feeling the hands around my waist shake with her amusement. At the same time, I learned the names of plants and animals, of rocks and hills and, eventually, in answer to my hesitant questions, her own story.

'My name is Leah,' she said after several attempts to worm it out of her. She wasn't giggling now. Giving someone her name was to give them power over her, even if it wasn't her real name. She told me that once but it was so full of clicks that I couldn't be sure she was making it up. 'Leah' came as a pleasant relief. I gathered it had been given to her by a Christian Mission.

'And what is your name?' she asked.

Without hesitation, I told her.

'Sam,' I said. 'My name is Sam.'

Pressing her face into my shoulder, she said how she had been captured when a child in an Ovaherero raid but she told me very little else except that she was treated almost as a slave, fetching firewood and water, finding pasture for the cows and being beaten if she failed in her tasks.

'So I saved you not only from a hanging,' I said, feeling her tears against my shirt.

There was a long silence.

'Saved me for what?' she said at last in a low voice. 'To be your servant as well?'

I hadn't thought about it. All I had desired was to be with her and I had never for a moment considered her wishes. All at once, I desperately wanted to do whatever she wanted.

'What do you want to do?' I said at last.

She raised her head and whispered directly into my ear.

'I want to go home.'

I thought about that.

'Where is your home?'

'With my people.'

So that was it. To make her happy – and that was suddenly my sole aim in life – I had to find the Nama and hand her over. There was of course the small problem that they were now at war with Germany.

Well, we were in her country anyway.

'Very well,' I said. 'We shall go to your people,' and I felt her hands grip my waist tighter.

There was silence between us after that but it was far from being uncomfortable. Things had been said but far more had been unsaid. A contract had been agreed.

That night, despite the risk of attack, Leah lit our fire even further apart than usual from the troopers and their sentries. She had a way with fire. There was no need for flint or lucifers. With a small bunch of dry grass and a few twigs, she made a fire the Bushman way. She rolled a pointed stick between her hands on another piece of wood until the friction gave birth to a wisp of smoke and then a small tongue of fire. We both fed the fire until it was a miniature blaze that would keep away predators. Without looking at me, she spread her blanket next to mine, took my hand and pulled me down.

I remember the crackling of the fire and the sparks curling up into the night like fireflies and her small lithe body warm in my arms. Oh, how I remember it.

~

They came out of the rising sun, their horses swerving between our tents and wagons, whipping up huge clouds of dust that blinded troopers and panicked horses, oxen and soldiers alike. They fired indiscriminately at men and beasts as the soldiers scrambled for their weapons while pulling on their boots. Mixed with the gunfire, I could hear the cries of men and the screams of wounded horses. Then, just as quickly as they had arrived, they vanished into the dust, leaving behind two of our fellows sprawled dead on the red earth and several others wounded. We had thought we were going to war but the war had come to us. It would be a different kind of war from now on.

First one, then another vulture glided down to a thorn tree, regarding with cold eyes the carnage below. The crimson streams of blood were the only colour in a grim landscape. The jackals and hyenas would almost certainly not be far behind. The burial details would have to work fast.

Leah had huddled behind me, whimpering as the bullets flew, while I was grateful that our fire had been some way away from the encampment. This had not gone unnoticed and while the troopers were clearing up the mess, including shooting the injured horses, several grim glances were fired in our direction. David approached, bare-headed, his young face now contorted with shock and anger. A trickle of blood was carving a track through the dust on his left temple. His pistol was in his hand. I stood up, my blanket still around me. Leah stayed behind me.

'What does your whore have to say about this?' he said hoarsely and waved at the destruction behind him. 'Her people did this. They killed some of my men. Give me one good reason why I shouldn't shoot her on the spot!' The hand with the pistol was shaking.

'I'll give you two good reasons,' I said softly so no one else could hear. 'One, she didn't have anything to do with this. She's been with us for weeks. You don't even know if they're from the same tribe. For all we know she could come from one of the tribes that have kept their contract with Germany. Killing her might add to the enemy. Second, if you so much as try to kill her, you'll have to kill me first. I'd like to see you try. My own pistol, underneath this blanket, is aimed right at your stomach.'

He could see from my face that I wasn't bluffing.

'If you kill me, my men will shoot you and the girl.' But the threat had gone out of his voice and his pistol no longer pointed at me.

'That would be a waste,' I said. 'We are supposed to be at war with the enemy, not with each other.'

Slowly, he nodded and started to turn away. 'Just keep her close,' he said. 'For her own sake. After this, my men will be on edge.'

'Very well. And tell your sentries to do a better job next time. Because there will certainly be a next time. These people are fighting like the Boer in South Africa. There will be no pitched battles: it'll be hit and run from now on. Be prepared.'

He glared at me. There was a long pause. 'I know you!' he said suddenly and stomped off.

What did he mean? 'I know you', that set me thinking. For some time I had nurtured a suspicion that David's desire to be with me was neither an accident nor just an act of friendship. In fact, looking back on it all, I felt fairly certain that he had been ordered to keep an eye on me from the start and that his fellows had kept a little apart from him not only because he was a Jew but because he was an Intelligence Officer. Then there was the matter of the pastor and Amelia. Were they real? Had they been installed on the farm to trap me? After all, it was David who had suggested that we go there with the sick trooper. If my suspicions were true, then David in his anger had let slip more than he should have. It was possible I would have to silence him to maintain my disguise. I should have to be on my guard even more or leave.

~

That night, in total silence, Leah and I packed our stuff and led our horse away from the camp. As we carefully picked our way across the stony ground, the sentries didn't hear a thing. Out of hearing, we mounted and rode off into the night and the unknown.

I had now burned my boats. The Germans would assume the worst and almost certainly follow us, even if only to avenge their fallen comrades. David would almost certainly assume that I was the spy he suspected. Webb, back in London, would be furious if he ever found out that I had abandoned my mission; if we weren't killed first, that is. We were on our own; and also, I realised as the dawn approached, at the mercy of any Nama sharpshooter.

Yet I still had that feeling of freedom, of having made the choice of my life. I wouldn't have had it any other way.

I think Leah felt the same way for as we rode along, she rested her head on my shoulder and crooned a wordless song. She sounded happy and when I twisted round in my saddle to look at her, she gave me the sweetest smile a man could ask for.

Having no chance of collecting supplies in camp, we lived off the land. Leah had a gift of knowing where we might find water, enough for us and the horse. As for food, she found enough roots and berries to keep us going. At times I longed for a hot meal but a fire would have sent a signal to everyone for miles around. At night we huddled together under our blankets for warmth. Neither of us complained.

Once, when we stopped to water and rest the horses, I was cupping my hands to light a cigarette when I felt a tap on my back. I turned to see Leah. She darted forward and prodded me again before jumping back. I had played this game before with my cousins when I was about eight. We used to spend hours in the garden laughing and chasing each other in and out of the trees until, exhausted, we'd flop down on the grass and start looking for four-leaved clovers.

I jumped after Leah but she was so quick, turning on the spot and changing direction, that I never managed to tag her in return until at last she relented and let me touch and hold her.

'You are slow,' she laughed, pulling clear. 'You run like an old man.'

I was too much out of breath to answer and lunged again at her and missed.

'You win,' I said.

'Yes I did.'

I think those were some of the happiest days of my life.

It wouldn't last, of course, we both knew that but it didn't matter.

When we escaped from the camp, we had no plan of action other than to get away as fast as we could. We had no local knowledge of the area and no compass: we had to rely on the sun and the stars to give us a sense of direction. Even then, we had little idea of which direction we wanted to go. In the event, we were guided by the need for water.

We had come away with very little food and only my water bottle and supplies of both in this land were hard to come by. Leah, however, had the ability to smell water together with the knowledge of the sort of places where it might be found.

In this manner we trekked from waterhole to waterhole but, apart from my water bottle, we and the horse could carry only what we could drink.

For food, Leah collected berries and on one occasion she dug deep into the soil and pulled up a root that yielded some sustenance but was bitter to the taste.

We desperately needed more to eat but even if there had been game – and we once saw some zebra – we dare not risk a shot for fear of it being heard by Germans or Nama.

On the day when we caught and ate a snake, I realised that we had to find a better source of provisions. But where? It was at that point that Providence took a hand.

Ten

Leah saw them first. They were lying in a small depression in the ground and when her slender hand pointed them out, my mind raced back to Hartmann's garden in Windhoek and, for a moment, I thought I saw a cluster of bleached human skulls.

'Eggs,' said Leah. 'Ostrich eggs.' So they were, large cream eggs, full of nourishment and ours for the taking. Except for the fact that they were being guarded by a very large ostrich that sat there, regarding us with a baleful eye. We ducked behind a rock and waited for it to lose interest in us.

'We must be careful,' said Leah. I knew that the birds had a vicious kick that could kill a man and that they could run at an impressive speed. What we proposed was, indeed, dangerous but the thought of a giant omelette made me determined to obtain at least one egg.

I led the horse some way away and tied it to a stunted thorn bush.

'We must make a plan,' I said but Leah had already thought of a cunning stratagem. I had the feeling this was not her first time as an egg thief. 'I will lead the bird away,' she said, 'and you must take one of the eggs and run back here.'

'How? You have just said they are dangerous.'

'I will dance for it.'

I had no answer to that. It was the strangest sight I had ever seen. Leah crept into the open some way away from the ostrich but with her arms and legs at awkward angles. Her body assumed the shape of an ostrich. She proceeded to caper about in a figure of eight, wagging her arms, kicking her feet in the dust and sticking her neck before her.

The ostrich spotted her, its long neck rising from the ground and her suspicious eyes fixed on the bizarre figure at some distance from her. Slowly, it rose to its feet and began to approach Leah who moved away while continuing to dance.

I was waiting for the right moment to make my move when music by Strauss insinuated itself into my brain, in time to Leah's dance. '*Strauss*', of course, is the German for 'Ostrich' and the music suited the scene perfectly.

Leah danced and strutted in her primeval ballet until she was some distance from the eggs and the ostrich was between us with its back to me. At what I deemed to be a safe moment, I darted forward, grabbed an egg and ran back to my rock. I was not quick enough.

The ostrich turned and was about to run straight towards me when there was a strange sound that I had heard before: the cry of a *strandwolf*. Immediately, the ostrich turned towards the new sound. Meanwhile, Leah had fallen flat on the ground. The ostrich could see nothing but again there was that eerie cry. This time I realised that it was Leah who had made the noise. Fearful for the rest of her eggs, the ostrich ran back to the clutch and stood there ready to defend them from the hyena.

Leah appeared beside me, panting and covered with the dust she had crawled through.

'Do you have the egg?'

'I do. Let's go!'

We picked up the horse and headed for a small rocky outcrop. Leah found a flat rock and I tested it with my hand which I immediately pulled away. It was hot enough.

Leah shook the egg hard to mix up the contents, took my knife and carefully inserted it in one end of the egg and began turning it until a hole appeared. She tipped the egg up and poured its contents onto the rock where they bubbled and sizzled. In no time at all, I was scraping off pieces of the omelette with my knife and sharing them with Leah.

'Delicious,' I said, licking my fingers. Leah smiled while doing the same. We were like two children eating forbidden sweets. I made to throw the egg shell away.

'No,' she said, laying a gentle hand on my arm. 'Do not break it. We must use it to carry water.' From then on we had her egg and my water bottle.

She fashioned a kind of sling out of twisted roots and a stopper from a pebble and slung the egg over her shoulder. It was time to move on.

The wonderful omelette did not keep our hunger at bay for long. We needed more supplies and there was only one place from which we could obtain a decent amount. A settlement, be it a farm or a group of houses. I said as much to Leah. She gave it some thought and then stood up sniffing the air.

'That way,' she said at last, pointing west. 'People are there.'

'How do you know that?'

She looked at me impatiently. 'I can smell the smoke of their fires.'

'German fires or Nama fires?'

She giggled. 'I cannot tell. But they are not far off. We can be there tomorrow, I think.'

That night we found shelter under some rocks at the foot of a ridge that reared up out of the veldt. We tied up the horse nearby and then pulled in branches of thorn tree to protect all three of us from predators. We would have to take our chances, as usual, with snakes and scorpions. We dropped off almost immediately.

I was woken by a loud gasp from Leah. I grabbed my rifle, ready to fight off the intruder, whatever it was. Only there was no intruder. Leah was kneeling by our blanket, peering up at the slab of rock that acted as the roof of our shelter. The early rays of dawn were poking into the shelter and splashing on the slab and Leah was tracing with her finger something she could see there.

'Look,' she said. 'We are not the first to be here.' She spoke softly, with the voice one usually uses in a place of worship. 'See, these were left here by the Old People.'

Now I could make them out. Someone from long ago, using fingers dipped in charcoal and red ochre, had painted pictures on the rock face. The first images I saw were of strange bulbous plants that neither I nor Leah could recognise. But the others were all too familiar: a giraffe, several antelope and a rhinoceros. Next to that was a scene of a stick-like man spearing a small antelope.

'For good luck in the hunt,' said Leah. 'I have seen paintings like this in other places, painted by the San. These are by their ancestors.'

Below that was the outline of a hand where someone long since dead had pressed his palm against the rock and sprayed red ochre around it. And then, at the end, were two figures, obviously those of a man and a woman together. Leah held her hand over her mouth and giggled.

'They are also hunting,' she laughed.

'Let's hope they found what they wanted,' I said.

She bent down to straighten out the blanket. Holding out a hand she pulled me down.

'Last night we slept under the protection of these pictures from the Old People and we must thank them.'

Later, as we packed up our meagre possessions, she again pointed at the paintings. 'They are a good sign. Today we shall find what we are looking for. We must go while the sun is still climbing the sky.'

The horse was beginning to look as under-nourished as us and we decided to walk for a while to give it some respite and that, fortunately, put us on the right trail. Leah had pointed out that the settlement, whatever it was, would be served by horses and oxen and that there would therefore be a trail of some sorts. All we had to do was find the trail and follow it. It did not take too long for me to find it. One moment I was striding best foot forward, the next I was cursing the universe.

'Damn and blast!' I cried while Leah again burst out into almost uncontrollable giggles. She seemed to be doing that quite often. It was one of the growing bonds between us.

I hopped about and finally was forced to sit down and remove my boot.

'Fresh ox dung,' she laughed, wrinkling her snub nose. 'From early this morning. And look, there is more. It is pointing the way for us.'

I knew it was fresh: it was sticking to my boot like glue. In a few hours it would dry out under the sun but now it was wet and offensively adhesive.

With my boot cleaner and less smelly than before, I remounted the horse with Leah behind me. At that height, we could see the ruts of the track straddling the piles of dung and soon after, we could make out the blue haze of buildings on the horizon.

'Listen,' I said. 'If the people living there are Nama, you will have to go and get food. Tell them your family are the only survivors of a German attack. Everyone is exhausted after walking for days with very little food or water and that you have come to look for supplies to take back to them.'

Leah considered this. 'They might offer to come with me,' she said.

'That's true but we shall have to take that chance. If they do, you will have to find some way of getting away from them.'

'And if they are German?'

'Well, I shall have to bluff my way in with a similar story only I shall say that I need to rejoin the German forces in the field. They will certainly not offer to come with me for fear of ambush.'

She gave me a solemn look and then suddenly embraced me. 'The spirits of the Old People will protect us,' she said. I hoped she was right.

No sooner had we gone more than a few hundred yards when I saw a puff of smoke by the side of the road.

'Down!' I cried, leaping off the horse. Leah followed me. Lying flat on the earth, still holding on to the horse's reins, I risked a look in the direction of the smoke. At the same time I became aware of a smell that was faintly familiar.

We both crawled towards the smoke. Where there was a fire, there might be food, I thought. When I was closer to the source of the smoke, I motioned to Leah to take over holding the reins while I investigated further.

The smell grew stronger until I suddenly realised what it was. Sulphur. This wasn't smoke from a fire. In fact, it wasn't smoke at all; it was steam!

As usual Leah had already reached this conclusion and was tugging the horse to follow her towards a small opening in the earth from which the steam was rising. It was a hot spring. The water was bubbling out of the ground and almost immediately sinking back from where it came leaving just a small pool around the spring. Leah was looking at it wide-eyed.

'Water!' she cried and put her hand in the pool, immediately snatching it out again. 'Hot water!'

I had heard of such springs occurring across the country, particularly in the south and one of the locally recruited German soldiers had told me there was a dead volcano some way to the north of us. In this case, the spring and its fellows were almost certainly what had attracted settlement here in the first place.

I tried to think of a way to scoop some water out. Despite the sulphurous smell, I became aware of how desperately dirty I was and how much I could do with a hot bath. Well, I wasn't able to have a bath but we could have a wash and so make ourselves more presentable when we entered the settlement.

I cast around and eventually found a piece of rock with a small depression in it, enough to act as a kind of basin. Eventually, with a sigh, I removed one of my boots and used it to transfer water from the pool to the rock. The boot would soon dry in the sun and any residual smell would be put down, if anyone cared, to lack of personal cleanliness.

We both stripped naked and although we had no soap, we took great delight in washing each other down. Before long we looked less like dust devils and more like normal human beings.

Once we had dressed, and feeling fresh and ready for action, we remounted and proceeded towards the settlement until we reached a small hillock that would act as a place to hide and from which to observe our destination.

I climbed to the top, lay down on the warm stones and took a long look. Through the ripples of the heat haze I could make out several European-style houses and, on one side, a round stone tower. Barricades had been built out of upturned ox-carts and some way behind them there were several horses tethered. At the barricades themselves I could see brown uniformed soldiers. *Schutztruppen*. The place was occupied by Germans.

Leah was concerned for my safety. 'They could shoot you before you reach there,' she said. 'I don't want to lose you.'

I hugged her. 'I'll be fine,' I said, with more conviction than I felt. 'You stay here and keep well out of sight. I promise I'll be back by nightfall.'

I climbed back on the horse and slowly walked it towards the barricades, armed only with my German rifle, my wits and with, what I hoped was my trump card, old Göring's letter.

As I drew closer, they spotted me. The sentries were clearly nervous and they raised their rifles as I approached. A machine-gun team ran to man their weapon. The nearest barricade showed signs of a recent attack with fresh bullet holes in the underside of the ox cart. Inside the barrier there were shattered windows in the nearest building and the stone tower had the scars of a recent fusillade. A glint of reflected sunlight from the top of the tower indicated the presence of a lookout with a telescope.

My main task was not to alarm the guards and I continued to saunter up to the barricade, carefully keeping my rifle visibly slung over my shoulder. '*Halt!*'

I did as I was ordered. A young soldier, holding his rifle in shaky hands, slowly advanced. A bandage under his hat showed he had been in action recently.

'What is your business?'

In such situations I had always found that the best course of action was to tell as much of the truth as I could. My bluff was to be simple and straightforward, relying on Göring's letter to do most of the talking for me.

'I am a civilian attached to the staff of General von Trotha,' I began in my best High German. 'Unfortunately I became separated from the column I was with when we were attacked by a band of Hottentot rebels. As a result I became lost in this unfriendly land. But God has seen to protect me and has led me to you. I require food, water and directions so that I can again be on my way to join our gallant troops.'

The pale faced soldier, who looked as if he were barely out of school, told me to wait where I was while he conferred with his superior officer. In a short while, the officer appeared. He was a different kettle of fish.

He was a burly and seasoned NCO and, by the depth of his tan, he could well have been recruited locally. I would have to go carefully. I repeated my story.

He did not look convinced and looked me up and down.

'How do I know you are not a deserter?' he growled.

'As I told you, I am a civilian,' I said.

'You are dressed like a civilian but you could have stolen those clothes from a farmer or some such.'

There was only one way to handle this, the Prussian way.

'Take me to your superior officer,' I barked. 'I have papers to prove who I am and who I am not.'

He tried to stare me out but I have played that game before and I rested easy in my saddle to demonstrate how confident I was. I raised an eyebrow at his lack of action and, true to form, his training told and he backed down.

'Very well. Wait here.'

As I waited, keeping an eye on the sentries who were still at full alert, I caught sight of another flash of light from the top of the stone tower. Suddenly, I stiffened. This was not a reflection from a telescope but from something else. A heliograph. The fort was in communication with other German forces. It was even possible that it had been in touch with David's patrol. In that case, he might have passed on information about my slipping away with Leah.

I had no choice but to stay where I was. Even if I wanted to beat a retreat, I could not outrun a machine gun.

The NCO returned with his superior. He turned out to be young and with the air of a fop but that, I knew, could be deceptive. At the moment he looked tired and harassed.

He eyed me up and down. 'Well?' he said. 'What do you want?' Again I repeated my story in a tone that implied I was his equal and then bent down from the saddle and handed him Göring's letter.

He took it and read it. He read it again.

'Very well,' he said at last, handing the letter back. 'We can give you some food and water but it won't be much as our own supplies are limited. Nevertheless, they should last until you rejoin your fellows. As for directions, well, the nearest body of our soldiers is that way,' and he pointed west. 'They are about twenty kilometres away. God go with you.'

He saluted me and issued orders to his men. Save for a lookout, the soldiers relaxed and the machine gun crew sat down and took out their pipes. In about ten minutes, a soldier pushed his way through the barricade carrying a canvas bag of food and a bottle of schnapps.

'To keep your spirits up,' he said.

I thanked him and turned to go. I looked up at the tower. Again there was a flash of light. I urged my horse into a trot.

I heard a shout behind me and looking over my shoulder, I saw a soldier leaning over the parapet of the tower and calling down to the men below. They stood up and pointed at me. I kicked my horse and broke into a canter and then a gallop. One or two shots whistled past but nowhere near me. The machine gun crew were still scrambling to resume their position but I was already almost out of range.

There was no way they would pursue me. For all they knew I would lead them into an ambush. Soon I reached the hillock where I had left Leah. I gave her the bag and bottle and she leapt up behind me. Avoiding heading west, we rode off into the safety of the open veldt.

A little while later, having made sure we had not been followed, we stopped under the thin shade of a thorn tree next to a small waterhole unerringly detected by Leah to examine the contents of the bag. After our diet of recent days, what we had was a feast. A large amount of biltong, that would keep us going for ages; a quantity of sausage that Leah sniffed at and rejected; a hunk of cheese, the thought of which made my mouth water; a large piece of bread that was still warm from the oven and, best of all, some coffee. Except that I had no container in which to make it.

Leah laughed at the problem.

'You want to cook the coffee? Then we steal a pot.'

'Fine. Excellent idea. But from where?'

'A farm, we will find one soon.'

As usual, she was right. That evening we came across a deserted farmstead. It had not been abandoned for long. The roof was still intact and there was glass in the windows. Animal feed was still stored in a barn. Presumably the inhabitants had fled to the town for protection. Inside, in one corner of what had been the kitchen, we found a small saucepan.

'I think we shall spend the night here,' I grinned.

There was enough wood around the farm to light a small fire. We ate bread and cheese followed by coffee. That coffee was the best I have ever tasted.

Later, we snuggled down under our blanket in the barn while the horse enjoyed a meal of abandoned grass and I asked Leah a question I had been meaning to put to her for a long time.

'Would you be able to tell me about your life before we met?'

She propped herself up on one elbow, her large eyes suddenly full of a deep sadness.

'Must I?'

'No, not if you don't want to.'

'Why do you want to know?'

'Because I want to know everything about you.'

She stroked my face. 'Later, maybe.'

We slept.

In the middle of the night, long before dawn, I woke to find her leaning over me, with tears in her eyes.

'I will tell you,' she said. 'But you must hold me as I do so.'

She nestled in the crook of my arm as she told her story.

'The Nama and the Ovaherero are now allies, fighting against the Germans but not too long ago they were enemies, fighting over land. There were many small battles between the two peoples and in one of these my parents were killed. I, too, would have died but I was rescued by a group of Gainin – you would call them Bushmen, or San – who brought me up as one of them and taught me so much of the San way of life. I learned about the plants and the animals and how to find water and roots to eat. Then my Gainin family were also killed.'

I had to ask. 'Who would kill the San? They were not involved in the wars, were they?' She didn't answer me, her whole being engaged with her past history and she continued with her story.

'They were killed by a white farmer because he found them on his land. Many whites think the San are lower than the animals. I was still young and the farmer took a fancy to me, the way he would adopt an animal, having killed its parents.

I became his servant, drawing water from the well, feeding the chickens, cleaning the house and doing whatever his woman told me to do. He was a tall man with a black beard and a big belly; she was a bad tempered Ovaherero who did nothing but beat me. She beat me when I was slow in doing things and beat me when I was good. She just liked beating me.

My master did not beat me, even when he was drunk which was a lot of the time, but as I grew older and became a woman, he started looking at me in a new way. His woman noticed and shouted and argued with him about me and then she beat me. When they were not fighting with each other, they drank together, making the British traders rich.

One day, while she was snoring in her room, he came to me and started to fondle me. I called for him to stop, hoping the woman would hear us but she was fast asleep. I managed to get away from him and ran into the farmyard and hid among the cattle. When he didn't find me he laughed and said he would get me later. That night I crept away from the farm.

I walked for miles until I came upon a group of Ovaherero women and old men. They told me how the war had started and that the men and cattle had gone north to meet their chief. They took me in and gave me shelter. They were very kind to me.

Then the Germans came and hanged them and you saved me.'

I held her as the tears ran down her cheeks and her body shook with sobs. Eventually, she fell asleep in my arms and soon after my own eyelids felt heavy and I dropped off.

A sudden noise woke us both. It was the click of a rifle being cocked.

Eleven

There were about a dozen of them on horseback, standing on a small hillock, all wearing broad brimmed hats and long jackets and with bandoliers slung across their shoulders. Their bronzed faces, high cheek bones and narrow eyes proclaimed who they were. Nama. Their overall demeanour and their obvious ease in the saddle reminded me of Cape Dutch commandos, guerilla fighters capable of living and fighting in this harsh terrain. They presented a more formidable foe, despite their numbers, than the Ovaherero.

The one with the cocked rifle was aiming at my heart, not at my head. He had no intention of missing. Another rode forward and pointed at Leah. His piercing eyes were like those of a bird of prey.

'Wait!' he said. His accent was different from Leah's but perfectly understandable. 'Who is that woman?'

Leah stepped out from behind me. She was still trembling.

'Has this man abused you?' More rifles pointed in my direction.

Leah shook her head and her small hand crept into mine.

'No. He saved my life. He is not like the other Germans.' Her grip tightened. 'He is mine.' Despite our situation, my heart lifted at her words.

'This man is not a German,' said a new yet strangely familiar voice. 'Lower your rifles.'

I turned to see one of the men ride forward. He spurred his horse nearer to me placing it between me and the rifleman and swept off his hat. Now I could see his burnt lined face, a face that I had last seen in British territory. I could see no sign of the ravages of alcohol that had been so apparent when I saw him last.

'Thomas,' I said, breathing easier. 'You're a long way from Walfish Bay and Mr Morrison.'

He bared his few teeth in a welcoming smile.

'So are you. What are you doing here?'

I shrugged my shoulders. The truth wouldn't hurt for once.

'We're running from the Germans. There's a forward column not far from here.'

The men all laughed and lowered their rifles.

'We know,' said Thomas. 'We gave them a little surprise a few days ago.'

'That was you, was it? You surprised us as well. Fortunately we were out of the line of fire.'

He continued to find this amusing. 'You were lucky, then. What were you doing with the Germans?'

'Watching, observing, noting. And what are you and your men doing?'

'We are at war with the Germans, Englishman. Just like the Herero.'

They hadn't heard then.

'The Ovaherero are no longer at war,' I said. 'The Germans have defeated them and those they have not killed they have driven into the Great Sand desert or will enslave.'

Thomas's face tightened in a grimace. His companions began exchanging worried looks and muttering among themselves.

'So the rumours are true,' said Thomas slowly. 'Now we fight alone. But it doesn't matter. We have no choice. We shall try to kill as many as we can before they kill us.'

One of the group called out. Thomas nodded.

'The Germans are not far off. Come with us.'

'Where are you going?'

'We are going to give them an interesting tour of our beautiful country. You shall see. Come!'

~

Before we set off, Leah removed a necklace from round her neck and looped it round mine. The necklace was made from tiny fragments of ostrich egg shell with a hole drilled in each piece and a shell as a central pendant. The whole thing was threaded on a leather thong. Once it was in place she stroked my cheek and smiled.

'Thank you,' I said as she swung up behind me on my horse.

She said nothing but gripped me with her hands and made a click with her tongue that made the horse neigh and follow the others.

We travelled over this stony desert at a speed slow enough to give the Germans a chance to catch us up. One rider was detailed to disturb the ground enough for even the most short-sighted trooper to follow.

'We are leading them to a place of ambush,' said Thomas. I looked around but could see no obvious position from where an ambush could be launched.

'Is there a ravine near by?' I asked.

'A ravine? Why do you ask?'

'Well, it would force them to travel in Indian file and it would then be easier to pick them off one by one.'

'No, there is no ravine but if there were, they would be wary and alert. We are leading them to a very pleasant place: a trap with very tasty bait. They will embrace the spot as if it is their own home,' he said.

I was puzzled by this but he refused to explain what he meant. He wanted me to see for myself, no doubt to give me a better opportunity to marvel at his cunning.

He was right. It was cunning.

~

The horsemen eventually pulled up near a low hill. Thomas beckoned me forward to accompany him as he dismounted. We, too, dismounted and followed. Over a small ridge we lay down and observed our destination. The trap.

'A farm?' I whispered.

'Yes. A German farm.'

It lay in a little hollow, partly masked by a small group of trees taking advantage of local water. A wind pump was clacking nearby. Some horses were stabled in an open-sided barn next to the main house. It was indeed a German farm that doubled as a military horse relay post. Tempting bait.

Thomas and his men had ensured that their trail ceased about half a mile from the post so that it appeared as if they had disappeared into thin air. Once the Germans realised that they had lost the trail, they almost certainly would rest at the post and change or water their horses before continuing their search.

'They will relax,' said Thomas, 'and when they have relaxed, we shall wake them up again.'

'And where will we be?'

'Up there,' and he pointed to a jumble of burnt rocks that formed a natural wall. Like so many features of this landscape they gave the illusion of having been shaped and assembled by some giant hands. 'Those rocks at the top there form a natural fort. We shall keep low among the rocks.'

'And the horses?'

He smiled. 'Do not worry. They will be muzzled and kept a little way off. Once the action begins, they will be brought to the other side of the hill, ready for us to move on.' He thought for a second. 'And you and the woman will come with us.'

It wasn't a suggestion but a command. He didn't say why but he didn't need to. Trust was a rare commodity in this war. I didn't blame him; recently I had stopped having trust in myself.

I thought I was fit but I was left behind as Leah and the Nama raced up the hill like sure-footed goats. Sweating and puffing, I slowly clambered up rocks that resembled giant steps. Just below the crest of the hill I was met by a bevy of grins from the guerrillas and a wry smile from Leah.

The leader muttered a command and we spread out so that each one of us had a line of fire. My rifle was handed back to me by Thomas.

'We need every gun,' he said. 'Now you are one of us. Use every bullet wisely.'

He was right. I had made my choice, I was one of them. I settled behind my appointed rock from which I could see the farm and aligned my rifle.

Leah wouldn't leave me and clung to me like a long shadow. She gave me some water as we crouched down and waited for David and his men. The sun was still high in the sky and there was little shade. Despite our dry mouths, I could feel the sweat pooling at my throat and under my shirt. One of the men gave me a hat; a German slouch hat with the rosette yanked off. I didn't like to ask how he had obtained it. I gave it to Leah and knotted a handkerchief over my own head much to general amusement.

I reasoned that we couldn't be too far from the border with Cape Colony and I started to plan how we might, under cover of any skirmish, borrow another horse and make a run for it. I didn't give much for our chances. Perhaps I could persuade Thomas to provide us with a map or even escort us there. I tried to calculate how far we were from British territory. As far as I could tell, the farm was deep in the south-east corner of the country so it was almost certainly not a great distance from the border. My musings were cut short by urgent whispers among the men. The Germans were coming.

A trick I had learned from a Zulu warrior in the south was to regard your own head as a rock and not move whatever happened. That way you could observe the enemy without a shot winging your way. My handkerchief was khaki and so my plan was to keep it on as a protection from the sun and to wait, resting my chin on a flat stone. Leah crouched out of sight beside me. We were both covered with dust. I gave her a quick smile before settling down. I could feel my heart racing and my mouth even dryer than usual as I felt the physical change from being hunted to the hunter.

I heard the jingle of their harnesses before the Germans came into sight in a cloud of dust. There were only half a dozen of them but I had no doubt that the rest of the column was not far behind with the machine gun and cannons. The Nama had to be quick. We gripped our weapons tighter and held our breath. Leah clutched at my arm.

One of the troopers dismounted to examine the trail but clearly found none of our tracks. There was some head scratching and discussion and then one of them, possibly David, pointed in the direction of the farm. We watched them make their way there and dismount, watering their horses, rifles slung over their backs. A farmer, unarmed, emerged from the house and greeted the soldiers. They were unsuspecting and vulnerable; it was the perfect moment to attack them.

What followed was like something out of Mr Hickok's Wild West Show except that it was real. One moment the German soldiers were relaxing, tunics off, pipes lit. The next they were reeling under a withering hail of rifle fire. Another soldier ran out of the farmhouse, rifle in hand, only to be cut down. It lasted only a few minutes before they were all sprawled on the ground, their terrified horses yanking at their tethers in an effort to escape.

We bounded down the hill, jumping over rocks and slithering down scree to where we were met by our horses brought round from the other side of the hill. One man rode over to the German mounts and led them away. The rest quickly gathered all the rifles and ammunition from the dead troopers before remounting, ready to ride off. I noticed that there was no looting from the pockets of the dead.

'Come,' said Thomas. 'We must go. The other soldiers will not be far behind and will have heard our gunfire. They will be here before we know it.'

As he galloped off, I was about to join him, Leah clinging on behind, when I noticed a movement from one of the Germans. I was about to ignore him when I caught a glimpse of his face. It was David. I don't know why but I turned my horse round and rode towards him.

I dismounted, rifle at the ready but he was too far gone to be a danger. I knelt down beside him. His young face and hair were smeared with blood and sand and it was clear that he was mortally wounded. I placed my rifle on the ground next to him. He opened his eyes at the movement and tried to sit up. A drop of blood trickled from the corner of his mouth.

'Hello,' he gasped.

'Don't speak. Here, have some water.'

'It hurts. I'm done for, I know it.'

'Nonsense. It's just a wound. Once you've been fixed up, you'll be fine.'

He looked me in the eye and gave a faint smile. 'We both know you're lying. Now listen, there's not much time. I've something to ask you.'

Leah was suddenly beside me.

'We must go,' she urged. 'More horses are coming. Germans!'

'One more minute. David, what do you want?'

'I know what you are.'

'I am doing my duty to my country,' I said lamely. 'You would have done the same.'

'No, no, not that. That's not important.' He coughed and more blood dripped from his mouth. He had to catch his breath between each word.

'Do you know the name of this place?'

I shook my head.

'It's just a farm and relay post.'

'True but it has a name. It's called Farm Jerusalem.'

He was growing paler by the second with the loss of blood. His voice dropped to a whisper and I had to bend lower to hear what he was saying.

'Mama was right. I'm going to die here. Now please do one last thing for me. I know what you are: I can always tell.' He tried to sit up but failed. I put my arms round his shoulders and lifted him gently. 'Thank you.' He fixed those brown soulful eyes on mine. 'Say Kaddish for me. Please.'

So I did. I hadn't said the prayer for the dead since I was small and the words came haltingly but I remembered them from across the years and Grandpa's funeral.

'*Yit'gadal*,' I began, '*v'yitkadash sh'mei raba*.'

I had barely finished before a cry from Leah caused me to look up. A group of German soldiers rode up just as I gently lay David back on the ground. I had just enough time and presence of mind to push my rifle under David's body. The troopers surveyed the carnage with mounting anger on their faces. The leader barked a harsh order. Two troopers pointed their rifles at me while another roughly grabbed Leah. She was still wearing my hat; a German trooper's hat that was roughly snatched away from her.

'We know where the bitch found that hat,' said one of them.

'No!' I cried and launched myself towards her only to feel a movement behind me and see the shadow of a rifle raised like a club. There was the sound of Leah screaming and then, nothing.

I don't know how long I lay there unconscious but when I came round, Leah was gone but someone else I knew was staring down at me as I lay bound on the bare earth. It was the highly polished boots that identified him.

'Explain yourself,' said Hartmann, 'and it had better be good.' The scar on his cheek was even more livid than usual against his sunburnt skin.

My head was aching and I could feel blood on my lips but my first thought for once was not of myself.

'What have you done with Leah?' I croaked. 'Where is she?'

He looked at me with one eyebrow raised as he lit a cigar.

'Your Hottentot whore? Your enemy whore? She is a prisoner of war and has been taken to where she should have gone in the first place. Now tell me why I should not have you executed as a traitor.'

I did what I do best. I lied.

'We were taken from our camp by a band of Nama guerrillas. They held us captive while they laid an ambush for the forward column and forced us to watch them kill our soldiers. In the confusion we managed to escape and while they rode off, we came to administer to our wounded. I was helping David when you arrived.'

Hartmann considered this but not for long enough. He tapped the ash from his cigar.

'That's most unlikely. Why would they bother to capture you? Why not execute you straightaway? What value would you be to them? No, I think your whore led you astray. You are a traitor and will be treated as such. Firing party!'

Two of his men dragged me none too gently to one of the trees by the farm and tied me to it. Four others were drawn up in a line ready to act as my executioners.

'Sir! Sir! This man is still alive!' A trooper was bending over David.

Hartmann strode over to the trooper and knelt down on one knee by David. His face was turned to me and he kept his eyes fixed on me as he spoke to Hartmann. I couldn't hear what was taking place or what was being said but a few minutes later it was all over and Hartmann closed David's eyes. The firing squad raised their rifles. Hartmann held up a hand and ordered them to stand down.

'Well,' he said as he approached me. 'It appears you were telling the truth. You can thank the Jew boy for saving your life. Untie him.'

So they untied me and gave me a horse.

'Where is the woman?' I asked.

'Forget about her,' said Hartmann. 'We have work to do. A native woman is of no consequence. Mention her again and I shall have you flogged. Is that clear?'

～

Over the next few weeks, under the close eye of two troopers, I travelled all over the south, chasing the Nama. This was much to my anger and frustration. Until I met Leah I had been content to take my time over my mission, allowing the winds of war to blow me where they wished. Now, I could not wait to escape from the Germans and discover where Leah was being held and then to find her and free her. I dared not contemplate the possibility that she was no longer alive. All the time I was either seeking to find a way of getting away or distressing myself with wondering what was happening to Leah. The more we rode across this stony waste, the more I felt time slipping away.

There were no pitched battles like Waterberg that had destroyed the Ovaherero. Instead there were literally hundreds of skirmishes in which the Germans, in order to match the mobility of the Nama fighting on their home ground, were forced to relinquish the use of cannon and machine-guns and the oxen that transported them. Most of these skirmishes were inconclusive, each one leaving a few dead and wounded from each side in its wake.

The enormous size of the rugged inhospitable country and the inexperience of newly arrived soldiers were clearly leading to a stalemate. The Germans were hampered by illness and fatigue and were very dispirited. It looked as if this sort of warfare could go on for years. I had no idea about the condition of the Nama but there were not many of them, only a couple of thousand, and they were losing men each day. I doubted if they could actually win. From what Leah told me, there was also the possibility of the different clans falling out with each other. One clan in Bethany had actually stayed neutral so far. It was a total mess.

All this time, I didn't care who won; all I was concerned about was Leah. I had to get away and find her. I had no idea what was happening to her and my dreams were full of terrifying images of her being abused, tortured and killed. Given what had happened to the Ovaherero, they were all possible, even likely.

There was only one way of finding out and that was through Hartmann.

Trading on our common activities in the South African war, I spent as much time as possible worming my way into his friendship once more. One night, as he sat by the fire with a cigar and a bottle of schnapps, I walked over to him.

'How do you think von Trotha will achieve victory?' I said, sitting down on a convenient rock.

He looked at me coldly. 'Isn't it obvious?'

'Not to me. After all, it's a different situation from up North. The Nama are more like the Boers. They specialise in ambush and surprise attack. They have great mobility. You will not bring them to battle.'

'Nonsense. The Hottentots do not have the bravery or the brains of the Boers. They are mere savages. The General will grind them into the rocks.'

'I'm sure he will. He's already proved his genius with his victory over the Ovaherero.'

He liked that and offered me some schnapps.

Slowly, over that night and several that followed, Hartmann thawed and became quite an expert in explaining to me how the General would soon bring the Nama to book. I did not point out that victory seemed remarkably elusive given the time and effort that his troopers were giving to the war.

'We can easily defeat them,' he said. 'If only Berlin weren't so flabby and cowardly. Instead of shouting our efforts to the skies, cheap politicians are complaining about the expense of the war and one or two of them are attacking our methods. Given half a chance, I would hang the lot and let the Kaiser have a totally free hand.'

One night, as we peed together into a thorn bush, I asked him what the plans were for the Nama once they had been defeated. Hartmann buttoned his trousers and walked back to the fire.

'We have been looking at the British and how they defeated the Boers. They couldn't win in battle against the commandos so they decided to use civilians as a weapon.'

'The concentration camps.'

'Exactly. As you know, they rounded up the women and children and put them into camps, where many of them died from lack of food and sickness. That helped bring the Boers to heel. We are already doing the same with the remaining Herero.'

I didn't mention that there was really no need for such camps as the Ovaherero had already been defeated. But I did ask why.

'Because we need them to build this country. The Herero are a physically strong race and we shall make them build roads and railways and help farmers with their cattle. It's all very logical.'

'And what about the Nama?'

Hartmann spat into the fire causing one log to hiss and sizzle.

'We have camps for them, too. But they are not a strong race and I expect most of them not to survive. There will be no more Hottentots once this war is over.'

I nodded as if in agreement. 'Where are these Nama camps?'

Hartmann looked at me stony-faced and then threw back his head and laughed.

'Are you still dreaming of your whore? Well, I'll tell you for all the good it may do you, or her.'

'Thank you. Where is she?'

'The Hottentots are in camps in Windhoek and Swakopmund but mostly in Lüderitzbucht.'

He scratched his chin and looked deep into the fire. After a while he sighed.

'Go on, go and look for her. I very much doubt you'll find her. Hard work doesn't seem to suit her race. Take your horse and go.'

Before he could change his mind, I packed my bags. The soldiers watched me. I think they were happy to see the back of me. It felt as if they regarded me as some kind of ill omen. Although I had no idea where it was or how far away it was, I decided to head for the nearest camp of the three mentioned by Hartmann. Lüderitz.

At last I was actually doing something. A small seed of hope still lurked inside my breast. I spurred my horse and headed away from the troops and out into the plains.

Twelve

A river. A genuine, real, flowing river. I could smell the water and suddenly I was aware of how filthy I was.

It was the Orange River, the border between German South West Africa and British South Africa. It was one of only two perennial rivers in the entire German territory, the other being in the far north, acting as the border of GSWA and Portuguese Angola. In between, nothing except waterholes and dry river beds hoping for a rare downpour. Not for the first time, I wondered what the Germans saw in this land.

My horse cared for none of this and was enjoying himself drinking. I had bad news for him.

Once I had crossed the river, I would be free of the war and all the horrors that went with it. If I wished, I could find a suitable point at which to wade across and once more be with my own people. I could even get a message to Webb, not that I cared any longer. However, that was not my wish. If I entered South Africa, I would be abandoning Leah. I had no choice but to remain within the bounds of German territory and continue my search.

First, however, I stripped off and trusting there were no crocodiles, I slipped into the cool water. My God it was good! I scraped off the dirt and dust and then lay on the bank, drying myself in the sun, contemplating how I was on the junction of two worlds in more ways than one.

When I left Hartmann, we had been patrolling not far from the border in order to stop Nama bands from travelling in and out of the country. Like so much in this war, it was an entirely fruitless manoeuvre. The border was about 550 kilometres long and the number of troops needed to guard it would be far more than the Germans had in the whole of the country. In addition, Hartmann had told me that they had no plans to move any more troops into the country. And then rumblings back in Germany about the cost and the drawn out nature of the war meant there was little stomach in Berlin for further conflict. I thought that Webb had his answer but so had I. If the border was that porous, then as we were near the lower reaches I thought I would cross it and follow the river to the coast to travel northwards to Lüderitz. It eventually turned out that that was a bad idea.

I dressed and pulled the horse away from the water. He was not a particularly friendly creature and I had accordingly named him Otto after Bismarck, the man who had decided to claim this land for Germany.

'Sorry, Otto,' I said as I remounted. 'It's not over yet.'

I rode by the side of the river as it wound its way to the Atlantic, taking advantage of the availability of water to keep Otto and me going. I camped by the river at night, with a large fire to keep off predators, and during the day I rode mile after mile towards the sea, the tantalising green strip of the south bank of the river constantly in sight.

It became clear after several attempts to find a boat of some description that the river was navigable in short stretches only. To cap it all, there were no boats. At one point I thought seriously about leaving Otto behind and trust to finding a boat to float me down the river to the ocean. However, I would need him to ride north from the river's mouth up to Lüderitz. And so I rode along the German bank for several days until the stony desert gave way to dunes. We were now on the final stretch before we would reach the river mouth.

~

One morning I tasted strong salty air and I rounded a bend to find the sea. The river fed into a large bay in which the breakers were crashing on to the beach. I dismounted and looked around me. Behind me was the river. Out to sea was an endless mass of menacing water. Both north and south was a long desolate line of beach stretching away for ever. I began to realise the impossible nature of the task I had set myself. I squatted down by the river gravels while Otto munched on a small clump of wind-bent vegetation. I had achieved nothing. There was simply no way I could travel up the coast to Lüderitz. There was no food, there was no water. I was in the same position as those poor souls who over the centuries had been shipwrecked on this coast and made it ashore only to realise they were doomed to die of thirst. If I moved away from the river, I would share their fate. There was nothing for it: I would have to travel back into the interior and find a land route.

I sat there for a few hours, playing the game of five stones with some quartz pebbles from the river, thinking of alternatives. There were none. From what I recollected of the terrain, I would have to travel up to the |Khomas mountains and from there to Lüderitz via Aus. It would take a week or two, maybe more, and meanwhile poor Leah was probably incarcerated in a German concentration camp. That didn't bear thinking about and once my horse had fed and rested, I pocketed the pebbles and prepared to set off.

I had one foot in the stirrups when I froze. In the far distance, to the north, were two figures and they were slowly approaching. I dismounted once more and waited for them. Eventually, through the curtain of spray, one figure emerged: a man and by his side what appeared to be a large dog, which struck me as strange until I realised it was not a dog. Otto was uneasy and pulled at the reins.

'Steady, boy,' I said. 'Steady.'

I could understand his nervousness for the animal was a large brown hyena, a *strandwolf*, similar to the one I had seen on the road between Walfish Bay and Swakopmund. I hadn't met a single person for days, not even a border guard, so I patiently waited, hoping I might get clearer directions as to the best route to Lüderitz.

As the man came closer, I could see it definitely wasn't a German but maybe a Bushman or a Nama with matted hair, dressed in greasy rags and smoking a pipe. A solitary individual strolling along the beach was strange enough even at the best of times. I had heard stories of a tribe living off shellfish and what could be found washed up from the sea but as far as I knew no one had seen them for years. Some said they were a branch of the Nama, others that they were a sort of Bushman. *Strandlopers*, they were called, beachcombers.

I waited, smoking a cigarette. The *strandloper* was taking his time but then, I guess that like the Prophets, he had plenty of time to spend. Finally, he came close enough for me to see his features and catch a whiff of him. I had once seen a dead seal putrefying on a beach down south and it had smelled very much like this individual.

The *strandwolf* lay down at a word of command but continued to watch the man as he and I met on the river bank. He certainly resembled a Nama so I said a few words of formal greeting in that language which brought a broad smile to his wrinkled face. He removed the pipe from his mouth, having first expelled two strong jets of smoke through his nostrils.

'Good day,' he said. 'Have you eaten?'

I had speared and eaten a fish in the river not long before so I nodded but he squatted on the sand and opened a leather bag slung over a bony shoulder. He produced a small melon, cut it open with an iron knife and offered me a small piece. It was slightly sour but refreshing.

In turn, I gave him a cigar that Hartmann had forced upon me before I left. He allowed me to light it, watching my lucifers with some surprise. His eyes widened at the blue spurt of the match but that didn't stop him accepting the flame with alacrity.

He gave a sigh of pleasure as he exhaled. The smoke went some way to masking the stench of his body.

After a period of polite silence, I broke with convention and told him my name.

'I'm Sam,' I said. 'Would you be offended if I asked you your name?'

He drew on the cigar. 'I have no name,' he said. 'Or if I have, I have forgotten it.'

'Forgotten your own name?'

'I have had no use for it for many years.' He glanced up and down the shore. 'Where are you going?'

'To the north, to the German harbour at Lüderitz Bay.'

His face darkened at the name and he spat into the sand.

'Why are you going there?'

I explained the situation, omitting nothing. He spat again.

'It is a place of pain and darkness,' he said, 'It is the home of the dead and the near dead. Not one of my people would willingly go there. You may be safe but you will need to protect your spirit. I shall show you how to get there and may you find what you want. Now look and take note.'

He stood up and picked up a stick from the river bank. The *strandwolf* stirred and growled but made no further move. The *strandloper* once more squatted and began drawing on a patch of damp sand.

'You must return back up the river until you reach this spot. It is where the sands end and the stones begin. There you must leave the river,' he said, making a mark.

He painstakingly drew a route, not as a map but as a series of pictures. He took care to indicate where I could find water and food, mostly in the form of melons. I had no paper and memorised everything. My life depended on it. He pointed out several significant landmarks and eventually I felt certain I could follow the route, having noted them all. The journey was going to be long and arduous.

'Thank you,' I said when he stood up to indicate he had finished.

'You will forgive me if I don't come with you,' he said, 'but they will kill me if they see me.'

'Who will?'

'Anyone,' he said and gave me a crooked smile. 'Soon we shall all be exterminated. Even now, I may be the last of our people.'

'So why did you not hide or run away when you saw me?' I asked.

'Because of that.' He pointed to the pendant round my neck that Leah had given to me what already seemed a long time ago. It was just a simple shell suspended on a leather thong between shards of ostrich egg shell.

'What about it?'

'That is a gift from a Nama woman who loves you and you wear it with pride. You would not harm me. Now, repeat to me my directions.'

I did so and he said he was satisfied.

'Go well,' he said, getting to his feet.

He carried on walking down the beach, where he was joined by the *strandwolf*, not once looking back. I watched him until he disappeared from view. I wished I shared his equanimity.

~

Otto and I were crossing a wilderness of rock and sand. Cinnamon-coloured mountains, with steep narrow passes, gave way to parched plains. Dry riverbeds criss-crossed the land. I saw no one for mile after mile as the sun glared down.

119

There were some signs of life, usually near the few water holes I found, following the *strandloper*'s directions. Without his guidance, I'm sure I would not have made it. It was the thought of Leah that kept me going and I was constantly fingering the shell on my necklace to remind me of my goal.

Through the heat haze, I occasionally saw some zebra or a few ostrich and once I caught a glimpse of a magnificent oryx, the most beautiful of antelopes. At this time of year, there was precious little vegetation apart from some stunted thorn trees and I was glad of the few bushes I did come across to feed the horse. Considering the nature of my task, I was tempted to re-christen him Rocinante, though even Don Quixote would have blanched at the task before me.

I estimated that we were about halfway to Lüderitz when I came, as planned, to another waterhole. As I approached I could see tracks in the sand at the water's edge. That was not unusual – animal spoor were to be expected – but I had not anticipated coming across the imprints of a pair of hob-nailed boots. No doubt they belonged to the owner of a small crude bivouac pitched just to one side and of a placid mule with a straw hat tethered under a meagre thorn tree. The ring of a hammer on rock suggested the occupation of the owner.

'*Goeie môre!*' I cried, figuring that Afrikaans was the nearest I could get to a neutral language. The hammering stopped, followed by the sound of slithering on rock. Then, round a small spur, appeared a huge pot-bellied man with an equally huge beard and a large hat. His flannel shirt may once have been grey but it was hard to tell as it was ingrained with sweat and rock dust. His filthy cord trousers were held up by an elderly pair of army-issue braces. In his hand was the hammer I had heard. A prospector's hammer.

He approached me with the other hand outstretched, his shrewd blue eyes smiling and assessing me at the same time.

'Pienaar,' he said and he raised an eyebrow on hearing my name. An Afrikaner – I had chosen the correct language. 'German?' he asked.

I nodded. I saw no good reason to tell him the truth.

'So how come you speak the *taal*?'

I explained some of my part in the war, without going into embarrassing detail. I also told him of how I was looking for my woman, though I said nothing of her race: Afrikaners have funny ideas that way. He smiled.

'*Ag*, the war is part of the past but we were comrades then so we can also be friends now. As for your woman, I am sorry for you. Perhaps you will meet up again if the good Lord so decides.'

Over a pot of weak coffee that tasted of the salt from the water hole, he told me of how he came to be in these dry and desolate mountains.

'After the war, I felt homeless and dispossessed as did many of my people. Some of them decided to move elsewhere looking for a new land. But me? I thought of the wealth in minerals in South Africa that are making people rich and I wondered if there might also be gold up here. I'd done a bit of prospecting on the reef so I decided to follow my nose.'

'And?'

He shook his head. 'No gold so far but I have found copper and some zinc so I live in hope. Now where are you hoping to go?'

'Lüderitz. I have heard my woman might be there.' I drank some more of the coffee. 'You know, if you strike water instead of gold, you'll have made your fortune. Perhaps you can confirm I am on the right path.'

'Hmm. Water? Do you think I am Moses? I'll talk about your route after supper, hey?'

He disappeared back into the rocks and shortly returned with a haunch of antelope. A springbok, I thought.

'I shot it this morning and hid it away from them.' He pointed up into the baked rocks.

There was a gap in the skyline where a river might once have flowed down the red burnt rock in a steep waterfall. Perched high either side of the dry bed were two scruffy baboon sentinels, watching every move we made. Just below, were the rest of the group, also looking in need of a brush and comb, with several females carrying infants on their backs. They screamed and bared their teeth as they saw the venison and continued to do so as we prepared the food.

'They'd steal anything and everything,' said Pienaar, 'and they can be vicious, too. They've resented me ever since I arrived and prowl up and down watching me all the time. Still, the fire helps to keep them away.'

Human beings must have lived like this in Africa for thousands of years, competing for food and water with the predators ranging around just out of the reach of the fire's light.

I assisted Pienaar in skinning the haunch and in spearing it on an iron bar over the fire once the flames had dimmed a little. The juices dripped on to the glowing embers with a fragrant hiss. The baboons screeched even more but kept their distance.

Pienaar cut slices from the bubbling haunch and speared them on to tin plates. We waited until they had cooled a little and then used our fingers to gnaw at the meat. In between mouthfuls, we exchanged yarns about the war and life in South Africa.

'When the *kommando* was disbanded, I returned home to find that my wife and daughter had died of typhoid in one of the British camps while I was fighting,' he said at one point.

It was the matter of fact way he mentioned this that was remarkable. 'You're not bitter about that?' I asked. 'Don't you blame the British?'

'Of course,' he said, licking his fingers, 'but it won't bring them back.' He tossed another log on the fire.

'No. We cannot undo the past, more's the pity. What is done is done. If I went through life holding a grudge, it would only kill me from the inside. But I won't go back.'

I helped him clear up and wash our greasy plates. We buried the remains of the antelope on the other side of the waterhole and covered them with branches of a thorn bush.

'They'll dig it up sooner or later but not right now. Good night to you.'

Pienaar squeezed into his little bivouac while, after seeing to Otto, I made do as I always did with a blanket by the fire. I threw a few more logs on to the flames and as ever, I thought of Leah and touched my pendant as I watched what looked like all the stars in the universe above my head before finally dropping off.

~

The shot echoed around the hills.

It was still dawn as, half asleep, I hastily rolled out of my blanket and reached for my rifle.

'Not to worry,' said Pienaar, striding over to the fire. He was holding his rifle. 'It was that big baboon, the leader I think. He came too close, looking for the remains of our supper. But, *allemachtig*, now he will feed the jackals; Nature always holds the balance. But first, to warn off the others.'

The rest of the group were screaming up on the rocks, baring their teeth but keeping their distance. He strolled over to the spread-eagled corpse and took out his knife. He knelt down and for a few minutes he sawed away and then stood back triumphant, holding the severed head high in the air and as blood dripped on the rocks, he called out to the baboons.

'There! Now you see who is your *baas*! That will teach you!'

He threw the head on the remnants of the fire where it bubbled and sizzled.

'Later I shall stick the skull where they can see it. That is the way of Africa. I will leave the body for the jackals,' and he threw the remains of the baboon over to the base of the rocks. 'Now for breakfast.'

I looked up at the high rocks. The sun was rising above them and the baboons were as active as ever. Some of the males were squabbling amongst themselves and I had no doubt that a replacement chief male would soon assume his place as the new leader of the troop.

'I hope you have plenty of bullets,' I said, drawing on my boots. 'They show no sign of retreating.'

'*Ag*, man, I don't need bullets. If they give me any more trouble I shall lay some poison. That will wipe out the lot of them. Coffee?'

I splashed some water on to my face and hands in a gesture to civilisation. Breakfast consisted of rusks which we dipped in coffee and a handful of biltong. It would certainly keep me going for some time.

'I must be on my way,' I said. 'Thank you so much for your hospitality.'

'It has been my pleasure. But I promised to give you directions to Lüderitz.'

'That is most kind of you but I have a map in my head and I plan to move from waterhole to waterhole in more or less a straight line.'

He grinned and brushed away a few crumbs from his beard. 'That's one way,' he said.

'Is there another?'

He drained the last few drops of coffee.

'You could always take the train,' he said.

I must have looked dumbstruck for he burst into laughter that echoed around the rocks and made the baboons scream and gibber with anger.

'Train?' I said at last.

He wiped tears from his eyes with a grimy red handkerchief. 'You must head for Aus,' he said at last. 'They've just completed the railway line. It goes straight to Lüderitz.'

'I hope we both find what we are looking for,' said Pienaar as I mounted my horse. 'By the way,' he added. 'I don't exactly have permission to be mining here. You know what officials are like. You won't split on me to the authorities, will you?'

'Certainly not. Again, thank you for your help and hospitality.'

He was still laughing as I rode away and watched me until I was out of sight.

Suddenly, Lüderitz seemed much closer. I had over a hundred miles to go, skirting the edge of the hills on one side and the near desert on the other, but I was full of new energy and hope. The quest was alive again.

It took just over two days. I won't say we galloped but we both felt a fresh surge of energy. Otto was striding out magnificently as if he too scented home. By night we camped by waterholes at the base of the hills, by day we pressed on through land that seemed unchanged since the earth was first created. Above our heads, the huge cloudless sky and the relentless sun reminded us how precarious life was in this part of Africa. We saw little game save the odd lizard and, once, a retreating sidewinder snake.

On the morning of the third day, not long after we had broken camp, I saw through the heat haze a puff of smoke ploughing its way across the horizon. It was a train. Then a couple of buildings loomed into sight. Aus.

It didn't appear to be a town or even a village. But I didn't care for all I needed was a train station and as I approached, I could see it, spanking brand new and ready to take me to Lüderitz. The rails were glinting in the sun like silver arrows, pointing the way towards the sea and, I desperately hoped, my Leah.

Thirteen

The thin steel lines looked as if they had been drawn across the desert with a ruler and pencil. It had an air of permanence, of the inexorable march of civilisation. One might imagine it as an attempt to bind the country together like string round a parcel. I wondered what it would look like after a season of sandstorms.

I was heading for the brand new station. It was a small white-washed single storey building, looking more like a European house, complete with sloping roofs and a chimney, than a railway station.

Next to the station, with its stack still leaking smoke, was the train, its steel body pitted with sand. The open carriages were being swept clean by two young black lads.

There was also a brand new military functionary waiting for me. I don't suppose he had many visitors. He was sporting an immaculate uniform, of which he was clearly extremely proud. His boots shone and his moustache curled upwards in another act of homage to the Kaiser.

The moustache bristled as I rode up and greeted its owner.

'Who are you?' was the reply.

I ignored this.

'I want a ticket to Lüderitzbucht.'

'Lüderitzbucht? What for? What business do you have there? Show me your papers.'

I stared down at him saying nothing until he almost imperceptibly moved to stand at attention.

'There is a war on, soldier,' I said at last, 'and I am on Army business.

Here is my authorisation.'

I passed him down the letter I had been given all that time ago by *Reichskommisar* Göring. It was now creased and grubby but it still had the power to cause the man to salute and click his heels. Not for the first time I wondered at the influence wielded by a man who had been a total failure in his job.

I gave him a curt smile.

'I need to stable my horse and a place to wash and shave.'

He was now eager to please and shouted to a young Nama boy to deal with my horse.

'By all means use my bathroom,' he said, 'and then perhaps you could join me for some bread and sausage and, perhaps, a beer? The train will not leave for over an hour and you have time to relax.'

His idea of relaxing was to give me a lecture about the new railway. The beer, however, was more than welcome and I drank two bottles straight off.

'It will not be long before the whole country will be unified by the railway system,' he said. 'As for this line, there are already plans to take it further south. First it will go to Keetmanshoop and then on to Karasburg.'

That would take the trains straight into the heart of Nama territory creating even more opportunities for German settlers. As if reading my mind, he launched into his views on the Nama.

'These Hottentots are not a strong race,' he began, prising a morsel of sausage from his teeth with a fingernail, 'I have these boys working here but for other than relatively light tasks, they are quite useless. I very much doubt they will provide good workers for our farmers. I see them all the time, doing very little although, to be fair, I must admit they have a way with horses.'

I accepted another beer in return for his views on breweries.

'It's good local stuff,' he burped. 'We opened the first brewery in this country in '01. Not bad, eh?'

'Tell me more about the, er, Hottentots. Are there many around here?'

'There are some here and there but during the war many of them died or were imprisoned and we are already hunting down the rest of them. Oh, there may be one or two scattered groups living in the desert but they are of little account.'

I took out a cigarette and he rushed to light it for me, declining one for himself.

'And their women and children?' I asked nonchalantly, puffing out a perfect smoke ring. 'What has happened to them?'

'Them?' he snorted. 'They are good for nothing. The Herero women are much stronger and are already helping to build our new colony. You will discover that in Lüderitzbucht. The Hottentot women are puny, on the other hand, and more or less useless. There is no place for them here. But it's a scientific law that the weak will be replaced by the strong. You will see evidence for this in Lüderitz.'

'Why in Lüderitz?'

'Oh, there is a prison for them there. We are in the process of transporting them there by train. They will have their own wagons, naturally.' He laughed out loud. 'They don't need tickets, of course!'

'Why not?'

He was still chuckling. 'Do we give tickets to cows or sheep?'

I wanted to smash his face in with a beer bottle and stuff the remnants of the bread and sausage down his fat throat. I was amazed by how much anger I was now capable of. But I still needed to know more.

'Is this prison in the middle of Lüderitz?'

He burped again and I could smell the garlic sausage on his breath. 'Can you swim?'

'I'm sorry?'

'Can you swim? The prison is on an island just off Lüderitz. It's called Shark Island. The prisoners are building a jetty or causeway there.'

He glanced at his pocket watch. 'The train will depart soon. It is never late. I will make sure you have a comfortable ride down to the coast. It is only just over a hundred kilometres. Now if you will excuse me.'

He adjusted his collar and went outside. Despite the beer I was stone cold sober and my mind was racing. Was Leah on Shark Island? If so, how was I going to get there? And even if I got there, how was I going to avoid the guards and help her to escape?

I couldn't really plan anything until I was in Lüderitz and the sound of a whistle told me it was time to start my journey. I made the stationmaster a present of Otto and boarded the train. It signalled its departure with a gush of steam and a blast on its whistle. I was more than ready to go.

It couldn't have been more different from my first train ride in this country. Then I was crammed in with a bunch of fresh-faced recruits who were eagerly anticipating a civilising mission to put down a savage revolt in a German colony. We were all for the first time discovering a vast sunburnt land that was in marked contrast to the neat green fields of Germany. Now I was alone in an open-sided carriage desperately hoping for a miracle.

The view from the train as it slowly rattled along was of a seemingly endless arid grassland. The stationmaster had said something grandiose about plans to graze sheep here but I couldn't see that happening. The clumps of tough yellow grass were at least a metre apart and looked distinctly unappetising.

As the train dropped down to the coast the brick-red land turned even more barren and sandy. I was once more on the fringe of the coastal Namib Desert. Even as we approached Lüderitz, a strong wind rose up and sand began to swirl around the train. In a matter of minutes it had developed into a small sandstorm.

The noise on the carriage roof was deafening as though the desert were hammering to be let in. And it came in through the open sides with a vengeance. I huddled down on myself, trying to turn my back to the wind but it came from all directions. I turned up my collar and covered my head with my arms but nothing could stop the flying sand from penetrating every crevice of my clothing and body, biting into my face and arms. It was in my ears and on my lips and I was continually spitting grit on to the carriage floor.

Then it was over almost as soon as it had started.

The carriage had aged overnight and its exterior had been scratched and scoured while inside there were little drifts of sand. I felt as if I had escaped being buried alive and it was a bruised and scratched British agent who entered Lüderitz.

With a screech of brakes and a clank of couplings, the train pulled up alongside a wooden platform that turned out to be Lüderitz station. As far as I could see there was no proper station as such. Indeed, there didn't appear to be any proper buildings at all although the foundations for several were just visible under a thin coating of sand.

So here I was. I had taken the next step. Despite all the time I had spent thinking about it, I still had no clear idea about what to do next except find the island and Leah. On the spur of the moment, I decided on the direct approach.

As soon as the train juddered to a halt, I jumped off, shook as much sand as I could from my clothes and hair and buttonholed the first person I could find. He turned out to be a soldier.

'Shark Island,' I said curtly. 'Show me the way.'

A civilian doesn't talk to a German soldier like that unless he has authority. The soldier moved with alacrity, showed me to the edge of the platform and dumbly pointed out the beaten sand road leading to the shore. I nodded my thanks and strode off as if I knew what I was doing.

~

Lüderitz was a tiny pimple on the arse of Africa and it took me no more than ten minutes to find the port. Ships were unloading more troops with their equipment. The German government must be spending millions on the war, far in excess of what they could hope to get out of the colony. For a second I recalled my mission. Would they try to recoup the cost by invading South Africa? Almost immediately, I dismissed the idea. They were already war weary. Then I shook my head to cast off my thoughts. Damn the Germans. Damn the war. Damn Webb.

It was already getting dark and the temperature was dropping sharply. It was too late to try and get to the prison island. I needed a base, somewhere to stay. After asking around, I found a soldier with a Red Cross armband who pointed out a rough building, almost a shack, near the centre of the town. Some foundations were being laid on an adjacent lot where a weather beaten sign said 'Kapps Hotel.' I knocked on the shack door.

I knocked three or four more times before I heard slow dragging footsteps and the scrape of a bolt being drawn back. The door opened a few inches and an elderly man peered out.

'Good evening,' I said in my best High German. 'May I trouble you for a few minutes?'

He peered up at me through thick scratched glasses and then pulled the door wide open and indicated for me to enter.

'Come in, come in,' he wheezed.

I squeezed past him into a small dishevelled room.

'What can I do for you?'

He was wearing a grubby waistcoat, dark shiny trousers and a collarless shirt that had seen better days. His face hadn't met up with a razor for some time and the few strands of grey hair on his head stuck up like a porcupine's quills.

'My apologies for disturbing you,' I said. 'I am here on official business but I have arrived too late to find accommodation. I am looking for a room for the night and I have been told that you might help. I can pay, of course.'

He hesitated and stroked his stubble.

'I have no authority,' he quavered. 'I am just the caretaker.'

It was then that I had the first of two ideas.

'I am due in Shark Island tomorrow but I cannot travel there tonight.'

'The Island? It is a prison, what business do you have there?'

I had my second brainwave, prompted by the armband of the soldier who had guided me here.

'I shall be seeing the camp doctor.' Well, if there was a prison, there had to be a prison doctor so it was a fair bet there was one on Shark Island.

The caretaker bit his lip.

'You mean Doctor Bofinger?'

There you go. 'Yes.'

He blinked once or twice and then said, 'I'm sure the family won't mind giving you assistance. After all, they are building the hotel next door.'

'The family?'

He sighed. 'The Lüderitz family. This is their property. Now sit down and I'll make some coffee.'

As I wiped the sand off my boots, I could hardly believe my good fortune. In one bound, I had found a contact on the island and found shelter with the first family of the town.

As if reading my thoughts, he told me they were away. 'You can use the box room,' he said. 'It's comfortable enough.'

I didn't care if I had to sleep on the floor. His own sitting-room was fairly Spartan but cosy enough. A small stove was already alight in one corner and he quickly moved two chairs near to it. There was a smell of cooked fish and I guessed that would be his staple diet.

He seemed to have forgotten about the coffee for he moved to a small cupboard and produced a bottle and two glasses.

'Schnapps?'

Later, after a supper of fried fish and bread, with more schnapps as dessert, the man who had revealed his name as Gustav, relaxed and settled down for a chat. I don't think he had many visitors.

'Thank God for the troops,' he said. 'I don't know what we would do without them.'

'Why? Is the town in danger?'

That set him off cackling. 'Danger? Oh my word, no. I'm talking about the money the troops bring with them. Many of them are stationed here permanently. You can see how the town is developing, new houses and shops being built all the time. That's why the hotel is planned. Before the soldiers came, we relied mostly on whaling. If only we could harvest *scheisse*, as the British do.'

I must have stared stupidly.

'Bird shit,' he explained. 'Guano. For fertiliser. They scrape it off some islands just north of here. Islands owned by the British. The birds roost there and crap money. Every now and then the guano is scraped off ready to be sold and the birds start all over again. It's almost money for nothing. Europe can't get enough of the stuff. I'd like some of the money that the British make. But, in the end, I prefer the soldiers, they need to buy things so that helps the shopkeepers.'

I saw an opening. 'What about the prison? Does that bring money to the town?'

He coughed and I poured him another glass. 'Well, it certainly saves money.'

'How does that work?'

'The prisoners are building a wave-breaker on the north side of the island. No one pays prisoners, see? So it's saving us money.'

'That's very business-like,' I said. 'Do you ever see any of the prisoners?'

He shrugged. 'I have no need to. After all, they never leave the island and I have no business there.'

He swallowed his schnapps in one gulp. 'But I know some of the guards.'

'Really?' I sensed an opportunity.

'Yes. They don't like the work on the whole. You see, it's not a pleasant job and you could easily pick up something nasty from the savages, though there are some benefits,' and he winked at me.

'Benefits?'

'You're a man of the world. Look, most of the prisoners are women and, well, soldiers will be soldiers, hey?'

Again I felt the heat of anger welling up inside. I needed to stay calm. 'At least they have a doctor,' I said.

He seemed to find this amazingly funny and he was still smiling when he finally dropped off in his chair. I made up the stove and leaned back in my own chair.

Gustav knew some guards. I could now see how I might get inside the prison camp. Things were at last falling into place.

I woke in the morning stiff from a night in the chair. There were still a few embers glowing in the stove and I blew them into life and added some more wood. Gustav stirred at the sound of this activity and licked his dry lips as he focused on his surroundings.

'Coffee,' he croaked. I put the pot on the stove and rummaged in his cupboard for something to eat. A small length of salami and some of yesterday's bread would have to do.

Waiting for the coffee, I looked through the window. Fog was still smothering the town so I would have to bide my time. Gustav was still thick-headed after the night before but the coffee revived him a little.

'So you know some guards,' I said. 'I'll say hello to them for you when I get to the island. How will I know them?'

He cleaned his teeth with his tongue. 'Well, there's one called Wilhelm. He's a grand fellow, always available for a chat and a drink. He's from Dresden, like me. You'd like him.'

I very much doubted that but the more people I got to know on the island, the better.

'What does he do at the prison?'

'He supervises the work parties. The prisoners are building a causeway to link the island to the mainland.'

'That's a responsible job.'

Gustav scratched his unshaven chin. 'Oh yes. Once they'd finished building the new railway, many Herero came here. Wilhelm says they are the strongest workers but lazy and he has continually to keep them at it.'

'Are there any Nama in the camp?' I asked casually. He looked puzzled. 'Hottentots,' I said.

He nodded. 'Oh, yes. Wilhelm knows all about it. He can tell you if you want to know.'

'I shall. I hope to see him while I'm on the island. What does he look like?'

Gustav spat into the stove. 'Wilhelm? Well, he's a bit on the stout side but you'll recognise him by his wooden leg. He lost his leg somewhere up north and that's why he's no longer on active duty.'

'Losing a leg? That's bad luck.'

'And it wasn't even a bullet,' cackled Gustav. 'It was gangrene from an infected mosquito bite, so they cut it off. Hurt like blazes, he says. He's upset that he doesn't have a medal to show for it, to show the folks back home. Still, now the Hottentots have surrendered, I guess he'll be off back home with lots of others. We shall miss their money.'

'They've surrendered?' That was bad news. It obviously had happened while I was travelling across the desert.

He nodded. 'Didn't you know? Most of the prisoners went to Swakopmund or Windhoek but some of them came down here by boat. There are over a thousand of them, Wilhelm says.'

All of a sudden, I wanted to get going. A glance out of the window showed that the fog was thinning. I stood up and thanked Gustav who would take nothing for his hospitality, then quickly packed my bag. I was anxious to meet Wilhelm and his wooden leg.

I set off through the cold streets down to the harbour. There I found a boatman who would take me across to the island. He charged a lot for such a small distance but I didn't quibble.

I scrambled off the other end to be met on the landing stage by a soldier with a rifle slung over his shoulder. He didn't look particularly vigilant and when I said I was there to see Dr Bofinger, he didn't ask for my papers but just pointed towards a group of wooden huts.

I felt as if I'd left one world for another. Almost immediately I came across a work gang of Ovaherero prisoners under the supervision of another soldier. He had both his legs so I nodded in his direction while having a good look at his charges.

They were a sorry lot. None of them looked fit or healthy and several of them were women. All of them were wearing only filthy rags though they were shivering in the morning chill. I thought that Dr Bofinger was neglecting his charges. They bent their heads in a kind of dumb salute as I passed. Looking closer, I could see fresh weeping scars on their bony backs where a whip or sjambok had been employed. It was then that I realised they were not prisoners of war. They were slaves.

I was almost at the group of huts when a soldier emerged still buttoning up his trousers. He had a wooden leg and the buttons were bursting on his tunic.

'Wilhelm?' I asked.

He burped with surprise and I could smell the beer on his breath.

'Yes. Who are you?'

'I'm a friend of Gustav but I'm also here to see the doctor.'

He broke into a broad grin. 'Welcome.'

'Can you spare a second?'

He chuckled. 'I've had my morning fun,' he said, thumbing over his shoulder. 'I'm not due on duty for another five minutes. Got a cigarette?'

'Fun?'

'The women,' he said. 'You can do what you like and it doesn't cost a *pfennig.*'

I resisted the impulse to punch him in the face. Instead we sat on a large rock, no doubt intended for the causeway. We both lit up.

'So what's it like working on Shark Island?'

He burped out a stream of smoke. 'Boring. Apart from the fun house.'

'Is that so?'

'Ja. It's the same every day. Keeping these creatures in order and making sure they don't slack. We have deadlines, you know.'

'But you are helping build Germany's new colony. It's all part of a grand plan.'

If his stomach could have puffed out any more, it would have.

'That's very true. You are a perceptive man. So why are you here?'

I told him of my language research, especially of the Nama. 'I understand you have some of them here.'

'That's right, in those tents over there but they are not much use. Not that it matters.'

'What do you mean?'

'We have orders not to bother too much with keeping any of this lot alive, especially if they can't work. There's plenty more where they came from.'

'So they are worked until they die.'

'That's about it. Very efficient, hey? I mean, look at that woman there.'

A skeletal Ovaherero woman, with a shawl of rags to keep out the spray and the cold, was sitting next to a shelter improvised out of sacking and driftwood. She was holding a shard of broken glass in her right hand with which she was scraping away at something in her lap. I moved closer then took a sudden step back.

'It's a head!' I gasped. 'A man's head!'

'That's it,' said Wilhelm, 'nothing goes to waste.'

For a moment, I couldn't speak. Wilhelm carried on regardless. 'You see that skull is probably her husband's. When she's finished cleaning it, the scraps will feed the gulls and we'll have a brand-new skull for Science.'

I wasn't the only one watching the woman. A group of soldiers were gathered around a camera and tripod, taking photographs of her.

'Are they the scientists?'

Wilhelm threw his cigarette on to the ground, stood up and adjusted his uniform. 'No, they will make the photographs into postcards which are in great demand back in Germany. I'm told they make a tidy profit.'

'But you said something about Science.'

'Oh, yes. Our fellows pack them up for shipping back to Germany for investigation.'

'What sort of investigation?'

'You'd better ask the doctor. He knows all about it. Now I have to go back on duty. Thank you for the cigarette. Good day.'

I mechanically took the proffered hand.

'By the way,' he added. 'We don't call it Shark Island. Me and the lads talk of it as Death Island.'

A shot rang out.

Fourteen

I dropped to the ground and turned my head just in time to see the second shot fired.

Near one of the rickety tents, an army sergeant was pointing his smoking pistol at an old woman. The wretched creature, who was stick-thin and obviously sick, was crawling towards another woman who was holding out a broken pan of water. He fired again and this time he hit her in the thigh. She screamed and lay there writhing in agony. The sergeant grinned as some of the soldiers taking photographs applauded the shot. He holstered his pistol and strolled away leaving the groaning women to bleed into the sand.

Here all the prisoners were women, many of them almost naked, all of them reduced to the status of animals in a slaughterer's yard. There was no sign of sanitation and some of them were lying in their own waste. The stench was appalling. I wondered what on earth the doctor was doing. Everywhere there were signs of his negligence.

His surgery or hospital was in one of the wooden huts on the southern edge of the camp. A wind-scoured red cross was painted on the side of the building. There was no sign of patients waiting to see him or of any who had been treated.

A guard was standing nearby and I gestured to the island as I approached. 'It's amazingly flat,' I said.

He nodded. 'We levelled it,' he explained. 'We used explosives and the prisoners cleared away the stone to use elsewhere. Some of it is being used to build the causeway.'

I estimated the island to be about a hundred acres. 'It must have taken a lot of explosive and a great amount of labour to reach this state. And there's obviously a lot still to do. And it's dangerous work.'

The guard, clearly bored, was only too eager to tell me more. 'You're right,' he said. 'Very dangerous but no one has been hurt. Except some of the prisoners,' he added with a smirk. It was a tale he had told before. 'Several of them were blown to pieces when a charge went off before it was ready. It certainly saved us the job of burying them.'

He chuckled at his own wit while I wondered yet again how easy it was for the unthinkable to become possible.

I knocked on the doctor's door.

'Come!'

I was expecting something like the cottage hospital near home. Instead, I found myself in what appeared to be a laboratory. Seated behind a long laboratory bench was a small man in uniform. His bald head was over-compensated for by a large walrus moustache. Without putting down the test tube in his hand, he peered at me over his wire-rimmed spectacles.

'Yes?'

I had my story ready.

'*Herr Doktor*,' I began as I handed over my letter. 'As one scientist to another, may I say what an honour it is to meet you in person. General von Trotha has told me about your fascinating work. He says it is of the utmost importance for the future of the colony and of Germany.'

He thawed. Who wouldn't? He put down his equipment and indicated a hard-backed chair next to his desk while scanning my latter.

'Ah, the *Reichskommissar*: a wonderful, wonderful man. He blazed a trail that we are all now following. I can honestly say he belongs up there in the pantheon of Germany's great heroes. You will take coffee,' he said.

While he fussed about shouting to an orderly in a back room, I had a quick glance round. There was a truckle bed in one corner but otherwise no indication of any medical services. No bandages, no ointments, no iodine, no surgical equipment. On the other hand, there was a strong smell of carbolic soap that served to mask most of the appalling reek penetrating from outside.

After the pleasantries were over, he handed me back my letter.

'Well, what can I do for you?'

'As you can see, *Herr Doktor*, in my field of linguistic science I need as many samples as possible of dialects and regional variations in my work on the Nama language. In this war, I can obviously not do my work freely in the field but as you have several Nama prisoners here, I was wondering if I could use them to assist me in my observations.'

He nodded sagely.

'It sounds most interesting,' he said 'and I can say without doubt that you have come to the right place. I, myself, in my own modest way, have also been using the inmates for my own researches.'

'Oh really! If you have the time, I should like to know about your work.'

He glanced at his pocket watch.

'Well, I have a few post mortem examinations to conduct shortly but I can briefly outline my work. And then you may pursue your own investigations.'

I sipped my coffee as he leaned back in his chair and cradled his fingertips in the approved manner.

'You have heard of scurvy?'

'Oh, yes.'

'Then as you know, it is a common problem for sailors on long voyages. The British discovered that eating limes could reduce the effect of the disease but my research is looking for a proper cure for scurvy that does not just rely on limes or lemons.'

'What line of investigation are you pursuing?'

His eyes gleamed as he leaned forward. 'I have isolated a number of substances that may provide the answer. My experiments so far are most promising, if I may say so. It is most fortunate that in this camp I have an almost endless supply of subjects.'

I tried not to show the sudden wave of nausea that leapt into my throat.

'Subjects?'

'Yes, fortunately we have specimens of both Herero and Hottentot here so I can determine the effect on separate races.'

'And what are the results for white subjects?'

He was horrified. 'That would be too dangerous!' he cried. 'The side effects can be devastating. No, I use just the savages. Now, if you will excuse me, I have those post mortem examinations awaiting.'

'Of course. Please accept my apologies for disturbing you. I am most grateful for your time. May I ask who the dead people are?'

'Oh, we have several prisoners die each night and my experiments help with my other research.'

'Other research?'

'Yes, I have an arrangement with Berlin.' He smiled with self-importance. 'You have heard of Dr Eugen Fischer? No? He was in this country looking at the deleterious effects of racial cross-breeding. I have had the honour of knowing him. He has definitely proved that the Herero are animals and that our German race is superior. I am, in my own small way, continuing with his work.'

Again I felt my gorge rise but managed to control myself.

'There is a vast investigation there,' he continued, 'into the physical and mental differences between ourselves and the sub-humans that live in this country. This involves a great number of scientific measurements, particularly of the cranium. My men get the prisoners to clean the skulls of dead prisoners and they then crate them up to go to Dr Fischer in Germany. In one or two cases we preserve the head itself, complete with features and we have had praise from Berlin for our efforts. I, myself, work on the brain. This involves extracting the brain from the skull – this is very delicate work – and then weighing it and recording the results. Speaking as one scientist to another, I think you will find this exciting work.' He reluctantly rose to his feet. 'Why don't you join me later for lunch? I can tell you more then. Meanwhile, please feel free to conduct your research outside.'

My mind still stunned by his words and armed with a clipboard borrowed from the good doctor, I went outside into the filth and stench to look for Leah. For all I knew, she had already been through the gentle hands of Dr Bofinger but I doubt that he kept records of the names of his victims. There was nothing for it but to walk around the camp hoping to catch sight of her among all the wretches that were still alive.

Where to start? Should I examine those lying under their shelters or see if I could spot her among the work gangs at the sea's edge? I could see a group of soldiers gathered at the north end of the island. A relatively new building stood there. I wondered what it was so I wandered up there to look at it. One of the soldiers noticed my interest and wandered over.

'What building is that?' I asked.

'*Ach*, that's the lighthouse,' he said with an air of pride. 'We built it well ahead of schedule. It will assist ships as they approach the harbour.'

I began looking at the faces of the nearest group of prisoners that the men were supposed to be guarding. The attention of the guards was elsewhere.

They were staring down with some interest at the sand below. One or two of them were pointing at a couple of objects floating out with the tide. Two others were attempting to take photographs. At first I thought they were looking at some of the seals that lived in these seas but then realised that they were not seals at all but headless human bodies bobbing in the water. They were on the water's edge, halfway between land and sea, where they had clearly been tossed from above with the intention that the waves would carry them away.

Even as I watched them, the tide began to turn and the bodies started to float out to sea. A shout broke out among the soldiers as a dark fin broke the surface and snapped at the bodies. One soldier slapped his thigh with merriment at the sight.

'So that's why it's called Shark Island,' I remarked to the soldier I had spoken to earlier.

'No, sir,' he replied. 'It's called that because of its shape. Normally there are no sharks here but this one has turned up recently. It's a very jolly coincidence.'

I could make out other bodies still half buried in the sand. Two hyenas were loping up and down the beach, waiting for an opportunity to snap at the corpses. This was how the dead bodies were disposed of, by being dumped on the beach until the tide dug them up and carried them away for the shark and hyenas and for the amusement of the guards. It was yet another example of German efficiency.

I pulled away and made my way towards a cluster of homemade shelters. No one seemed around but as I went closer, I could hear a low hum from inside.

'No, sir, no, no!'

A soldier had left the shark and was running across the camp towards me. I stopped and turned to meet him.

'What is it?'

He breathed heavily as he pointed at the tents. 'Danger, sir, they all have the fever.'

I looked at him and then back at the tents. 'Fever. What fever is that?'

'I don't know sir. All I know is that those inside are dead or dying. You should keep away.'

'Thank you. Thank you.'

He saluted and started on his way back to the sharks and as he did so, I realised that the hum from inside the tent was the sound of thousands of flies. I moved further away.

So the choice had been made for me. If Leah was in there then there was nothing I, or anyone else, could do for her. I hesitated then walked away and started to look over the work gangs.

~

There were several of them, again made up almost entirely of women, straining on long ropes attached to trolleys full of rock. The first I approached was formed of Ovaherero women. So was the second. And the third and fourth. It was only the sixth that contained some Nama women. Even if Leah was not there but was somewhere on the island, surely one of them would have heard of her.

They flinched as I drew closer and carried on hauling the truck. An overseer cracked his whip and they flinched again.

'If you want to have one of them, wait until tonight,' he cried.

I waved my clipboard at him and looked important. I was an official on official business. Immediately he nodded and lit a cigarette. The women released their load and stood still.

None of the women was Leah. I went up to one whose eyes flickered in my direction. Turning my back on the guard, I pulled aside my shirt to reveal Leah's necklace.

Her eyes widened and her mouth opened but she looked at the guard and closed it again.

'I am looking for a Nama woman called Leah. Have you seen her?'

Hearing me speaking in her own language, she forgot the guard.

'Who are you? Where did you come from?'

'I have little time before the soldier interrupts us. Do you know Leah? Just nod.'

She slowly nodded. I breathed out. She was here and she was still alive.

'Where is she?'

The woman pointed to a work gang some way away against the sea wall.

I thanked her and moved on, pretending to write on my clipboard. The guard cracked his whip again and the work gang picked up the ropes and once more heaved until the loaded cart was slowly under way again.

I forced myself not to run. 'You're supposed to be a German official,' I said to myself, 'so move with dignity and arrogance. Take your time. Leah is not going anywhere.'

Heart pounding, I moved from group to group, making senseless notes on my clipboard and all the time inching towards the work gang that the Nama woman had pointed out to me. As I grew closer, I could see it was made up entirely of slight Nama women, pulling twice the normal size load. And there, at the end, her head bent and breathing heavily was the object of my search. My Leah.

For what seemed a lifetime, I stood there, stock still, staring at her, my brain almost paralysed, unable to think of anything. The crack of a whip brought me back to reality. All those weeks of searching for her had not been in vain. I had found her. At last we were together again.

She still hadn't seen me and I pulled myself together. This was what I had been waiting for. I had work to do.

A grinning guard was leaning against the sea wall, smoking a pipe. I went up to him with a stern face.

'How many loads have they shifted so far today?' I said, without introducing myself.

'Er, three or four,' he said, knocking out his pipe.

'I'm not surprised. Do you know anything about civil engineering?'

'Sir?'

'I assumed not. If you did, you'd know that if you overload a vehicle, it will perform badly. It will take longer to make one trip than with two smaller loads. You are making what is known as a false economy. Have some of this rock unloaded. Now!'

He snapped out an order and the women laid down their ropes and began unloading the cart. I tried not to look at Leah straining under the weight of a large rock.

'Good. Now let me check the strength of these women; each should have been chosen to give balance to their haulage capacity.'

'Sir!'

Now I could talk to Leah.

She had already seen me but stayed where she was, head bowed. She was nothing but skin and bone. Her entire body was a ghastly white from the dust and the rocks. There were sjambok scars on her legs and back, some of them fresh. Again there was that flash of anger spurting up like a lit jet of gas. I strolled over to her.

'Put down that rock,' I ordered in German. 'Answer my questions.' And then, softly, in Nama, 'I am here to take you away but not right now. I will be back to fetch you.'

One swift look, a ghost of a smile and then her head was lowered again. She started shivering again. I like to think it was partly from excitement and hope.

I asked a couple more questions of some of the others and then moved away.

I was so elated, it was difficult for me to keep a straight face. I had found her. After all my travels and troubles, I had actually found her. I could barely believe it. Now I was free to think that I could achieve anything. All I had to do was to find a way to get her off the island. I was sure I could do it. I was sure I could do anything. Perhaps Bofinger could supply the answer over lunch. Meanwhile, I took a look round the island's edge. It didn't take long to see that the natural barrier of the sea and the hyenas, together with the barbed-wire fence at the entrance to the camp, showed that there was no chance of walking or swimming away. But there had to be a way. It broke my heart to leave her again but without looking back I went off to see the good doctor.

Bofinger's soft hand smelled of carbolic soap. He was smiling broadly and had obviously had a happy morning among the dead. He had removed his white coat and was now wearing a jacket and waistcoat.

'Come inside,' he said. A table had been cleared of medical equipment and was now covered with a crisp white tablecloth. I noted that three places were laid.

He busied himself with glasses and bottles for a pre-lunch beer.

When we were seated, he raised his glass in a toast. His moustache was immediately coated with a creamy layer of foam. He glanced at his watch.

'English?' he said.

I stayed very still. Under cover of the table, I reached for the knife in my boot. 'I beg your pardon?'

'Do you speak English?'

All my senses were alert. Where was this going? 'Yes, of course,' I said.

He beamed. 'Very good! We have another guest for lunch, an Englishman who doesn't speak much German. I have some English so I thought that we should converse in that language.'

I relaxed my grip on the knife. 'It will be my pleasure,' I said. And that is exactly what it turned out to be.

Fred Cornell said he was a diamond prospector but right now he was very well turned out in a tweed suit and spoke with an educated accent. His beard was neatly trimmed and his eyes sparkled with intelligence. We declared we were both extremely pleased to meet each other and sat down to a lunch that was served by an awkward young soldier.

The smell of the meal could not quite mask that of carbolic soap and the acrid odour of the camp seeping into the room. Bofinger had placed a record on his gramophone and we chewed our rather tough beef and swallowed the over-cooked vegetables to the strains of Beethoven's Violin Concerto.

During coffee, Bofinger expanded on his work.

'As one scientist to another,' he said, 'I should be most happy to welcome you back here to further your research. I shall issue orders to the guards to give you complete freedom of access.'

'You are most kind,' I replied. 'I shall inform Berlin of how cooperative you have been.'

Bofinger's eyes gleamed behind their glasses.

I could tell that Cornell was not impressed though he said nothing. He seemed relieved when I steered the conversation towards camp security.

'Have any prisoners ever escaped from the island, *Herr Doktor*?'

He chuckled and waved his cigarette in the air.

'Not a single one,' he said. 'Between the sea on one side and the desert on the other, where would they go? In any case, we have a strong garrison in town so there is no chance. Oh, and of course there are the dogs, German hunting dogs. They are very well trained. More coffee?'

That was that, then. However, there was one factor on my side. The Germans thought they had ruled out any chance of escape and that meant their complacency could work for me.

Cornell and I left together. I stopped after a few paces and bent down on the pretence of tying my bootlace. My real intent was to attempt to catch a final glimpse of Leah. She must have had the same idea for somehow she had placed herself in a position from where, despite her workload, she could maintain a watch on Bofinger's surgery. Instantly, across that grotesque landscape of inhumanity, our eyes connected. A trace of a smile lit up her ravaged face while I risked a brief nod of my head in return. A promise had been renewed. Then she returned to her burden and I stood up. I had the feeling that Cornell may have seen me but I had already decided that I didn't really care. In any case, he was unlikely to mention anything to Bofinger or any of the German guards. All I received was a quizzical look that could have meant anything.

As we stepped into the boat, he made me an offer.

'You know,' he said. 'If you're here for some time, there is a spare room in my lodgings in town. You're more than welcome to share them for a while.'

I had taken a liking to the fellow, not because he was a fellow countryman but because he seemed to have a spark of humanity in him. He had not needed to speak up for me to detect that he disliked the doctor and, more important from my point of view, detested what was going on in the camp.

'How did you get to know the good doctor?' I asked him as we left the boat and strolled through the town to his place.

'He wants to be rich and believes that the mineral wealth of South Africa might be repeated here. I think that he hopes I will somehow open up an Aladdin's Cave of wealth for him so that he can retire here.'

'And will you?'

'Not a chance. Come in.'

An idea was beginning to germinate in my brain. Cornell disliked the doctor almost as much as I did. Had I found an ally? Then I noticed something that threw a new light on Cornell.

~

Before leaving London, Webb had tried to give me some identification.

'All my agents carry a secret sign of who they are,' he said. 'It's always useful in the field and it will offer you some protection if by chance you happen to fall into the hands of some of our fellows who might think you are a German.'

'No, thank you,' I'd replied. 'My experiences in the South African war taught me not to carry anything that might give me away. The only way to stay alive in this clandestine business of ours is to trust no one. I'll take my chances and do without.'

'Are you sure? Look, here is mine.'

Webb raised his right hand and showed me his little finger on which was a small gold ring with a garnet set in it.

'It's our badge,' he said with not a little pride. What he meant was that it showed he was a member of an exclusive club. How the British love their clubs.

'No badges,' I said firmly. 'They can only bring one harm.'

I was quite wrong.

On the little finger of Cornell's right hand was a gold ring inset with a small garnet winking at me like a fresh pomegranate seed.

Fifteen

This changed everything. Unless it was a massive coincidence, Cornell's ring meant that he, too, was one of Webb's agents.

I said nothing until we were inside the comparative safety of his quarters although my mind was racing with all kinds of implications.

From the outside, Cornell's lodgings were little different from any other of the port's buildings. On the inside it immediately was apparent that he was one of those people who, wherever they happen to be, can transform a mere room to a home from home. There was a comforting sweet smell of pipe tobacco and several bottles of good whisky on a table near the fire. One bottle, I immediately noticed, was of Glenturret. A rifle was propped up in one corner and a miner's pick-axe in another.

Once we were seated Cornell lit his pipe and rattled the embers in the fire until he managed to rekindle a flame which he then fed from a pile of driftwood stacked neatly by the fireside.

'Drink?' he said.

I looked him straight in the eye. 'I fancy a glass of Glenturret.'

'Excellent choice,' he said. 'I'll join you.'

While he was making the drinks I took a deep breath and started on the path that could lead to hope or despair.

'I note you're wearing a ring,' I began. 'I don't like them myself but I know someone who does. Strangely enough, his is exactly the same as yours.'

He turned and looked at me. 'Really? An odd coincidence.'

'Oh, I don't think so. He's a fellow named Webb,' I said as he handed me my glass. His face was expressionless as I continued. 'He works in

London and, here's another strange thing, there's another chap I know who also has one; name of Morrison in Walfish Bay. Incidentally, he also gave me a Glenturret. Cheers!'

'Ah,' he said and stood by the fire, manifestly weighing things up in his mind. I sipped my whisky and waited.

'And you don't wear a ring,' he said at last, no doubt still unsure if I were a member of the club.

'No, I refused. Anything like that is far too dangerous.' I didn't need to say why.

He raised an eyebrow and drew on his pipe. 'I see.'

We let that hang in the air for a while.

'What were you doing over there on the island?'

'I might ask you the same question.'

Finally it was time for the fencing to stop.

'Yes,' I offered. 'I'm one of you, working here undercover and under orders from Webb.'

My directness seemed to disconcert him.

'We should stay mum,' he murmured. 'Sharing information is strictly against the rules and all that.'

'Then it's going to be a quiet evening.'

We both burst out laughing at the same time.

'To be serious, this is not a normal situation,' I began.

'Go on.'

'This island; I find it abhorrent. It's not an internment camp like the ones we built down south for the Boers but an extermination camp.'

'We?'

I took a deep breath. 'Yes, we British.'

'Ah, I thought as much. I wanted to make sure. Go on.'

'The Germans are deliberately working those poor devils to death and then, even after death, they are mutilating their bodies. That shouldn't be a secret, the whole world should know about it.'

I must have raised my voice for he looked at me strangely for a second or two and then stood up to make sure the doors and windows were firmly closed.

'Look, you're right of course.' He hesitated. 'All right. It'll come out soon enough. But say nothing until you read about it in the newspapers down south.'

'The newspapers?'

'Webb decided that's how we're going to do it, not directly from our Government but from the newspapers in South Africa. So nothing, please, until then.'

'Very well. You have my word.' Of course I was going to agree; I hadn't forgotten that I needed Cornell's assistance.

He settled back in his chair.

'I really am a diamond prospector. I've spent a great deal of time looking for them in the south. However, I'm not primarily looking for them here; I'm not even sure there are any. Not in great quantities, anyway. No, I'm in this country on behalf of you know who to report on German atrocities during the war and publicise them via the press down south. The aim, of course, is to reduce sympathy for them among the Boers.'

He replenished my glass and his own.

'And that's about it. I've more or less finished my report and I shall be leaving for the Cape shortly.'

That was my cue.

'My work here is also finished.' I told him about my mission and how Webb was concerned about German designs on South Africa. 'Frankly,' I said, 'from what I've seen and heard there is no sign at all of that happening. The Germans have spent huge sums on this war and they have tied up enormous numbers of troops in a country where it is unlikely they will ever get their money back. What is more,' I added, 'there are calls in Berlin for the troops to be recalled and there is even disquiet in their Parliament – but not from the Kaiser – about von Trotha and his extermination policy towards the Ovaherero; he may also have to return. No, I think the south is pretty safe.'

Cornell laughed.

'Webb is a bit of an old woman at times, over cautious and all that.'

Now was the moment to pitch my case and try to jockey Cornell into helping me.

'How are you getting back to Cape Town? Across the Orange River?'

He knocked back his whisky.

'No, I'm travelling in comfort. I'm booked on a boat to the Cape via Walfish Bay, leaving the day after tomorrow.'

He held up his empty glass and pointed at mine.

'Please. This is very kind of you.' I hesitated. 'May I come with you?'

He raised an eyebrow.

'Do you need my permission?'

'No, but I need your help.'

There, I'd said it. The die was almost cast.

'This sounds intriguing. What are you after? Money? I can lend you a little but I'm not particularly flush right now. Or is someone chasing you?'

'No, money's not a problem. I've spent hardly a thing of my own since I first came here. I've been living off the country most of the time. I might even be able to give Webb some change.'

He laughed again at that. 'That'll please him. He has a reputation for being a little tight.'

'And,' I continued, 'as far as I know, no one is after me. No, it's a rather big favour I'm asking.'

'Very well, ask on!'

I told him everything. I held nothing back about Hartmann, David and, most of all, about Leah. I made my feelings about her quite clear. I felt surprisingly relieved to tell someone about the past few months.

He sat quite still, except for toying with his glass.

'And,' I concluded, 'I want your assistance to help get her out of that dreadful place and down to South Africa.'

At that, he shifted uncomfortably in his chair but said nothing for some time. I let him think about it. After what seemed an hour but could have been only a few minutes, he put down his glass. He wiped his jaw with his hand.

'She's a native, you say?'

'Yes. Is that a problem?'

'And you want to get her off the island and smuggle her on board a boat?'

'I thought we might say she's my servant – she's very slight and could be made to look like a boy.'

'And how do you plan to get her away from the Germans?'

At least he hadn't yet refused to help.

'I was hoping you might have an idea.'

He coughed and scratched his head.

'I think a frontal assault is out of the question,' he grinned. His humour raised my spirits only for them to be dashed almost immediately.

'Nevertheless, old chap,' he said gently. 'I'm not sure we should try. I mean to say, if we're found out it could start a diplomatic incident. The Germans are bound to kick up a fuss. You know how touchy they are about us, anyway. They showed that during the South African war. And they really resent our ownership of the guano islands. At a pinch they could walk in and take over Walfish Bay. They'd love a proper harbour.'

'They don't have the troops,' I said, 'and would they really go to war with our Empire over the abduction of a native woman? Hardly.'

'Wars have been fought over less,' he remarked, 'but even if the Germans were to do nothing, there is the matter of Webb. He'd be incandescent if he found out. We're supposed not to exist and any sort of exposure would give ammunition to all those who think our work is underhand and ungentlemanly.'

'Who is going to tell him? I certainly won't and I doubt that you would.'

He grinned sheepishly. 'I wouldn't blab, no.'

He hesitated. 'There's also the fact that if we were helping our own, well, we might be forgiven. But she's not a British subject.'

I knew what he meant by that. She was a native, a black, a kaffir – I'd heard all the words before during the war in South Africa. I'd used them myself. But I had one more card to play.

I reached in my pocket and pulled out one of the pebbles I had picked up at the spot where I'd met the *strandloper*. I had carried them all the way from the river's mouth to Lüderitz. I handed the pebble to Cornell. To the untutored eye it looked like a rough piece of quartz but not to him. He stared at the stone, turning it over in his fingers before going over to a sideboard and extracting a magnifying glass. For a long while he closely examined the pebble. Eventually he turned to me and said in almost a whisper, 'By George! It *is* a diamond! And a bloody big one at that!'

Of course it was; I'd recognised it as soon as I had picked it up. One of my uncles was in the cutting business in London and Amsterdam.

'Yes, it's a diamond and it's yours if you help me. I know where there are more; many, many more, just lying around. This country is rich with them, only the Germans don't know it. At least, not yet.'

He again rubbed the diamond between his fingers and then tossed it up into the air.

'And if we fail?'

'It's still yours.'

He whistled. 'She means that much to you?'

'She does.'

He bit the inside of his cheek. 'Well, I absolutely detest the Germans and what they are doing in that infernal camp. The whole place deserves to be wiped off the face of the earth.'

'Then you agree to help me.'

'I think we'd better make a plan,' he replied.

I was fairly certain that he would agree. After all, I wasn't asking him to be a traitor. And, let's face it, in our line of work, it's the excitement and the challenge that keep us going. A diamond is an extra bonus. You clearly don't do it for the pay or pension and there are certainly no medals.

'We don't have a lot of time,' I said. 'People are dying on the island every day from starvation and overwork. Leah is not strong and I wouldn't want her to end up on a slab in Bofinger's mortuary or to see her head packed up in a box heading for Berlin.'

Even as I spoke, the answer how to liberate Leah leapt into my head. Cornell had come to the same conclusion at much the same time. We looked at each other and suddenly we were both galvanised into action.

Cornell jumped to his feet and paced around the room.

'We must do it tomorrow first thing,' he said. 'We shall have to work fast between the first lifting of the mist and full daylight. That will reduce our chances of being seen. Now we need to spend time on the details. I've some paper and a pen so that we can take notes.'

We used the rest of the day and most of the night deciding on our moves, drawing plans and listing what we had to do. It wouldn't be easy. We would face unexpected problems at each stage but that was what we were trained to do. We were both experienced enough to know it was axiomatic that plans will go wrong as soon as they are implemented. But we made the plans anyway.

We went to bed red-eyed and with our mouths raw with the taste of whisky and tobacco but excitement kept us going and the next day saw us eager and ready for action. Now I knew how Daniel felt going into the lions' den.

There was a heavy sea mist over the town that morning. It clung to our clothes and hair and we were thankful for our thick coats. I shivered and thrust my hands deep in my pockets. There was condensation on the hat that Cornell had lent me and it wept onto my face.

The air was thick with cold and damp and we could taste the salt on our lips. Leah and her fellows were bound to be shivering in their rags and tattered tents and some of them almost certainly would not have survived the night. Today Dr Bofinger would have more specimens to dissect and package for Berlin. I felt sick with worrying that Leah might be among them and that our plan might fall at the first hurdle.

It was the air of death around the camp and my fear that Leah would die that had given me the idea.

'A box,' Cornell had said, voicing what we had both hit upon. 'We bring her out in a box.'

I'd nodded excitedly. 'In one of Bofinger's boxes. We empty its … its contents and get Leah to hide inside.'

'And,' added Cornell slowly, 'he's sending his boxes by sea to Berlin. If we can switch boxes at the harbour, we could do it. The box containing Leah would go instead onto my ship and on to Walfish Bay.'

In essence, that was the plan.

'It's chancy,' I said, impatient to be going, 'but it could work.'

'Have you considered,' said Cornell slowly, 'how she will feel about being placed in a small dark box? Do you think she will be able to go along with it?'

I confess I had not thought of that, being so wrapped up in our plan.

'You are right,' I said at last. 'She might well be terrified. But we have no choice.'

So having planned that Leah would leave the island in a box, we just had to hope it wouldn't become her coffin.

There were few people about. The blind mist was making everyone and everything shapeless and anonymous. We couldn't risk revealing ourselves by hiring a boatman even if we mollified him with cash. But we knew that the day before, the link between the island and the mainland had been closed with a last load of rocks and although not formally completed, one could clamber across. No doubt there would be guards but the early hour and the fog would give us the chance we were banking on. Cornell took a mouthful from his flask and then handed it to me. I took it so as to help banish the mist tingling in my throat but not too much for we needed our wits for what lay ahead.

We could hear the sea before we saw it. Then, through the wall of mist, I could make out the shadows of the rocks that were to be the land bridge. Even at a few yards, it would be difficult for anyone to pick us out. Cornell and I glanced at each other and nodded. Then, as we had rehearsed, I took a deep salty breath and began to clamber over the rocks. The mist made them wet and slippery but they were of a size that enabled us to reach from one to the other without losing our footing. I was more concerned about making a noise that might alert any guard. So it was slow and careful does it. We stopped only once when we heard a clink of metal on a rock. Then there was the quick spurt of a match. We bent lower and moved across the rocks away from the guard. And then we were over them and tip-toeing across the sand to the sea wall. We followed this around intending to locate the doctor's hut. We thought we had found it but feeling round the walls of the building, I realised it was a sentry hut belonging to the soldier smoking by the rocks. I was about to move on when I saw a blanket hanging inside. I leant inside and snatched it and then we were off into the fog.

Suddenly, there was a loud splash and for a second we froze where we were before dropping to the ground. Slowly I crawled to the sea wall and glanced over. Through the mist hanging over the water, I could just make out a sleek head and a flipper. I returned to Cornell.

'A seal,' I whispered. 'Come on, let's go.'

Our first stop was the hut where we had dined the day before. We crept round to the rear where boxes were stacked, some of them empty and some of them labelled and waiting to be sent for shipping. One of the latter was of a size that would contain a small person. We prised it open with the crowbar we had brought with us. The crack of the wood echoed around the rocks and we froze to the spot.

'It's all right,' whispered Cornell who had been straining to hear any sign of alarm from the guards. 'Carry on.'

I again inserted the crowbar but this time covered the box with the blanket. The protest of the nails was now muffled and we were able to prise back the lid with no fear of discovery.

Inside were several round objects wrapped in sackcloth. Almost certainly they were heads but we had neither time nor appetite for checking. Instead, we swiftly threw them over the wall and into the sea. In my head I said Kaddish for them, no matter what their faith.

With the next stage of the plan over, we set out on the most important step so far. Finding Leah.

We knew roughly where her tent lay and following the wall round, we soon came to where I estimated we needed to move towards the tent. It was the coughing that guided us. The mist was slowly lifting but it was still thick enough to hide us.

I drew back the flap of the first tent. The stench of unwashed bodies and faeces hit me full in the face. No one moved and there wasn't a sound, not even a whimper. I put my hand over my nose and mouth as I peered inside. The mouth of the first person I saw was open but there was no steam of breath. The same was true of the others, none of which was Leah. This was a tent of the dead.

I swiftly moved on to the next. This time the inhabitants were alive, but still no Leah.

We found her in the fourth tent, shivering under a scrap of cloth. I bent over her. She opened her eyes. They were larger than I remembered and the skin was tighter over her face.

'Leah,' I whispered. 'It's me.'

Her hand, as small as a child's, slowly reached up to me. I clasped it eagerly. It was as cold as the grave. We were not a moment too soon. She would not have lasted another day.

'We have come for you,' I said. 'We must leave now. There is not much time. The guards could discover us any moment.'

She was so weak that she could barely get to her feet. I put my arm round her waist and helped her out of the tent. There was no one about as the mist swirled around us. Leah shivered and I wrapped the blanket around her.

Cornell took her other arm and between us we headed back to the doctor's hut. As we did so, I quietly told her what we were going to do. She stiffened but carried on.

'We will leave you with water and some bread,' I said. 'It will be uncomfortable for you but you will soon be off this hateful place. Be brave. Be strong. I shall be waiting for you at the other end.'

This seemed to give her strength and when we finally reached the hut, she made no objection when we gently laid her in the box with the blanket and provisions. As we lifted the lid above her, she gasped and her eyes blinked with fear. I bent down and kissed her on the forehead and adjusted the blanket. Then for the first time she smiled weakly and lay there quietly as we nailed the lid back on having first made enough gaps in the planks to give her a supply of air. We added the box to those also labelled for Berlin but marked it with an extra scratched H on each side and left her. I turned back for one last glance at Leah's box. I hoped it would not be too long before she would be resurrected.

The fog lasted long enough for us to clamber unseen back over the bridge of rocks. A few minutes later we were in Cornell's house, warming our hands round a large mug of coffee.

'I'll go out again as soon as the fog lifts completely,' he said 'and check when the boxes leave the island.' Cornell was eager to earn his diamond. I promised myself I would give him an extra one once we had retrieved the box.

'Breakfast?' he said. 'I have eggs, cheese and milk so I could knock you up an omelette.'

Suddenly, I felt ravenous.

'I'll give you a hand,' I said. I needed to do something, anything rather than just sit around waiting.

By the time we had polished off the omelettes and wiped the plates clean with yesterday's bread and swallowed more hot coffee, I felt a surge of optimism. We had taken the first important step towards Leah's freedom.

I could barely contain my impatience and for the umpteenth time I went to the window and pulled back the curtains to glance outside. Finally, I found that I could make out buildings across the road and passers-by on their way to work. The fog was lifting.

'Very well, old chap,' said Cornell, pulling on his hat and coat, 'I'll pop down to the jetty to see if the boxes are leaving the island.'

'Don't you think I should come with you?'

'No. I have genuine business with my boat so I won't arouse suspicion. You have no reason to be there. But as soon as things start moving I'll come and fetch you to give me a hand with the box.'

While he was gone, I washed up the breakfast things and tidied the room. I also made sure that my meagre possessions were packed and ready at hand in case we had to make a quick departure.

Sooner than I had expected, Cornell was back. His eyes were bright with excitement.

'So far it's going according to plan. They are moving the boxes off the island,' he said. 'It's time to go.'

Sixteen

We made our way through the misty streets, walking at an infuriatingly glacial pace so as not to arouse suspicion among the other shadows around us. We said nothing to each other in case we were overheard. This suited both of us as Cornell was laconic at the best of times while I was saving all my energy for the task ahead.

I rehearsed in my head what had been agreed between us. We had decided on a very simple plan that meant there was less that might go wrong. In essence, my task was to distract the guards while Cornell searched among the boxes.

The worst aspect of this strategy for me was the fact that I had to wait. Outwardly I was calm but inside my mind I was in a raging fever of impatience. After all this time, I was within reach of rescuing Leah yet I had to control my urge to run towards her. Slowly does it, I said to myself, slowly does it.

As we approached the shore opposite the island, we could see the ghosts of figures moving through the mist and hear the groans of their exertions. Again I felt like that character in the Greek myths who descended into Hell to reclaim his lost love. Well, this was certainly a Hell but I fervently hoped I would have more luck than he did.

And underlying my impatience was the constant throb of anger – anger at all those who had brought my Leah to this horrid place. If I had my way, I would raze it to the ground and people like Bofinger and Hartmann would end up on the wrong end of a firing squad. But that would be for later, if ever. Now was the time for action.

The work party was unloading the boxes from a flat-bottomed boat that had crossed over from the island. It was mainly composed of Ovaherero women grunting under the strain of carrying the boxes to a rapidly growing pile on the sand. Another group was loading them on to a sled that they would haul the short distance to the harbour. In charge of them all was just one German soldier, a soldier with a wooden leg. Corporal Wilhelm.

I took this as a good omen. Perhaps after all we had a better chance than even of pulling this off. We would need to wait until the boxes were actually at the harbour to make the switch. Cornell had a label in his pocket ready to attach to the marked crate.

The sun was now appearing as the mist evaporated but there was still a strong chill in the air. The women, dressed in their rags, were shivering despite their exertions. Even Wilhelm was hunched up against the cold.

For a moment he didn't recognise me and held up his hand to stop my advance. As I grew closer, however, he saw who I was and when I took my flask out of my coat pocket, his face creased into a huge grin.

'You are too kind, sir,' he said, putting his rifle aside and reaching for my flask. 'My leg aches in this weather and there are times when I long to be back home. I miss the green fields and the white women. Here it is a miserable desert. I sometimes think the top brass don't realise that we guards are also in prison.'

'Perhaps this will warm you up as well,' I said, taking out my tobacco pouch.

He handed me back my flask, wiped his lips and moustache and took the pouch. He fumbled in a pocket of his uniform for his pipe. Out of the corner of my eye, I could see Cornell. I moved so that Wilhelm was between us with his back to the boxes. Cornell was now obscured from Wilhelm's line of sight. I glimpsed him walking up casually to the work party that was unloading the sled. He was doing his part. I returned to mine.

Wilhelm took several puffs to get the pipe going as my matches were proving difficult to light.

'Curse this damp,' he said.

By now Cornell was nonchalantly moving from box to box. The natives paid him no attention. Then he stopped and bent down. He had located the box containing Leah and slapped on his label. He stood up, caught my eye, and nodded slightly.

'And,' said Wilhelm, 'conditions on the island are not good and getting worse. There is sickness all the time among the prisoners and it will not be long before it spreads to the guards, mark my words. Then we'll all be in trouble.'

Cornell had disappeared, no doubt on his way to the ship, leaving the marked box on the sand.

'If that is the case,' I said, 'then it is lucky that Dr Bofinger is on the spot.'

Wilhelm pulled a face.

'Anyone who is sick and goes in there seldom comes out,' he whispered. 'The natives never do. He's not the best doctor in the world. If any of the lads are sick, especially with the clap, we go to the doctor in the town.'

Cornell had returned with a couple of natives from the ship. He pointed to the box and they lifted it up and carried it off. The Ovaherero women made no move to stop him. They didn't even look at him but stood there waiting for orders.

'Take my leg,' continued Wilhelm. 'It aches, especially in the morning but Bofinger won't help. He's too busy cutting up bodies. Useless man.'

I stood up, sick of hearing his voice and could not wait to get away from this wretched place. 'I must be off,' I said. 'It was pleasant to have a chat with one of our brave fellows.'

Wilhelm smirked and rubbed his stubbled chin. 'Well, thank you, sir, for the schnapps and the smoke,' he said. 'I, too, must get back to work. There is no rest for the wicked,' and he shook my hand before turning to the work gang and shouting at them to return to the island for more boxes.

Keeping at a safe distance, I followed Cornell and the men carrying the box. It would not do to create any kind of link between us until we were on board.

When we reached the port, I waited as they boarded a barge to take them out to the ship anchored in the bay. I was achingly desperate to see Leah again but caution made me take a small boat following the barge. My rowers smelled of garlic and brandy and fortunately were not at all inquisitive. The sight of a gold coin no doubt helped them stifle any questions and row faster.

At last, we hove to alongside and I climbed the proffered ladder. I could see Cornell ahead of me and I made haste to catch him up.

'Is she well?' I asked stupidly, as I matched his stride.

'No idea,' he said, pipe clenched between his teeth. 'We'll have to wait and see. We're nearly there,' he added, like a parent speaking to a small child, but he meant it kindly.

Then he stopped. 'Here we are,' he said.

'You'll need this,' he said as we entered, handing me a crowbar. I was ready to use my bare hands if necessary but I took the tool with alacrity. I frantically hammered it between the planks of the box with the heel of my hand. Was she still alive? Had the air-holes been large enough? Had the blanket been sufficient to shield her from the cold? I even had a momentary panic wondering if we had picked the right box, although the impact of rancid body odour was proof enough. All these questions raced through my mind as I pushed and prised and wrenched at the box.

We were in a cramped and windowless store room next to Cornell's cabin, well away from the prying eyes of the crew who were, in any case, fully occupied readying the ship for sea. The throb of the engines reverberated throughout the ship.

I frantically tugged at the plank and suddenly it came away with a creak and then a tearing sound. I flung it to one side. And there she was.

The first thing I saw was her eyes fixed wide open. For a heart-stopping moment I thought we were too late. Then I noticed traces of colour on her cheeks. At that moment she blinked and a half smile crossed her gaunt face. She let out a huge sigh as if she had been holding her breath since we'd nailed her up, and then she began coughing.

Between us we tugged away at the remaining planks revealing her blanket-covered body. I noticed that the food and water remained untouched. It was as if, akin to holding her breath, she had not dared to move since we had nailed down the lid.

'What must she have been feeling, being cooped up in there?' exclaimed Cornell. 'It reminds me of all those tales of poor creatures being buried alive.'

Cornell went to his cabin and soon returned with some warm water, soap and towels. He tactfully left us alone while I lifted her unresisting body on to a table. She felt as light and as vulnerable as a bird.

She never took her eyes off me as I gently peeled back the blanket and then removed the foul rags covering her frail body. She was nothing but skin and bone and the sjambok welts on her arms and legs seemed like vicious ritual scarring.

She whimpered a little as I gently washed the scars and dried her face and body but when I stopped, she raised a stick-like arm to indicate that I should continue. I took my time and when I had finished, she looked human again.

I carried her to my cabin and laid her on the bunk and covered her softly with clean sheets. Her head against the pillow seemed so beautiful that I bent down and kissed her on the forehead. Again she smiled, at the same time reaching up to stroke my cheek.

'Sam,' she whispered. 'Sam.' She coughed and then closed her eyes. She was asleep before I had left the cabin, locking the door behind me. She was now safe and I meant it to stay that way.

Below decks the air was still and stale as if it had been breathed by too many people. The odour of hot oil from the engines permeated everywhere. Already I longed for the clean air of the desert.

On deck, I said as much to Cornell. 'She needs to be up here,' I said. 'The air down there in the cabin will serve only to assist microbes to breed.'

'Perhaps,' he said. 'But the crew will be unhappy if there is a woman on board. You wouldn't want the boat to turn round and drop her off, would you?'

~

Over the next few days, as we steamed north, I fed Leah mostly soup as she couldn't keep down solid food. She slept a lot and, although I loved seeing her few smiles, she said nothing more. I knew that, given time, she would slowly gain strength and return to normal but I had no way of knowing if she would ever fully recover from her ordeal. Every day I cursed those who had caused her to suffer on that wretched island. Hartmann was first on the list of those I damned to Hell.

Cornell was full of good spirits as I went up on deck for a cigarette. We were sailing parallel to the coast but keeping a safe distance from its treacherous currents and hidden rocks. The sky was unremittingly blue and cloudless while the shore seemed to be made of nothing but sand. Nothing could possibly live there and I said as much to Cornell.

'Well, apart from the odd scavenger living on dead seals or whales, you're absolutely correct. The Germans have commandeered hundreds of square miles of nothingness just to compete with us and the other European powers. As you pointed out, it's cost them a packet already and I doubt it'll ever pay for them. On the other hand, I don't think they have any appetite for going south, unless of course we go to war in Europe. Then who knows what will happen? No, they'll have to make do with this place, much good may it do them.'

'And,' I added, 'their reputation as a civilised country will have been shot to pieces, especially once your report hits the headlines.'

He nodded in agreement.

'How many more days to Walfish Bay?'

'Well, we're battling against the currents but it should be tomorrow or the day after.'

'Good, because Leah really needs to see a doctor, she's still very weak.'

In fact, she was even worse than I thought, because that night, she developed a heavy fever and diarrhoea. I spent all night wiping her with a cool face cloth while constantly carrying her to the ship's heads, holding and cleaning her up. On one of these visits, a crew member, who looked and sounded like an Angolan Portuguese, caught me in the corridor with Leah in my arms.

'What are you doing? Those are for whites only,' he growled. 'Toilets for blacks are down below. Take your boy away.'

'Get out of my way,' I said mildly, 'or I'll cut your throat.'

He went off muttering to himself but he was no hero and I had no more trouble from him or anyone else. Considering Cornell's warning about how superstitious sailors are, especially about having women on board, I was relieved that he would return to his shipmates and pass on the news that Leah was a boy.

As we approached Walfish Bay, Leah's condition grew worse. She had developed a nasty looking rash and her fever had returned. Cornell looked at her through the cabin door, while holding his handkerchief over his nose.

'I don't like the look of her,' he said. 'We can't keep her on board if she stays like this. There's the problem of it spreading to the crew.'

'She's not moved once from the cabin, except to go to the bathroom,' I said, 'and as for me I'm feeling fine though I've been with her all the time. It won't bother the crew.'

We went up on deck and I breathed in the sea air while Cornell lit his pipe. He was still worried.

'Healthy people sometimes pass on infection without being harmed themselves,' he said. 'No, it's Walfish Bay for her if she doesn't recover soon. In any case, she should see a proper doctor.'

I couldn't fault his logic. We could always get another ship from Walfish Bay once she'd recovered.

'Very well,' and I threw my cigarette over the rail into the swell of the sea.

I returned to my cabin to check on Leah only to find her in acute distress. She was writhing on the bed clutching at her emaciated stomach and her face was contorted with pain. I rushed to her side and held her hand. It felt as dry and hot as hell.

Eventually she calmed down as the pain subsided a little. I stroked her sweat-soaked hair.

'Don't worry,' I said emptily, 'we shall soon be at Walfish Bay where we can go on shore and you will be treated by a real doctor and lie in a soft hospital bed.'

I supposed she had never seen a hospital except for the ghastly mockery of one run by Dr Bofinger. She stared at me, not comprehending what I was saying or what was happening to her.

'I'll fetch you some soup,' I said but she shook her head and grasped me by the wrist.

'Sam,' she whispered. I knew she was asking me not to leave her so I stayed there with her all day and all the next night until the following day when we pulled into Walfish Bay.

~

It was another beautiful day as I carried her ashore. The flamingos were still striding stiffly in the bay and a skein of cormorants heralded our arrival on British soil. Cornell sent a crew member ahead to find a doctor and he returned with directions. We received some odd looks as we made our way through the hard sand streets – two white men carrying a native boy – but no one stopped us. Cornell accompanied us to the doctor and then disappeared to report to Morrison, no doubt anticipating a glass of malt whisky.

The receptionist, a young man with a harelip and a Cape Dutch accent, raised an eyebrow as we entered the empty surgery. Before he could say anything I tersely informed him that this was an urgent case and that I was not to be fobbed off. He scuttled inside and presently indicated that we should follow him.

The doctor was British, unshaven, and smelt of carbolic soap and brandy but he had a kind face. His white coat barely met across his enormous gut.

'Doctor Ridge,' he said, thrusting out a large hand. 'What can I do for you?'

'How do you do, doctor,' I replied. He looked taken aback at my British accent. There was a long mirror on the wall and I had a glimpse of my appearance. With my tanned face, long unkempt hair and two days of growth on my chin, I looked more like a desperado than a British don.

'Yes,' I explained. 'I must apologise for the way I look but I have been in German South West, caught up in the war there.'

'Of course, of course. Now what have we here? Allow me to examine her.'

He pointed at the truckle bed at the side of his office and I gently laid Leah on top of it. Her huge eyes stared up at me from her bone-stretched face.

'What are her symptoms?' A northern accent – Bradford, I thought. At least he recognised that she was a woman.

'She has fever, diarrhoea, and a rash. She can't eat anything.'

'Let me see the rash.'

He took one long look. He said nothing but took a step backwards.

'Right, thank you. Please cover her up. Come outside, I'd like a word.'

I laid what I hoped was a reassuring hand on Leah's arm and left the room after the doctor.

He was surprisingly kind and gentle.

'Where has she been that could explain her condition? She's extremely undernourished.'

I saw no reason why I shouldn't tell him. So I did, with much emphasis on her ill treatment on Shark Island.

He frowned and shook his head. 'I've heard stories coming out of

German territory, stories of atrocities,' he muttered.

'She is but one of many,' I said, 'But the most important thing is, can you cure her?'

He chewed his lip. 'She's very sick. I'm almost certain it's typhoid and in her weak condition there's little chance of recovery. You could take her to the hospital but they don't have an isolation ward for blacks. I'm afraid you must prepare for the worst. The best thing you could do is to make her comfortable before she, um, she goes. It's only a matter of a day or two. Luckily for you, you're fit and healthy so it will have passed you by. You might even have had a dose but it would at most have given you some discomfort.'

He looked at my face and touched me on the shoulder.

'There'll be no charge. I'm sorry. She can't stay here and I suggest you take her out in the sun somewhere. '

I moved almost mechanically, stunned by what he had told me and carried her outside just as Cornell turned up. I lay her on the ground in the shade, covered by the scarlet blanket that the doctor had given me. I explained what the doctor had said and he visibly flinched.

'Typhoid?'

'I need to get her away from here.'

He pulled himself together.

'Morrison has ordered you back to Britain. And I have to return to Cape Town. Webb isn't pleased that you have not completed your mission. I'm sorry, old chap but I had to make my report.'

'Bugger Webb and bugger the mission. I need to take care of Leah.'

'Well, I'm afraid that I've done all I can. Orders and all that.'

'Surely you can help me get some transport.'

He hesitated.

'Where do you intend to take her?'

'I have no idea.'

Leah must have heard me for she stirred.

'Sam,' she breathed. 'The !Kuiseb River.'

I must have looked blank.

'Take me.'

'You'll need some kind of cart,' said Cornell. 'I'll see what I can do.'

At that very moment, another voice spoke in Nama behind me, a voice that I had heard before. I also became aware of a powerful smell of fish.

'I have a donkey cart, my brother.'

I turned and there stood a figure that I had last seen near the mouth of the Orange River. It was the *strandloper*.

'What on earth are you doing here?' I managed to ask.

Cornell, meanwhile, took advantage of the *strandloper*'s arrival. 'I'd better be off,' he said.

'Thank you for all your help. I couldn't have reached this far without you. Here.' I reached in my pocket and pulled out another diamond.

'That's not necessary,' he mumbled but I forced him to accept. He said his farewells and with a final glance at Leah, made a hurried departure.

The *strandloper* walked over to Leah and said a few words. I couldn't hear her answer but it seemed to satisfy him.

'Let us go,' he said and motioned to the other side of the road where his donkey cart was waiting.

'Where are we going?'

'To the !Kuiseb River. That is her wish and it is a fit and proper place.'

I lifted Leah up on to the cart and sat down beside her.

'How did you come to be here in Walfish Bay?' I said.

He looked over his shoulder and once again there was that smell of old fish.

'She called me,' he said and flicked his whip at the donkey.

Called him? In what way? She hadn't seen anyone other than Cornell and me since we got her off Shark Island.

'What are her signs of sickness?' he called. He nodded as I told him. 'There are ways of curing her but nothing is certain, she is not strong. The village is the best place for her.'

The cart soon left the hard-packed streets of the town and headed for the river bed. Like most of the year, it would be dry and offered the most convenient way of travelling through the desert.

On our left was the bare, barren rock of the desert. On our right were towering pale rose-pink sand dunes. In between, like a line carved in the landscape was the dry bed of the !Kuiseb River.

'The wind blows the sand all the time,' said our guide, 'but the river is wide and stops it crossing over. So much of it falls in the river itself.'

At one point, I caught sight of a sudden movement out of the corner of my eye. I looked over my shoulder and there was the *strandwolf*, racing to catch us up. It then trotted alongside as we progressed down the valley.

Any other time I would have been fascinated but I was feeling queasy with the bucking and swaying of the cart. To make things worse, the sun was getting stronger and my mouth was dry. Above all, I was impatient to get Leah to, well, to wherever we were going.

'Is it far?'

'Not far at all. It's just up ahead.'

Sure enough, as the cart bumped and trundled round the next curve in the river, there before us was a small Nama village, consisting of several dome-shaped huts of branches covered with animal skins. I could see a small group of figures watching us approach. A little further on, separate from the village, was a small freshly-painted house and church that I guessed was a missionary outpost.

It was at this point that I felt the first cramps in my stomach and the pangs of fever. I immediately broke out in a huge sweat and just as we pulled up at the village, still grasping Leah's hand, I felt myself blacking out.

Seventeen

Someone was singing to me. It was a song without words and almost without tune. It went on and on, expanding and filling my head until I thought it would explode.

I tried to see who was singing but my eyes were hot and heavy and after a few seconds the blackness returned.

The next time I returned to the world, the singing had changed to a distant chorus of whispers. I strained to hear what was being said but, again, the effort was too much. I thought I felt the pressure of someone's hand on mine.

At one point there was drumming as well, relentless and insistent, but I must have been imagining it for just before I lapsed into unconsciousness I realised the drumming was synchronised with the boom of my own heart.

I finally came round, as weak as a newborn lamb, but fully aware of who I was. A few drops of water dripped on to my forehead and then something soft and cool was gently pushed between my lips. I slowly and painfully opened my eyes.

I was lying in the shade of a grass matting shelter and yet I was burning hot. Trickles of sweat were pooling in the small hollow in my chest.

'Drink this,' said a woman's voice, 'it will chase away the fever.'

'Leah?' I croaked. 'Is that you, Leah?'

The woman bent forward, an old half-naked woman with a look of concern on her wizened features.

'Where's Leah?' I said, pushing the drink away. I must have spoken in English for she stood and left me. I tried to sit up but I felt as if a ton weight was pressing on my body and I sank back on the mat, breathing heavily. I heard the old woman's voice and then that of a man. I could see neither of them but there was a strong smell of decaying fish. The *strandloper*.

He was holding a small cup made out of an ostrich egg.

'You must drink this,' he said.

'What is it?'

'Drink.'

But I had more questions. 'Who is that singing? Do they never stop?'

He grinned. 'No one. No one is singing...'

'But I can hear them! Listen.'

'What you hear is the singing of the sands.'

As I tried to focus on my surroundings, I realised he was right and that the wind and the constant movement of the dunes were creating a kind of wild susurration filling the air of the river bed.

'And what is in the cup?' My voice seemed to be coming from a long way off.

'It is medicine made from the leaves and root of the bitterbush. It will help your stomach and your fever. Drink.'

I took a cautious sip. The name was apt for it was as bitter as anything I have ever drunk. It stuck in my dry throat and I retched and spat it out. He hissed and drew swiftly back avoiding the stream of liquid.

'You must drink it,' he said, waving away a couple of flies, 'try again.'

Again I attempted to sit up. This took what seemed to be all my strength but I was able to swallow another sip of the revolting liquid. This time I could just about keep most of it down. I couldn't be bothered to wipe my chin and collapsed back on to my sleeping mat, my eyes closing again. Just before I dropped back into sleep, I suddenly realised I had forgotten to ask about Leah and then there was only the song of the sands whispering in my ears.

$\sim$

Later they told me I had been in and out of fever for two days. I was drained of strength and attempting to stand up unaided was a major effort. The first time I tried it, the *strandloper* rushed to assist but I limply waved him away.

'I'm all right,' I gasped and immediately sat down again. I took a deep breath, 'But how is Leah?'

He squatted on his haunches and looked me straight in the eye. He licked his lips. Even before he spoke I knew what he was going to say.

'She was not strong enough,' he said simply. 'She died even before she reached this village. Now she is with her ancestors.'

'But ...'

'It is over.' He tapped me on the knee. 'When we leave someone, we do not look back. You must do the same. Neither of them can come back.'

I wasn't sure I had heard correctly.

'I'm sorry? Neither of them? What do you mean?'

He frowned. 'You did not know?'

'Know what?'

'She was with child. The women here say it died with her. I am very sorry, please.'

I lay back on the mat, my heart racing. I wanted to speak but could not think of anything to say.

'I never said "goodbye",' I said at last.

He smiled sadly. 'She was still holding your hand when she left us. You cannot want more than that.'

'Where is she ...?'

'I will show you tomorrow, when you have more strength. Now eat this.'

He handed me a piece of melon, which I now realised was what the old woman had put in my mouth earlier.

'It is *!nara*,' he said. 'It grows wild here.' It was the same kind of fruit that he had given me when we first met.

'Sleep,' he said, before leaving.

After he had gone, I lay there for a long, long time staring into nothing. There had been a child, our child, and they were both dead. My mouth was dry and my heart was empty. I couldn't even say Kaddish for them. Eventually I slept.

~

Their grave was simple. Just a small mound covered with stones in the sand at the side of the dry river. A bush had been planted on the mound. There were hundreds of them growing in the river bed. The sun hurt my head and eyes as I tried to come to terms with her death. The *strandloper* was standing beside me.

'She will be protected from jackals and hyenas and the river, even in flood, will not reach her. It will not be long before it will be hidden entirely and no one will be able to find it again.'

'What is that plant on her grave?'

'It is bitterbush. It helped cure you and maybe it will cure her somewhere else.'

The *strandloper* silently moved away, leaving me by the side of the mound, having again urged me to look forward.

'They are now safer than we are. Let them rest while you begin thinking of where you are going next.'

I still couldn't say anything to her, even in my mind. With bowed head I stayed there between the desert and the dunes for maybe an hour alone with my thoughts. The sun was high in the sky and the only shadow around was mine, falling across Leah's grave. There was an aromatic smell coming from the bitterbush: it smelled better than it tasted.

Finally, I took a deep breath and then returned to the village from where I could hear the faint sound of drumming.

There seemed to be a party going on as I entered the village. Three men were dancing in the middle of a large group, their feet raising spurts of dust. A third was drumming with a stick on a hollow log. The women were tending a large fire on which they were roasting an animal, its fat dripping and hissing into the flames. An old man was sitting on a rickety three-legged stool, plinking out a tuneless melody on a thumb piano. Children were squatting on the sand, mesmerised by the dancing men. At other times I would have been entranced by the rustic simplicity but right now, having just left Leah's grave, it all seemed out of place.

The *strandloper* once again seemed to have divined my thoughts for he loomed up behind me.

'You think they should not be happy because you are sad,' he said.

I nodded.

'Well, those three men have caught two porcupine. They are now dancing to show us how they tracked and hunted them down and dug them out of their burrows. This is very dangerous work and they might have been killed but we are happy because now we all can eat and eat well. And,' he continued, holding up a filthy hand to stop me interrupting him, 'they put their luck down to your arriving in the village. The dance is also in your honour.'

'But Leah is dead.'

'That is true but would it be less true if we did not celebrate our successful hunt?'

I had no answer.

'Then come and join us. You will have the choicest part of the porcupine.'

I sat down on the bare sand with the children and watched the dance of the hunt and, when the meat was ready, joined them in feasting on the roasted porcupine.

All the while, the single notes of the thumb piano played its tune of sadness and joy.

~

Over the next few days my strength gradually returned. The villagers took great care of me although they normally kept at a respectful distance. One day, however, three snotty-nosed children, naked except for a band of shells around their waists, approached and shyly offered me some berries. They were surprised and then delighted when they heard me speak their language and it was not long before they were chattering away to me and asking questions. Not once did they mention Leah. Their laughter was the best tonic I could have asked for.

At one point they pointed over my shoulder and scampered away. I turned to see a white man approaching from the small church. He was tall with a heavy beard and he was sporting a large straw hat. His tinted glasses made him look as if he were holidaying in the south of France rather than living in the desert.

He tipped his hat as he approached. I bowed and we exchanged handshakes.

'The Reverend Karl Martin,' he said in faultless High German. 'I have heard from my congregation,' – and he gestured to a woman following behind him, dressed from neck to toe in a western dress – 'that a white man is living in the village.'

I smiled and nodded, suddenly wishing he would go away.

'May I be of any assistance to you?' he continued. 'I fear these poor heathens have little to offer you.'

I stiffened. 'They have saved my life,' I said, 'and although they have little, they have shared it with me.' I did not mention Leah.

'Of course, of course. Er, will you be staying here long? Tomorrow is the Sabbath and you are welcome to join us for divine service. So far there are few of us for these people are slow to accept God's word.'

'That is kind of you,' I replied 'but I leave tomorrow morning.' I had intended this as a deception but even as I spoke I knew it was true. It was time to go.

The minister tilted his head in acceptance and we again shook hands.

'Safe journey,' he said, 'and may God go with you.'

I thanked him, at the same time thinking that God had not been much in evidence recently.

I was packing my bags. The villagers gathered round and pressed small gifts into my hands. A bracelet made from bits of ostrich eggshell, a miniature bow and arrow, and a small skin bag bulging with fresh, nutritious !nara seeds. One small child gave me an ostrich feather and another, the quill of a porcupine. Leah would be in good hands.

The *strandloper* offered me a ride in his cart and still feeling weak I accepted. We waited until dusk in order to avoid the unlikely event of meeting a German border patrol. The villagers, especially the children, waved until I was out of sight. He dropped me off at the outskirts of Walfish Bay and immediately drove away without once looking back.

The town was falling dark when I walked slowly into the streets. There was already a hint of sea mist as I threaded my way towards Morrison's house and what I expected would be a flea in the ear.

'What the hell have you been up to?' he growled, as he opened the door.

'Good evening,' I said. 'May I sit down? I've been sick and I'm still a bit feeble.' The smell of the oil lamps grabbed my throat and immediately I felt the bile grow in my stomach. I managed to hold it in.

'You're in trouble, big trouble,' he replied but he pointed to a chair. 'Drink?'

'It'll probably knock me out. But I really don't care so yes, please.'

His eyes narrowed and he bit his lip and stared at me for a second before going for the single malt bottle.

'Webb has been in touch,' he said. 'He's not happy.'

'Bugger Webb.'

'And I've spoken to Cornell.'

'I guessed you would. What did he say?'

'He said you were a damned fool.'

I managed a sort of smile. 'That's not news. Did he say why?'

'Not really. He said something about a woman. He didn't go into detail.'

I mentally blessed Cornell; the diamonds must still be working their magic.

'He was right. There was a woman and she's dead.'

He paid me the compliment of not asking any more questions. Instead he rustled up some bread and cheese and replenished my glass.

Afterwards, with the warmth of the whisky in my belly and a cigarette between my fingers, I summoned up some more energy.

'So what's got Webb's back up? He must know by now that Germany has no intention of going south.'

'Aye, he does.'

'Something else is bothering him? I mean, he left me no way of getting in touch with him. A heliograph wouldn't reach London.'

He laughed at that.

'All I know is that he's in a bit of a stew. He wants to see you as soon as you get back. Before you see anyone else.'

'All right, I can live with that. Now I need to find a ship to get home.'

Home. Is that what it was? Right now it felt like a far-off foreign country.

'I'll do what I can. There are some ships in the harbour and one of them might be going that way.'

'You'd know damned well if one of them was London bound. That's part of your job.'

He threw back his head and laughed again.

'Aye, that's true. There's one going the day after tomorrow. I'll get you a berth.' He paused. 'I guess you'll be going as yourself. I mean as one of us and not as a German.'

I sighed. 'I'm past deception. I just want to get it over with.'

175

'Fair enough. I think you'd better bed down here tonight and not where you went last time. The fewer people know about you the better. And you'd be advised to keep your head down while you wait for the boat.'

I was faintly surprised. 'What on earth for? This is British soil.'

'British sand, anyway. Look, the word is that there are one or two German spies in the town keeping an eye on us to see if we make any military moves. So we don't want them to see anything out of the ordinary. One of them may recognise you. Just stay out of sight for a wee while until the time comes.'

He sounded and looked serious. Clearly, the game was spreading. And it was no longer a game.

I went to bed with the taste of whisky clinging to the roof of my mouth. My head ached and I longed for the air of the desert but that was already behind me. I tried to smile as I thought of Leah. It was the nearest I could get to praying. I spent the night dreaming of dead kisses. Once I woke and thought I heard her laugh but it was just a noise in the street.

In the morning I stared out of the window at the fog veiling the town. There was not much incentive to go outside. I would wait. Before Morrison went out he produced something resembling coffee and it felt good. I could eat nothing beyond a few dry biscuits.

I went back to my bed and lay there composing the half-truths I would tell Webb. I must have dropped off and on waking, and feeling decidedly better, I suddenly felt ravenous and went into the kitchen for something to eat. There was nothing and I had developed a fancy for something sweet; the image of a bar of chocolate swam into my mind. Before long the fancy turned into a strong desire and then an obsession. I put on my coat and borrowed a hat with a large floppy brim to help conceal my face.

It was pretty cool outside and the mist still lingered here and there but several people were out and about buying bread. I knew I could achieve anonymity in a crowd so I followed a couple of empty-handed people towards a small store. It looked as if it sold everything and that surely would include chocolate.

There were three or four customers already waiting so I took the opportunity to look around for where the chocolate might be. And then I heard a voice I knew from the past.

'Give me cigars.' The voice spoke in English but the last time I'd heard it, it was using German.

I didn't turn round but glanced in a mirror advertising cigarettes. He had changed his appearance somewhat and grown a full beard, now looking more like the King than the Kaiser, but it was his voice I recognised. He had assumed a sort of Cape Dutch accent, no doubt acquired during his time there, but he couldn't conceal his German vowels. Hartmann.

I immediately recalled the times he had called Leah a whore and the number of people he had ordered to be hanged, all in the name of a superior culture. He represented all that I hated about the past months. Anger welled up inside me as I decided it was time to show him some culture of my own.

The fact that he was probably a spy made it a little easier but I didn't really need a reason, I already had plenty of my own. It was surprising how clear my mind was and how quickly I decided what I had to do.

I waited until he left the store and keeping at a safe distance I followed him down the street, all thoughts of chocolate forgotten. Something much sweeter was almost in my grasp. I had no idea what I was going to do but that didn't matter. I had to finish it.

He turned off the street into a small alley in which some of the morning fog still lingered. It couldn't have been more perfect. I had plans for a dramatic confrontation in which I would reveal myself to him before a fight to the death. Unfortunately I had no weapon on me. Then I had a thought. Of course I had a weapon.

In my coat pocket I still had the diamonds in the small skin bag. They never left my person. Without removing my hands from my pockets I curled three fingers round the neck of the bag. I quickened my steps that were already muffled by the sand underfoot and then took a swift final two paces preparatory to smashing him over the head.

'Sir!'

I whirled round as did Hartmann. A young black lad had appeared out of a doorway. I guessed he was another of Hartmann's perverted conquests. Hartmann took a step back and then gave a roar and in the best traditions of the German army, charged straight at me. I had to think quickly and suddenly called out to him in Yiddish:

'You don't remember me, General?' On principle I always promoted officers when I addressed them; it never did any harm.

He stopped in his tracks.

'Do I know you, Jew boy?'

I reverted to German but with a Yiddish accent. 'I have brought you the diamond.'

'What diamond?' He was peering through the mist at my face but my newly acquired hat maintained my anonymity.

'The one you asked for.'

He advanced further.

'I asked for it? Show me.'

I extended my closed and empty left fist. He bent forward as I slowly opened it. With my other hand I swiftly pulled the bag of diamonds from my pocket and swung it at the side of his skull. He collapsed without a sound. I leant over and hit once more for luck. I quickly felt his wrist. Nothing. No pulse, no blood. The lad was still standing there, his mouth open in shock.

'Run!' I hissed. 'Run all the way to Hell.'

I pulled the body into the doorway. I wanted to hang him high and leave him dangling there just as he'd hanged so many but there was nothing suitable to act as a hook so there I left him lying like a carcass on an abattoir floor.

My mind was quite calm throughout the attack. I had witnessed too many deaths during the wars in German South West Africa and too many horrors in the camp on Shark Island for me to feel guilt at my actions. The death of Hartmann was not so much an act of vengeance as a restoration of right against wrong.

As I strolled away, I thought I heard from the direction of the sea, the long wild cry of a *strandwolf*. I went back to the store and bought a bar of chocolate.

Morrison was not pleased.

'I told you not to go out!'

'I think you only advised me. However, I needed some chocolate to restore my energy. Would you like a piece?'

'No, thank you. Now look, I've managed to get you a berth on a ship bound for Britain. It leaves with the tide tomorrow morning. You'd better be on it.'

'Don't worry, I've no intention of staying.'

He calmed down a little and over a pot of coffee changed his mind about the chocolate. We shared it as we spoke.

'Will Webb know I'm returning?'

'Well, the undersea telegraph operates to London so I've sent a note that way. How long it will take is anyone's guess so you could still surprise him by turning up on his doorstep.'

I didn't care whether or not I surprised Webb. I was no longer the man he had sent out to Africa. There was a pub near my parents' house called 'The World Turned Upside Down' and I had often wondered as a child what the name meant. Now I knew. Nothing would ever be the same again.

Bearing in mind the *strandloper*'s words, I did not look back. The other passengers clustered around the rail at the stern watching the flamingos and pelicans against the sea and the sky while the sand dunes receded into the distance. I realised I hadn't seen a proper cloud for what seemed a lifetime.

I was in my cabin taking a shower, giving myself a clean shave and putting on the clothes Morrison had bought for me. When I returned to London I wanted to merge with the crowd, become anonymous again, before taking on Webb and my family. And, perhaps, Julia.

I then planned to sit on deck reading a book I had borrowed from Morrison on Gaelic place-names in the Scottish Highlands. The hope was that it would clear my mind of the horrors of my stay in German South West Africa. Hope. It was a start.

Eighteen

It was raining. Since I'd landed in Britain, the rain had been almost continually stair-rodding down and I loved it. I had forgotten how invigorating a downpour could be. Even though I was on my way to see Webb, I decided not to hail a cab and keeping my umbrella rolled, I happily succumbed to the rain. I was smiling as my shoes squelched through the puddles. A bedraggled pigeon hopped out of my way as I crossed Trafalgar Square and headed for Whitehall.

I'd been anticipating this meeting since I had boarded the ship in Walfish Bay. As the stars floated by in the clear southern sky and I said farewell to the Southern Cross, I looked forward to the stars back home being obscured by the rain-filled clouds. Except for the cloud named Webb.

I pictured him sitting there in his pokey little office, surrounded by files and maps, waiting to attack me because I'd disobeyed orders. As if I cared. In fact, I was looking forward to a confrontation with the fellow. There was no way he could understand the horrors of the war or the death of Leah and the child and yet he would delight in digging out some petty regulation that he'd accuse me of disregarding. Well, his regulations could go hang and he could go hang with them. I was going back to my studies.

The voyage had been a welcome monotony of regular meals and lying on my bunk. The study of Scottish Gaelic place-names lasted me up the coast of West Africa and across the Bay of Biscay, punctuated only by the occasional bout of seasickness. I put the book down when I saw the thick grey clouds above Britain. I was home.

Webb was expecting me. I'd phoned his office from my hotel and using my best public school English asked to speak to the head of Archives Research Unit.

'Who shall I say is calling?' said the man at the other end in an equally refined accent. Genuine, I think. Talk like the king and always be polite, that's what my father had taught me about doing business in Britain. I didn't mind, I'd had enough of shouting in Africa.

'My mother was Hannah,' I said, using the agreed password. And Hannah's son was Samuel. Webb's idea; he had always been more aware of my background than I had.

'One moment, please.'

There was a click and Webb came on the line.

'You're back.'

'Yes.'

'Tomorrow afternoon. Two o'clock. My office.'

That was the extent of my welcome back and I didn't care a jot. Webb was now an irrelevance in my life. I was almost at his office, weaving a crooked path through the traffic of horse-drawn cabs while avoiding the dung lying in glistening piles in the road.

The man on the door in the top hat consulted a list of names and then allowed me to take a lift to the fourth floor. I shook the rain off myself like a dog and left a puddle in the lift. Webb's office door wasn't as I remembered it. He'd moved. The door was opened by a middle-aged corporal who I assumed was the owner of the upper-class voice on the telephone.

'Do come in,' he said. 'The Colonel will be with you in a moment.' He returned to his typewriter. Colonel? So he had been promoted. I wondered why.

I could see another door near the window. Well, well, now Webb had a secretary and a larger office. Apparently the spy business was booming but not on account of anything I had sent him. Which, no doubt, was why he wanted to see me.

A buzzer sounded on the secretary's desk.

'He will see you now.'

I'd spent years in Africa enduring all kinds of horrors on his behalf and now I was being treated like a patient waiting to see the dentist. I knocked on his door.

'Come.'

I waited. Again he called out. His secretary looked up in consternation and began to speak but I waved him into silence. There was the sound of footsteps and Webb opened the door.

'Good morning,' I said and walked past him into his office. I felt better already. I took a seat without being asked, leaned back and lit a cigarette.

Webb stood watching me for a few moments while stroking his moustache.

'Why are you being such an arse?' he said mildly.

I wasn't quite sure how to respond to that so I said nothing. He sat down opposite me and steepled his fingers.

'You always were cocky,' he said in the same even tone. 'That was part of your charm. Now you're just being a bore.' He leaned forward. 'I know all about what happened in German South West Africa.' He paused. 'Including that final incident with Hartmann.'

I hadn't been expecting that. Something was brewing, he was being far less antagonistic than I'd expected. I must have shown my surprise as I stubbed out my cigarette.

'You're not quite as clever as you think,' he smiled thinly. 'Did you really believe we wouldn't keep an eye on you in Walfish Bay? Morrison isn't our only agent there.'

My mind was racing. Who could possibly have witnessed Hartmann's death, apart from ... Good lord, was that it?

'The boy? Hartmann's boy?' I recalled the shock on his face, his sudden fear and desperate flight down the alley.

Webb nodded. 'Don't worry,' he said. 'We were about to deal with Hartmann ourselves. He was getting too close with one of our, shall we say, vulnerable military personnel stationed there, someone who was in possession of rather sensitive information. So you saved us a job. Another cigarette?'

While I lit up and rearranged my thoughts, he shuffled the papers on his desk.

'I assume Cornell has reported on the possibility of a German expansion into South Africa,' I said at last.

'Oh yes. Thank you for that. Good job, by the way. Well done.' He hesitated. 'I could bend the rules and give you a medal if you like.'

I shook my head. He seemed relieved.

'Well, there's no chance now of the Kaiser turning south. His parliament, such as it is, is most unhappy with his costly little war. No, his mind is elsewhere. He's busy building battleships and increasing the strength of his army in Europe. It'll soon be a match for that of his cousin, the Tsar. Not to mention his other cousin, King Edward. Things aren't looking too good.' He looked up. 'Now tell me more about the German military posts.'

I asked myself why Webb was going over this stuff all over again? Surely, with the war more or less over, he had to be convinced by now that the Germans were not going to invade British territory? It was only when he pressed me once more about troop dispositions, particularly those in the south, that the truth hit me. What a fool I'd been! I held up a hand and interrupted him in mid-sentence.

'I've been looking at this the wrong way round,' I said, getting to my feet. 'You weren't really interested in the possibility of a German invasion at all, were you? Rather, you were preparing the way for a possible invasion of German territory by us. Is that it? You were asking me to probe the German defences and that's why you were not worried about the lack of communications: my sending back information on the war was not your main objective. You were planning for a war in the future. You've been playing me like a fish on a line.'

Webb sighed. 'That's my job, old chap. Do sit down. And that future war you are talking about may happen sooner than you think.'

'You lied to me!' I cried, banging his desk with my fist. 'I've seen all kinds of horrors and all the time you were tricking me.'

The door flew open and the corporal rushed in, alarm on his face and a large revolver in his hand.

'Colonel?'

'It's all right,' said Webb calmly. 'Just leave us alone, will you?'

The corporal closed the door behind him.

'Now look,' said Webb. 'Do sit down, there's a good fellow. I know you've been through a lot but it was all in a good cause. Let me explain.'

I resumed my chair and lit another cigarette.

'Despite the surprisingly intelligent policies of the King, the Kaiser is making all sorts of belligerent noises and if war does break out in Europe, you can be sure that it will also spill over into our overseas possessions. German East Africa and German South West Africa would almost certainly be part of any conflict and we must be ready for them. You were a part of our preparations, as was Cornell.'

He let that sink in. 'Shall we continue?' he said at last. 'For the time being the German Protectorate poses no threat, it's elsewhere that is giving those upstairs some cause for concern and that is where you come in.'

'But I've just got back!'

'I know and you deserve some leave.'

'Leave? I'm not in the Army!'

'Sorry, force of habit, old chap. Anyway, you're entitled to a break, whatever you see yourself as and when you're ready I've another job for you.'

Why was he being so sympathetic, so nice?

'I'm not sure I want another job.'

'Fair enough. I know you've had a jolly tough time.' And then he surprised me more than ever. He scratched his head and suddenly looked me straight in the eye. I hadn't noticed before how blue his own eyes were, an innocent cornflower blue. He dropped his voice.

'Why don't you tell me about her?'

I caught my breath. I felt as if he'd punched me in the stomach and I had difficulty breathing. For a second I held his gaze and then, to my utter surprise, I found myself sobbing.

Ever since I'd come round in the Nama village, I'd not wept. Even on the voyage home my feelings had been in suspension and now, to a spy chief of all persons, I was letting my feelings tumble out, my shoulders shaking with my tears.

He sat there in total silence while I described our first meeting, our shy discovery of each other, our separation and her final ordeal in the camp on Shark Island and then the death of her and the child.

'She gave me this,' I said, wiping my eyes with the back of my hand as I revealed my necklace.

He nodded. He allowed a short silence to develop before standing and going over to the window and looking out at the rain. He lit another cigarette.

'I understand,' he said. 'I was in India with the Madras Lancers. In my case there was a native girl.' A pause. 'She was of a very high caste and her parents disapproved. I never saw her again.' He sat down.

We stayed there for some time, smoking and sharing our sense of loss.

A knock on the door broke the silence.

'Come.'

The secretary entered, 'I'm sorry, sir, but Captain Hillier is here.'

'Of course. Give me a couple more minutes.'

I stubbed out my cigarette. 'I'd better be going,' I said.

'Of course. Take as long as you like but I do have a job for you. I just want you to think about it.'

'Think about what? You haven't told me what the job is.'

'Nor have I.' He sniffed, looked over my shoulder at the wall and coughed. 'The Germans are cosying up to the Ottoman Turks in a way that might threaten our interests in the Middle East. It started back in '98 when the Kaiser visited Jerusalem dressed up like some kind of modern crusader. He looked ridiculous, of course, but the Turks seemed to like it. They'd made no end of effort to clean the place up in his honour.' He stared up at the ceiling. 'So, how do you fancy going to Jerusalem?'

Epilogue

It was still raining as I splashed my way back to Charing Cross Station. I was on my way home. My parents had no idea I was back in Britain. They had no access to a telephone and a telegram might have worried them unnecessarily. I could have sent a letter or a postcard but I thought I would give them a pleasant surprise.

Nothing seemed to have changed. The path leading up to the front door and the door itself were as I remembered them. Even the mezuzah by the front door bell proudly announcing a Jewish house was the same although perhaps a little more polished by the fingers that had stroked it. I touched it myself before ringing the bell.

'Samuel! It's you!'

My father, greyer now, reached out and hugged me tight. Was he shorter than before? Or just a little stooped? His veined arm clutched mine and he led me inside.

'Mother, it's Samuel. Our boy has come home!'

The house smelled as always of roast dinners and lavender. My mother bustled out of the kitchen to hug me, all apron and newly-baked bread, covered me with hot tears.

'Samuel! We thought you'd gone for ever.' She stepped back and examined me. 'My, how brown you are. Now, come and have some tea.'

Later, after more hugs and tears and cups of tea, I gave them a brief sketch of my years in German South West Africa. I omitted the nastier bits and said nothing of Leah. That could wait.

And then my father, despite the rain, took me into the garden and up to the orchard cobbled with fallen apples.

'We can't eat them all or even give them away so we let them stay and rot to nourish next year's crop. Now look at my walnut tree, hasn't it grown since you were last here?'

He hadn't asked any more about what I'd been doing but I guessed he was just wishing to renew the bonds between us by continuing from the normality where we'd left off.

'I've started a small vegetable garden, see? There are carrots, spring onions, garlic and potatoes. Next year I'm going to try eggplants in the greenhouse. I know we don't eat them but I like the colour. Of course, you haven't seen my greenhouse. It's over there on the south wall.'

It was his way of intimating that he and mother had stopped wandering and had put down roots and that I should do the same.

'I don't remember that yellow rose,' I said.

'Of course you do. I planted it when your mother's sister died.'

'I'm sorry.'

'Don't worry. It happens. Look at me, sometimes I feel I've forgotten more than I ever knew.'

In the afternoon, they told me all about the family, including relations, most of whom I could barely remember, still living in Germany.

'Except for Uncle Leo,' said my mother. 'He got out of Russia by applying for Turkish nationality. No doubt it cost him a bit but he got his passport and went to Germany and then came here. He's up in Manchester, a Jewish Turk in Manchester.' While she was still chuckling, I stored that piece of information away for possible future use; Jerusalem was held by the Ottoman Turks.

When it began getting dark, my mother lit the candles and produced the homemade bread and bottle of kosher wine that always mysteriously appeared on a Friday evening in this supposedly agnostic household.

After supper I asked if they had heard from Julia.

'She's married,' said my mother in a tone that said I'd somehow lost something.

'Really? Who's the lucky fellow?'

'Someone in insurance,' said my father.

'A nice steady job,' added Mother. 'More potatoes?'

After pudding, my father lit his pipe while I took out a cigarette. Mother refused our help in clearing away and washing up so I knew something was brewing. I sat back and waited.

'Mother's not well,' he said at last. 'And I'm not getting any younger. It'll not be long before we can no longer look after ourselves. You may have us on your hands.'

Before I went to Africa, I'd have been uncomfortable with this chat. I'd always seen myself as, called myself, the Wandering Jew. Settling down? Responsibilities? Not for me. But now I was looking at my mother and father in a different light.

'I love you, Papa,' I said, 'and Mama. Of course I'll look after you.'

'You must look after yourself as well,' he said.

'That's right,' said Mama. I'd not heard her enter the room. 'You need a wife who'll look after you.'

I resolved to put that off for as long as I was able. However, I prepared for the future as best as I could.

~

I sold some of the diamonds to my cousin in Amsterdam and with the proceeds I was able to make life for Mama and Papa more comfortable.

I took up my old research post – they seemed surprisingly pleased to see me but later I learned that Webb had pulled a few strings – and picked up from where I had left off with inter-departmental battles and pressures to publish. I had drafted an article about Nama clicks on the boat and submitted it for publication.

At home I slowly took up household duties from Mama and Papa, easing them into retirement. I helped Papa in the garden, with me doing the digging and mowing and Papa pruning and dead-heading and giving me instructions. I also gave Mama a hand in the kitchen, washing up and putting things away and when she allowed me to do this without demur, I knew she was really ill.

I even went to worship at the shul with Papa although neither of us had been since I could remember. He found me an old and shiny kippah for my head and when we entered, we were welcomed with hugs and Yiddish. I still felt an outsider but Papa loved it and after the service even started arguing with his cronies about the merits of Zionism. Papa was against it.

'Nonsense,' he'd say, smiling over his glasses. 'It's arrant nonsense. Herzl is just a dreamer.'

'No, no,' said his new friend, Marks. 'Every nation in Europe, from Russia to France, wants to get rid of us. They all hate us. If they don't want us, we must have a home of our own. It's as simple as that.'

'We have a good, safe home in this country,' my father said. 'No one here wants to kick us out.'

And the same conversation took place each time they met.

He had also changed his musical tastes and now listened to Mendelssohn on his new gramophone.

'The old queen's favourite,' he said.

So I settled down as they wished me to and I made some improvements such as installing a telephone. But sooner than anyone expected, everything changed. Within eighteen months, Mama was dead of cancer of the pancreas and Papa followed her soon after. 'Cardiac Infarction,' the death certificate had said but doctors do not consider grief to be a possible cause of death.

After the funerals and the effort of clearing and arranging the renting of the house, I sat down on the last packing case in the empty front room in the house where I'd spent so much of my life, looked at the light rectangles on the walls where the pictures had been and suddenly felt the need to get away.

I had to go out. I went to my office and then to a second-hand bookshop in Bloomsbury, not far from the British Museum. I often went there for solace, rummaging among old books and pamphlets in the dusty shop that smelled of history and mildew. At last I reluctantly tore myself away with a sigh and made my way back home. My route took me past the Registry Office and as I approached the main entrance a man and a woman emerged. I stopped in my tracks and stared at them for I knew them both.

Lucy Goldstein was a friend of my cousin Ruth in Germany. Rumour had it that she had been divorced from her husband and now I had proof. She was hanging on the arm of a man I had never expected to see again. The last time we'd met, he'd been ordering a hanging. It was General von Trotha, the butcher of German South West Africa.

He was in civilian clothing but there was no mistaking that stiff military bearing and his equally stiff moustache. He was smiling into the eyes of Lucy. Neither of them spotted me and stopped gazing at each other only long enough to hail a cab. So he had married a Jew. What would Hartmann have made of that?

I made my way back home not knowing what to think, except that the world never stopped spinning and throwing off the unexpected.

Back in the echoing house I sat down and did what I suppose had been at the back of my mind for months. I rang Webb.

'Tell me about Jerusalem,' I said.

Author's Note

This story is a work of fiction but the historical background and several of the characters are all too real.

1. Heinrich Göring was the first Governor-General of German South West Africa and the father of the infamous Herman Göring of the Nazi Third Reich.

2. General von Trotha was indeed responsible for instigating the genocide of the Ovaherero and Nama through his notorious proclamation, and for other atrocities. He married a Jewish woman, Lucy Goldstein, in London in May 1912.

3. Dr Bofinger and his mentor, Dr Eugen Fischer, carried out medical experiments on inmates of the concentration camp on Shark Island and the skulls of prisoners were sent back to Germany. Some of these were returned to Namibia only in 2011 after a long-standing campaign initiated by Traditional Authorities in Namibia.

4. The battle of the Waterberg took place much as I have described, although I have taken one or two liberties with the timing.

5. Walfish Bay is, of course, the current Walvis Bay.

6. Fred Cornell was a diamond prospector and a writer who reported on German atrocities in South Africa. In the Great War (the First World War, from 1914 to 1918) he was the first to inform the South African government that German forces had entered the Cape.

7. The Union of South Africa, at the request of the British Government, entered German South West Africa in 1915 and defeated the German forces.

Details of these events may be found in some of the books in the bibliography. Any errors of fact are mine and mine alone.

Select Bibliography

1. *The Kaiser's Holocaust* by David Olusoga and Casper W. Erichsen (Faber & Faber, London, 2010). A readable, affecting account that gives much detail.

2. *Peter Moor's Journey to Southwest Africa* (translation: Archibald Constable and Company, London, 1908). A popular novel in Nazi Germany revealing the German colonial viewpoint.

3. *Genocide in German South-West Africa: The Colonial War of 1904–1908 in Namibia and its Aftermath* edited by Jürgen Zimmerer and Joachim Zeller (Merlin Press, Monmouth, 2008).

4. *Germany's Genocide of the Herero: Kaiser Wilhelm II, his General, his Settlers, his Soldiers* by Jeremy Sarkin (UCT Press, Cape Town, 2011).

5. *Die Kämpfe der deutschen Truppen in Südwestafrika* (Ernst Siegfried Mittler, Berlin, 1906).

6. *Shark Island, 1904–1907: A Historical Overview* by Casper W. Erichsen (Archives of the Anti-Colonial Resistance and the Liberation Struggle (AACRLS), Windhoek, 2007).

7. *Kriegskarte von Deutsch-Südwestafrika* (Berlin, 1904; reprinted 1987 by National Archives SWA/Namibia).

8. *The Boer War* by Thomas Pakenham (Futura, 1982; reprinted 2015 by Little, Brown Book Group).

9. *Urgent Imperial Service* by Gerald L'Ange (Ashanti Publishing, Rivonia, 1991).

10. *First World War in Namibia* by Gordon McGregor and Manfred Goldbeck (Gondwana History, Namibia, 2014).

11. *Fotografische Erinnerungen an Deutsch-Südwestafrika* by Bernd and Holger Kroemer (Glanz & Gloria Verlag, Namibia, 2012).

12. *The Glamour of Prospecting* by Fred C. Cornell (David Philip, Cape Town, 1992, second impression. Distributed by the Springbok Café, Springbok, Western Cape).

13. *Mama Namibia* by Mari Serebrov (Wordweaver Publishing House, Windhoek, 2013).

14. *The Scattering* by Lauri Kubuitsile (Penguin, Cape Town, 2016).

Printed in the United States
By Bookmasters